RACHEL KENLEY

Melusine's *Daughters*
Book Two

WAVES OF
Desire

For more information contact:
Riverdale Avenue Books
5676 Riverdale Avenue
Riverdale, NY 10471
www.riverdaleavebooks.com

Design by www.formatting4U.com
Cover by Scott Carpenter

Digital ISBN:978-1-62601-393-3
Print ISBN: 978-1-62601-394-0

First Edition July 2017

Dedication

For my husband, Mark,
for being by my side no matter where the current takes
us

And all the women connected with
Mama Gena's Mastery 2017 Class,
I could never have written this book without the love,
support
and understanding of my wonderful Sister Goddesses.

I brag that I wrote this during my time with you
as I learned to open myself up more completely to my
own emotions.
I am grateful you have come into my life.
I desire many more occasions for us to be together and
connect.

Aquatic Races

Oceanides - A general term referring to all the sentient beings who live in the ocean. Unlike their human counterparts, they have access to magic and ways to enhance it. The races can and do mix, although the resulting offspring are not always accepted. There are several races mentioned who differ from their mythological counterparts. The Oceanides mentioned in this series are:

Mermaids and Mermen—Best known of the Oceanides. Male and female can change between the traditional fully human form and half human/half fin form. Can easily swim long distances. Lives on land. Prefer warm climates for their homes.

Rusalka—Former human who now lives as mermaid or merman after their lives were almost claimed by the ocean. Occurs when the human is changed by a healer at the time of death.

Kelpie—Water horse with ability to shape shift into human-appearing form as well as a half human/half horse form. Tend to be born male which is why there is a fair amount of interbreeding with other Oceanide creatures.

Sea Dragon—The mixed race offspring of a mermaid/merman and a kelpie. The resulting race can shapeshift into three different forms: their bottom half into a traditional mermaid fin, their entire bodies into a horse form, or a combination of horse upper half and fin lower half. The last is how the race gets its name.

Lamia—Serpentine creature with the ability to be all snake/eel in appearance or half snake/half human. Not a particularly peaceful or diplomatic race.

Leviathan—Vicious and violent creature. Lives in colder climates and destroys it enemies by putting the sharpened bones of its victims within whirlpools and riptides. Rarely, if ever, seen by humans, but the basis for many of their myths about sea monsters. Squid like in its natural form.

Angler Witch—Thought for a long time to be legend. Lives in the deeper parts of the ocean where no sunlight reaches. It is not known how many exist. Isolationists by nature.

Character List

Amina, mermaid. Wears the powerful green sapphire known as Stone of Strength in a bracelet on her right wrist. It is one of three that were created generations ago from Melusine's Band. A natural empath, the magic in the bracelet enhances her abilities and connections to others. Works as a counselor and ambassador within her government.

Jonathan, human. Head of security at Suadela Resort for the last two years. Former New York City cop. Left his job after his partner was shot during a domestic violence situation.

Lyria, mermaid. Amina's cousin. Wears the clear sapphire, Stone of Clarity. Healer. (Her story is in *Waves of Pleasure*.)

Fiero, sea dragon. Son of a mermaid and a kelpie. Considered an abomination by many full-blooded merfolk and only tolerated by the kelpie. Determined to find all three bracelets so that he can unite them and rule over all the Oceanides.

Costin, merman. One of four Quadrant Governors, heads of government. Inherited title which will go to his oldest son on his death or abdication. Uncle to Amina, Lyria and Eden.

Betta, mermaid. Wife of Costin. Aunt to Amina and Lyria. Had the gift of vision and prophecy but has blocked it.

Zia and *Zan,* mermaids. Twins. Younger sisters of Costin. Zia was Lyria's mother and the previous wearer of the Stone of Clarity. Zan is Eden's and Amina's mother and previous wearer of the Stone of Strength.

Eden, mermaid. Amina's older sister by four years. Wore the Stone of Strength from the time she was thirteen until she was twenty-four. Renounced her heritage and lives as a human. Can no longer use magic, shape shift, and has cut herself off completely from her family.

Nerine, daughter of a mermaid and a lamia. Known for her magical abilities and being difficult to find. Sells potions and spells to those who can pay her—and find her.

Balban, kelpie. Fiero's uncle and guardian since the death of Fiero's father. Supporting his nephew to find the bracelets and take over the rule of the Oceans.

Sofia, human. Teenager (age 16) and native of the island of Jariz. Works at the Suadela Resort. No father and her mother has died leaving her in charge of her younger brother, Raul.

Raul, human. Young boy (age 11) and brother of Sofia. Fascinated by the street gangs who profit off the rich tourists who come to the island where he lives.

The Legend of Melusine's Band

Long ago, when the Earth formed, it was divided in two—the areas of land, and the areas of water. Each was populated by a vast number of species. Those who came to rule on land were humanoid and they had no magic, nor did they believe in it. Those who had rule over the water were the Oceanides and in addition to their shape-shifting abilities, they had magic.

For much of early time the two species lived separately, each vaguely aware of the other. As the humanoids increased in number so too did they increase violence. The Oceanides took to hiding themselves and their gifts. Unknown to the humanoids and cloaked by magic, there were many islands and kingdoms where the Oceanides lived out of water.

It came to pass over many generations that magic was stronger in some Oceanides than others, especially the mermaids. While their men had some, that which developed in the women was more powerful. There came a time when the men sought to lessen the strength of their women and encouraged them to meet and mate with human males.

Although there were some strong love matches and marriages that succeeded, story has long told of how ruinous this turned out to be for both the humans and mermaids. After a time, however, tales of love gone wrong faded into distant memory, replaced by fear or foolishly forgotten completely.

One day a mermaid was born who came from a long and powerful line of unbroken magic. Her name was Melusine.

Melusine's father was king of the merfolk and her mother came from the ruling class. Melusine was told from an early age that it was important she marry one of her own kind, preferably someone with the right background. Upon her 18th birthday, Melusine was given an intricate golden necklace, thick and filigreed with gems and minerals from all parts of the sea, an inheritance from her mother's family. She grew in beauty, knowledge, and magic, her strengths and gifts creating a time of great abundance and joy for her people.

However, when her father grew ill shortly after Melusine's 20th birthday it seemed likely she would ascend the throne unwed. Once the word of this spread, the beautiful princess became a target for any and all distant male relatives.

Fearing for her life and freedom, the king set his army against their enemies, and Melusine fled to her private island and waited for word that it was safe to return. On a stormy night a ship crashed against the rocks near her retreat. She saved the men she could, one of whom was a prince. Using her magic, she cast them safely home. Remembering what happened, the prince went to the water's edge of his own home every day looking for the sea maiden who saved him. Eventually Melusine revealed herself to him, believing his actions showed a caring heart.

Sadly, she was mistaken.

The prince was an ambitious man, a third son, and not truly in line for the throne as his oldest brother was already married and had an heir. He had heard tales of the magic water creatures and, once he met Melusine, he believed if he could win her as his wife, he would be able to use her magic to take over his brother's kingdom. He hid his intentions and wooed Melusine. Innocent and giving, she fell in love with the human and soon they were married. Her mother worried about the match, but her father decided it was for the best and was relieved Melusine would be protected.

So that her husband could be with her both in and out of water and rule by her side, Melusine gifted him with a magic amulet. At its center was a unique gem forged by her magic from the three different sapphires she took from her necklace: the clear Stone of Clarity, the Stone of Strength which was a deep magnificent green and finally, the pink Stone of Love. The three stones together enabled him learn and practice magic.

When her father died a few months after the wedding, Melusine was ready to lead her people and she was grateful to have her prince at her side. At her coronation, to acknowledge her husband as a co-ruler, she magically removed one strand of gold from the necklace and placed it around her husband's wrists. Once it was there, magic closed it so the band had no beginning and no end, as she believed their love to be. Outwardly, the prince always showed support and found ways to help her rule even as he continued to make other plans and gain followers of his own among the Oceanides, to whom he promised wealth and power once he assumed control.

All was well until Melusine gave birth a year later

to triplets, three daughters. It was then that the Prince showed his true nature. Furious not to have sons, he locked Melusine in her room swearing she would be his prisoner until she bore him as many male heirs as she had daughters. He must have heirs if she was to help him take over his brother's kingdom. To ensure her compliance, he threatened to have her daughters killed if she didn't do as he commanded. He told her that her magic, like her body, was his to command and she would do as he said or suffer the consequences. To prove his power over her, he tried to take the band from her neck, but to both their surprise it repelled him.

Still, she knew the band and magic were not enough protection. Petrified for her daughters' safety and horrified by her own unfortunate choice, Melusine meticulously planned her revenge. Each day she painfully pulled out her magic and imbued it into the gold threads of her necklace. She ate little and hardly noticed what her husband did to her body. Growing weaker by the day, Melusine decided to do what she must to protect her daughters and destroy the prince.

Finally, her work was complete. She waited for him to come to her that night and played the role he wanted her to play. She was soft and sweet. Offering words of apology and love, promising to do all he wanted, give him all he asked for. As he lay on the bed, she straddled him and placed her hand on the amulet, which allowed him to live in and out of water. With the last of her energy, she forced magic through the amulet and shattered it back into the three original separate stones. Instantly, the Prince screamed gasped for air. Even though they were on land, it was as though all the waters of the ocean filled his lungs.

Before long there was banging and shouting on the other side of the door. Her husband's final yell had brought his guards to her prison. Knowing these men were on his side and fearing what they would do to her or her daughters, she did the last thing she could to protect her children and her kingdom.

Taking the three stones from the amulet, she wove them into the band that now held nearly all of her magic. Finally, she called back the thin gold strand that was around her dead husband's wrist and worked it into the bracelet where it glowed before settling into place. She magically broke the necklace into three bracelets, each with one of the stones and sent them to her daughters. She would give them her magic to protect them—body and heart.

With her final breaths, Melusine created the promise of the jewels. In every generation three women would receive the bracelets. Each woman would have her own gifts which would benefit and protect their people. In addition, the magic in each would show each woman her heart's true match. The bracelets must be kept separate and would always keep her daughters safe. However, should the day come that a great threat endangered her people, it could be stopped only if all three women worked together with the men who loved them.

The bracelets traveled through time, passed down only through the matriarchal line, from mother to daughter or eldest niece. Outside males and females tried unsuccessfully to steal them for the purpose of reuniting the three, for the power they held was unimaginable, but all failed.

It is said that each woman gifted with a bracelet

will lead an extraordinary life but must be careful to whom she gives her heart. Should she promise herself to the wrong man, the bracelet and its power and protection will desert her.

Prologue
Once Upon a Time...

Fifteen years ago—Governor's Compound

Someone was shaking her awake.

"Betta, please wake up, please." It was a familiar voice. More softly she heard, "I hope she's alright. I'm worried. This one hit her so hard."

A woman's voice. A safe voice.

"I think she's coming around," said a second person. Also female. Slowly her mind put together the sounds with the correct people. Zia and Zan, her twin sisters-in-law, two halves of a rainbow.

Betta reached out and touched something soft. A blanket. Her other hand touched a piece of furniture. The couch. She was lying on the couch.

With those pieces of information, the rest of the memories came flooding back.

The three of them had been enjoying lunch on the patio outside Zia's suite. Betta remembered thinking how lucky she was not only to have married such a good man in Costin, but that his sisters had welcomed her as family and friends. She was an only child from a less populated part of the Oceanide world, and she was grateful fate had put her in the path of such a wonderful and loving man.

Costin was the quadrant's Governor, an inherited title which made him leader of the Merfolk and many of the other sentient ocean dwellers in their quadrant. His sisters wore the clear Stone of Clarity and the green Stone of Strength in bracelets created by Melusine herself. Costin's family members were direct decedents of this famous princess which is why the bracelets, worn only by women, were bonded to his sisters. Had Betta given birth to daughters, those may have passed to her children, but she delivered two sons to her husband.

Zia's daughter, Lyria, was the oldest in her generation and would eventually wear the Stone of Clarity. Zan had two daughters, Eden and Amina. Eden, younger than Lyria by only a few months, would wear the Stone of Strength. The bracelets were originally a set of three, but the third, the Stone of Love, had appeared to an unknown descendent generations before. Legitimacy was not much of an issue for Oceanides, so it was likely it was bound to a daughter produced from an affair. Unfortunately, no one knew who or where she was.

Betta always hoped that whoever had the bracelet appreciated the gifts as Zia, a healer, and Zan, an ambassador, did. Love had changed Betta's life. Costin had come to her isolated part of the ocean because he had heard about a mermaid with the gift of prophecy. He came to ask for help and, instead, had fallen in love and asked for her hand. All Oceanides had magic of one form or another, some strong, some weak, with certain gifts or strengths appearing in individuals.

It was Betta's magic which had caused her blackout today. Fortunately, it wasn't often she was hit with a prophecy that rendered her unconscious.

"Zia? Zan?" she said softly.

"Thank the gods, you're awake," Zia said.

"You scared us, Betta."

"Yes, I can see that." Her sisters-in-law rarely hovered over her, but there was no other word for the way they were crowding the couch. "How long was I unconscious?"

"Not long, maybe 20 minutes, but one moment we were talking, the next you were shouting."

Betta took a deep breath. "And what was I shouting?"

"At first it sounded like unclear warnings," Zan said. "Phrases—'Don't go there.' 'Don't do that.' 'Stay away, there's no need to see him.' 'It's dangerous.' 'You have to stop.' Things like that."

"And then?"

The identical women looked at each other. Zia continued, "You said 'Without the three, we lose the sea.' Do you know what you meant?"

Betta's visions came to her when she was sleeping or resting, almost like a dream, and she remembered them. She could see them as they unfolded before her, almost as if she was a part of it, and she could relay what she saw to others. But when she received a prophecy, which was rare, she completely blacked out. It was as though the revelation overcame her and, if there was no one around to hear it, it was lost. All she retained were flashes of images.

Sadly, she had no control over when and where her gift manifested. She often wished she had a stone like her sisters-in-law which could enhance and focus her gift, but that was not to be. Today was a prophecy and, fortunately, there were witnesses.

"Tell me again what I said and, if possible, exactly the order I said it."

They did their best to repeat back what she said. As they did, she saw a few images. She couldn't be certain, but she had a good idea of what the prophecy was about. "It's the bracelets. Melusine's three bracelets. I could see them. Clear, green, pink."

Zia and Zan put their hands to their wrists in the same manner and at the same time. Betta would have been amused if it weren't for the worry in their eyes, caused by what she had seen. Zia asked, "Are they in danger? Are we?"

"Yes, but I don't know when and I don't know how. Only that all three bracelets must be found, must be together or someone is going to take over the oceans and it will be deadly for all who live there."

The three women sat in silence holding hands until Costin crashed into the room.

"Where is she? Is she okay?" He was a large merman who held great power and status among his people, but the concern on his face showed only a man worried about the woman he loved. Zia and Zan moved out of the way so he could sit and hold his wife.

After a short time fussing, Betta and the twins told him what had happened and what they believed the prophecy meant. "What do we do now, Costin?" Betta asked.

"I don't know. It's clear we need to find the mermaid who wears the third bracelet. The family histories haven't revealed anything when we've looked before, but that doesn't mean there's nothing there. We'll look again. We'll find and talk to the oldest Merfolk. Someone must know something." He took a breath, brought Betta's hands to his lips and kissed them. "We will find her and the bracelet."

Bella smiled at her husband. She knew he believed what he said, but something told her the cost would be high.

* * *

Six months later no leads or stories had uncovered the whereabouts of the third bracelet. Betta wondered if she had misinterpreted her prophecy or perhaps something had changed and what she saw was not to be. Time had a way of altering things. Still, the uneasy feeling she'd had since that day had not entirely left her.

That night she woke up screaming. "Zia! Zan! Come back! Don't go!"

Costin was immediately awake, turning on the bedside lamp and pulling her to him. "What is it, my love?"

"Your sisters. They are in trouble. They are somewhere I didn't recognize. It was dark. Cold. Terrifying. They have gone to find information about the Stone of Love."

"I'm certain they're fine."

"You are doubting me? Saying my vision was a dream?" Her voice held as much anger as fear.

Costin realized this was serious. "I will go check on them."

5

"You won't find them. They're not here."

"Do you want someone to stay with you?"

Betta was about to say no, but then another thought came to her. "Bring me Lyria, Eden and Amina."

The color drained from Costin's face. He nodded and left the room.

Minutes that felt like hours later the girls joined their aunt on her bed. "What's wrong, Aunt Betta?" Lyria asked.

"I've had a vision. It concerned your mothers. I didn't see it through to the end, so I don't know how things will turn out, but I am worried."

"They are in danger," Eden said. The girls knew their aunt and her visions. Eden didn't need to ask it as a question.

"I am afraid so. I don't know how bad the situation is or the outcome. Your Uncle has gone to find where they went. Do you know when they left?"

"Early yesterday," Eden said. "They told us they hoped to find the mermaid who wore the third bracelet."

Betta nodded. "Yes, that is what I thought this was about."

"But they are going to be alright, yes?" Amina asked. She was so sweet, so small, Betta thought. She was only four years old. Too young for this much fear, too young to lose her... Betta wouldn't think about that outcome. She'd woken too soon. She hoped that was for a good reason.

As they sat there in silence Amina began to sing. "I am unwritten, can't read my mind, I'm undefined. I'm just beginning, the pen's in my hand, ending unplanned."

"That's very pretty, honey. Where did you learn it?" Betta asked.

"I heard it on the radio." It was one of the ways Oceanides knew what was happening with humans, in case their actions threatened the oceans. "A woman named Natasha Bedingfield sings it." Betta smiled. Amina loved music, especially human music. "I know I'm supposed to prefer our music, but sometimes I like other things, Aunt Betta."

"I know. I think it is just fine. You should always be open to the things in the world around you. And you have a lovely voice. It's wonderful when you sing."

"Too bad it's exactly what humans think mermaids do," Eden said. "Sing and brush our hair all day long."

"Well it would be silly for you not to brush your hair, wouldn't it," Betta said and Amina laughed. "And as for what humans think of us, I don't think you should ever let that influence what you do."

Between one breath and the next, and before Amina could answer, Lyria and Eden both screamed and jumped off the bed. They stared at their arms, then looked at each other and the screams started again.

"Girls, what is it? What's happened," but the cold wave that passed through Betta's body told her the answer before she saw what had upset the girls. Their screams had turn to cries. They held out their wrists.

On Lyria's right wrist was the Stone of Clarity. On Eden, the Stone of Strength. Betta knew what that meant.

Zia and Zan were dead.

* * *

Ten Years Later—Five Years Ago

She didn't mean to, but Amina screamed when she woke and saw the bracelet on her wrist. She must still be dreaming. She had to be.

She closed her eyes and put her head back on the pillow. She tried to remember what she'd been dreaming about and then thought about what the day might hold. She was planning to head out into the Atlantic, visit with Lyria and perhaps see if should could find a pleasant, physical diversion.

When she was ready, she opened her eyes and tried waking up again.

It didn't work. The bracelet with the green Stone of Strength remained on her wrist.

Which meant her older sister, Eden, was dead or had renounced her mermaid heritage. Either was bad.

Her first call out was to Lyria. She didn't need anything other than her thoughts.

Something's happened to Eden. As cousins, they had a strong telepathic link that was easy to use for connection. Telepathic speech was handiest when swimming while talking, but it also worked well for contacting each other over a distance.

Good morning to you, cousin. The voice sounded sleepy. She'd woken her cousin.

Did you hear me? Something. Has. Happened. To. Eden.

Something is always happening to Eden, Lyria said. It was true, Amina's sister wasn't the most drama-free mermaid, and she did like attention and

8

creating problems. Since their mothers' deaths, Lyria had taken the responsibility of the bracelet seriously. Eden had become more reckless, frequently acting out and taking unnecessary chances. She resented the band and any restrictions placed on her. She would disappear for days without telling anyone, then reappear with no explanation or apology.

But the bracelet's arrival meant this wasn't the usual situation.

Let me try this again differently. I am wearing the Stone of Strength.

You're what?

Amina winced even though the sound got no louder in her head. She could picture Lyria's face and body language. Wherever her cousin was right now, she was standing and pacing.

You heard me.

That's not possible.

Amina looked at her right arm. *I assure you it is.*

I'll be there as fast as I can.

Fast was less than an hour. Amina hadn't left her room. In fact, she was still sitting on the bed when Lyria knocked and came in without waiting for an answer.

"By the seas, it's true," she said as her eyes went directly to Amina's wrist.

"No, I was kidding about this just to see how fast you could get from your island to mine. I thought it would be fun to remind you of the night our mothers were killed and suggest that the same thing had happened to Eden."

"I'm sorry. I didn't doubt you after you told me about the bracelet, although I admit there was a part of me that was hoping it was a practical joke. Oh, Amina, what happened?"

"What do you mean 'what happened?' It was on my arm when I woke. I didn't feel anything during the night or dream anything unusual, not that I remember. But when I opened my eyes, it was the first thing I saw. And I screamed—which seems to be the typical reaction of the women in our generation when we get the bracelets. Goddesses above and below, why can't we receive these bracelets the way we're supposed to, when the previous wearer is old and gray and ready to pass it on?"

"I'm so sorry," Lyria said. "I know it must be quite a shock."

"Thank you. I do understand your response, though. I tried to prove to myself it was a dream by attempting to go back to sleep." They sat in silence staring at the intricate piece of jewelry. "It's not a dream, is it?"

Lyria gave a heartfelt and sympathetic sigh, sat next to Amina and pulled her into a hug. "No, my sweet. It's real. Something has happened to Eden, and although we need to find out what that is, it won't change the situation. The Stone of Strength is now yours."

Amina fell back on her bed and tested out a few colorful human curses. They didn't help. Looking up at the ceiling she said, "Remember when we were kids? And I envied you and Eden the beautiful bracelets and the attention it gave you? Remember when I wished for one of my own? I used to dream that the Stone of Love would appear on my arm and make me important like the two of you were."

"I remember."

"I take it back. And I want Eden to take this back."

"You know that's not possible. She has died or disavowed. It doesn't matter which. She cannot have it back and you cannot relinquish it, except in the same way. I know you don't want to give up your life as a mermaid, and I will not even speak of the other."

Amina sat up. She knew what this meant, but she wanted to stay in denial for as long as possible. She and Eden had inherited their mother's gift of empathy. The Stone enhanced the gift first in their mother and then in Eden, who hated it from the beginning and did everything she could to avoid the work that was expected of her. Of course, when your ability to feel the feelings of others is enhanced as you—and they—are trying to deal with the death of your mother that is understandable. Unfortunately, Eden never recovered from the loss of their mother or embraced the gifts of the bracelet.

Amina thought about what this meant. She would have to have a bonding ceremony, and since she was past her 18th birthday it would be scheduled as soon as possible. And once that happened Amina's life would change forever.

She would do what Eden first avoided and then ran from. She would join the Council as Head Councilor and act as advisor and ambassador for her people.

They sent word to their Uncle Costin and Aunt Betta, who were waiting for them at the Governing Compound when they arrived a few minutes later. Aunt Betta wrapped Amina in a smothering hug and when they separated, Amina saw tears in her eyes.

"Is Eden dead? Did you sense something?" Amina asked.

The older woman shook her head. Their Aunt Betta no longer had the gift of prophecy or vision. She had repudiated her gift the night Zia and Zan died. Since then she only had the occasional sense that something was about to happen, and if the sense became too strong Betta self-medicated with soothing teas and potions which caused her to fall and stay asleep until the feeling passed. It was unfortunate not to know more, but no one argued with her. She had nearly gone mad with grief when she lost her sisters-in-law. Costin thought it was better to lose the knowledge of the future than lose his wife.

"I've sent out messengers to see if we can learn what happened. If she's denied her heritage or..." Costin didn't finish—couldn't finish the sentence. It wasn't necessary.

The rest of the day happened in slow motion for Amina. It was like the way sounds were muffled when she was underwater. There was no time to wait for her to become accustomed to the idea that she wore the Stone of Strength and had an important role to play in the Quadrant's government, one that had been relatively unsupported because Eden never fully committed to the job.

Within hours of the band's arrival, Amina was sitting in Eden's former suite at the government compound trying to learn the names of the people she'd be working with, along with trying to make sense of the schedule of things that needed to be done. Everything was a priority. Amina couldn't believe how much had been left undone or completely ignored. If she wasn't worried about her safety, Amina would have cursed Eden to the Angler Witch.

Part of her was grateful to be so busy. Every time things were quiet for a moment she remembered first her grief about Eden, and then her grief over what she was going to be giving up because of her.

No more taking off to have fun at human resorts whenever she wanted.

No more long shopping trips and sneaking away to see movies, one of her favorite human pastimes.

No more helping only when and who she wanted.

By the end of the day, Amina was more exhausted than she could ever remembered being, but she did have an idea of what needed to be her first priority and what could be assigned to others. No one thought she would be able to do everything immediately but, even without her empathy she could sense their needs and expectations. She didn't want to let them down the way her sister had.

She was wondering if it was safe to leave for the sanctuary of her office when Lyria came in along with some staff that brought dinner. Her stomach growled when she saw the food.

"Thank you," she said. "I'd completely forgotten about food."

"I remember what it's like to be new to the position, even if I did have some time to prepare," Lyria said. Because they were so young, Lyria and Eden only did some work when the bracelets came to them, not taking over their current roles until they were older. "Make sure to drink, too."

"Yes," Amina laughed, "hydration is so very important."

13

They ate and Amina discussed her day, running some ideas passed Lyria and getting input on people Amina could rely on and others who she might want to replace if she didn't feel the person was a good fit. They were finishing up, sitting on the couch drinking tea, when there was a knock and Aunt Betta came in.

Amina felt her emotions but there were so many, she couldn't pull out one she could focus on. "You have news about Eden."

Betta nodded. "It is good. Eden is alive. She is living among and as a human."

"Has she chosen to mate with one?" Lyria asked.

"No, not yet anyway. Her choice had nothing to do with a male, which I personally think is a good thing, and only to do with her own desires to start another life away from this one. She grieves but she is also content with her decision."

"I can't see her."

"None of us can ever see her again."

In that moment the enormity of the day fell on Amina like a tidal wave and, falling off the couch, she burst into harsh, deep sobs.

She was only slightly aware of Betta and Lyria sitting by her side and hugging her. Her emotions were so strong, so intense that she didn't pick up on anyone else's as she allowed herself to drown in her feelings.

Not even when her mother and aunt died did she cry this hard. In her grief she gave up singing, since she associated it with that night, but never did she allow herself to fall into despair. Tonight, falling wasn't necessary. Despair had been waiting for her and she let it envelop her.

She cried. She screamed and she rocked back and

forth. She yelled out for her sister and her mother and didn't stop crying until someone passed a crystal across her forehead and she lost consciousness.

When Amina woke she was disoriented and groggy, unsure of how much time had passed. Her aunt was in a chair by her bed. She must have dozed off while reading because the book was still in her lap.

"I'm thirsty," she said and startled her aunt awake.

"Oh, thank the Goddess. We were so worried."

"What happened?"

"You were distraught, inconsolable."

"That I remember."

"We were so worried. Lyria asked one of her assistants to bring a crystal with a calming potion on it but it knocked you out completely."

"For how long?"

"It's been nearly two days. Lyria thinks because your feelings were so intense, the potion was enhanced."

"They were. And they should be," Amina said, her voice becoming angry. She sat up and tried to get out of bed.

"Wait, *asteri mou*," Betta said, calling Amina her little star. "You haven't eaten and barely moved in two days. Let me help you."

"I think," Amina said, "that you have helped me more than enough."

Clearly not expecting her niece's anger, Betta took a step back. "What's wrong?"

"I cannot believe you are asking that. What is wrong? You knocked me unconscious without my permission. You shut down my grief, my emotions. You turned me off like some electronic toy." Her voice rose with every sentence. Betta paled hearing the outburst.

15

"I'm so sorry. We were concerned for your well being. You were so upset."

"Of course I was upset. My sister was gone, lost to me forever. The emotions swirling around me all day long were of grief and anxiety and confusion. I finally have a moment to take in all that has happened, all that *I* was feeling and you made me stop. You. Made. Me. Stop."

Betta tried to say something but nothing came out.

"Get Uncle Costin. Get Lyria. Get anyone you think is important to me and my well-being and bring them here immediately."

Betta nodded and ran from the room. While she was gone, Amina drank the water that had been left for her, then finished the entire pitcher and she slowly walked around the room. In under an hour her request had been granted.

Without preamble she said, "Don't you ever, *ever* take away my emotions or the process I am going through to deal with them again." She saw Lyria begin to open her mouth. "No, cousin. Not one comment. None of you understand my gift so I will explain it to you. I feel. I feel a lot and all the time, now more than ever. It is not easy to handle the emotions sometimes, but I am capable of doing so. However, you do not have the right under any circumstances to decide that what I am feeling is too much. I don't think you realize, but you truly could have killed me with your potion."

"It wasn't that strong," Lyria started.

"Which part of 'not one comment' was not clear?" Lyria shrank back and said nothing further. "Perhaps the potion wasn't that strong, yet it knocked me out for two days. Had it been any stronger you could have lost me. I am *supposed* to feel things. And since you were all very busy with your own anguish 15 years ago, I assume you didn't notice that I tapped down my emotions then. Well, two nights ago, all that I have gone through and lost came rushing back. I needed that grief, and you took it from me. You cannot and will not do that again. I will find ways to feel all I need to feel, to take in emotion and release it. You will never stop me or change how I choose to manage my gift. If I need help I will ask for it and if I do not ask, then do not give it." She took a deep breath and let in their feelings of shock, hurt and fear. Good. They needed to understand. "Do you have any questions?"

They shook their heads 'no.'

"Good. Please remember, just because you may be uncomfortable with the intensity of my emotions, doesn't mean they are not exactly what I want or need." She took a deep breath. "I assume there is food here for me to eat. Someone probably took care of that for when I woke up, yes?"

Betta answered, "There is."

"Thank you. Then there is nothing else I need tonight. I think you should all go."

They turned to leave but Costin stopped. "When do you think you will return to the compound?"

Amina thought for a moment. Part of her wanted to say "When I'm good and ready," but she'd put them through enough tonight with her brutal honesty. They weren't expecting it, and they would have to digest it in their own way, in their own time. In the meantime, there was work to be done. "Tomorrow afternoon."

She was as good as her word and after lunch she

17

was back in her suite arranging meetings and pouring through notes and letters of concern. Lyria came by toward the end of the day to make amends and to be certain that their relationship hadn't been permanently damaged. Amina assured her it had not. They were cousins as well as friends and she loved her always, but there would be serious problems in the future if Lyria didn't take her words seriously. Lyria assured Amina she did.

At the end of the day, Amina was starting to understand the priorities and responsibilities of her position. She had some moments of regret that she'd spoken so harshly to her family, but mostly she was proud of herself. She had never done anything like that before, never even considered it, but she was clear and it had to be said. She wondered if things would have been different for Eden if she had found a way to do the same—truly feel her emotions, release them.

Three days later, in a hastily created event, Amina officially bonded with the Stone of Strength. It was hardly necessary after what she'd been through and what she knew in her heart to be true. She was ready. She felt it. She knew it. She hadn't expected or wanted this position, but now it was hers and she was going to be successful and helpful. Unfortunately, that was also the night she broke Lyria's heart, but that was the occasional cost of bringing true emotions out where anyone could know them.

Her work was important. Her emotions were important. She intended to do this job and do it well. Feelings were powerful. They were her power, and no one was going to get in the way of her using them.

Chapter One

Present Day

There was a naked woman sunning herself on the beach.

One of the things Jonathan Barrett liked most about his morning jog was that it was one of the only times of the day he wasn't around people. His job as head of security at the Suadela Resort and Spa meant full days of talking, interacting with guests and worrying about their problems. Early morning was his solace from people.

But this morning there was someone else enjoying the sun and solitude. At first he wasn't certain what he was seeing, perhaps it was a trick of the light. As he got closer, however, he was certain it was a person and as he got closer still it was clear he'd come across a gorgeous, naked woman. It seemed wrong to disturb her, after all there was no one else around this early in the morning—most guests slept in after a long night of dancing, partying and hooking up—and she certainly wasn't bothering him.

The beach, which was leased to the resort, was dotted with furniture, some in groups, some alone.

19

There were cabanas for privacy and those who wanted extra amenities like televisions, and lounge chairs open to the sun for comfort, some arranged around fire pits which were lit in the evenings. For their more adventurous and outgoing guests, there were four-poster canopied beds. Public acts of sex weren't permitted, but almost everything else was.

Nudity on the beach was also not permitted.

Brian, his high school friend and the assistant Rooms Division Manager of the resort, told Jonathan this was something guests tried all the time, but wasn't allowed, yet. The resort hoped to get a permit for it in the future and if they allowed it prior to going through all the proper legal—and likely illegal—channels, getting the license could be put in jeopardy. Jonathan usually didn't believe in making exceptions, but the beautiful woman with the long red-gold hair deserved one.

She was exceptional. The closer he got, the more details he noticed. In addition to her beautiful hair, which rested by her side in a long braid, she had long arms and legs and he could detect the outline of muscles, even in her relaxed position, which mean she was in very good shape. Staring at her legs, he estimated she was probably about 5'8", maybe a little taller, and he couldn't help but think how well that could fit against his 6'1" frame. A lot of his friends preferred petite women, but he'd always had a thing for taller ones. Her fingers were clear of nail polish, and she had an astonishing natural beauty about her. All he could see that adorned her was a thin gold chain around her waist, accenting how small it was, how nicely her hips flared out.

Damn, she was sexy. Everything about her was appealing. Arousing.

But she wasn't allowed to be out naked on resort property.

When he was closer, he heard her humming. He didn't recognize the song, but it was beautiful. Clearing his throat and hoping not to startle her, he said "Excuse me, miss, but this isn't a nude beach." There was no response so he walked a little closer. "I don't mean to bother you, but even though it's early, you're not permitted to sunbathe naked on this property."

She took a deep breath which raised her breasts, which were full and real, but other than that she gave no acknowledgement she'd heard him. As he walked next to her, he saw she was lightly tanned all over, but there were no lines to mar the perfection of her skin. Either she'd found the best tanning salon in the world, or she regularly laid out in the sun naked. Something told him it was the latter.

Finally, he was close enough to cast a shadow over her face. She turned to him and opened her eyes. He was momentarily dazzled by their deep green color.

"You can't sunbathe naked here."

"I'm not naked," she said in a soft, sexy voice that sounded as though she'd just woken from a wonderful dream. "I'm wearing this." She held out her right arm which he didn't see before, he was too busy looking at her sexy figure, and the sunlight caught the facets of the jewels in her bracelet. It was as stunning as she was. Heavy but delicate at the same time and like nothing he'd ever seen before.

"I don't think that counts."

"Too bad," she said sitting up and turning toward him. She looked at him closely and he felt frozen by her gaze. Her body was luscious but in the moment all he could do was look into her eyes. Fathomless, and the color was like something out of a painting or a video game with a goddess for a heroine.

He didn't know how long she stared at him before she said, "Pain. Loneliness. Loss. Grief." She said each word singly, slowly. "I am so sorry."

Before he could come up with a response to her disturbing summary of him, she shifted to sitting on her knees. Then she raised herself up so they were facing each other and put her arms around him, then kissed him full on the mouth.

There was nothing hesitant about her touch. One moment she was looking at him and seeing into his soul, the next she was pressed against him, clearly not caring that she was naked, that he was fully dressed, that they were in a public place, or they hadn't really met.

He didn't care either.

His arms moved of their own accord and wrapped around her body. He pulled her closer to him so he could feel the heat of her skin through his shirt. He was instantly hard. He couldn't remember reacting to a woman this fast since he was in high school and had no control over his body's responses. But this reaction, although fast as those early days—if not faster—was different. Something in him cracked. Something in him wanted to open up and drink her in completely.

The feel of her mouth and now her tongue was beyond intoxicating. She tasted of salt and sea, of sunshine and something elusive and desirable.

She touched him as she kissed him. Her hands

moved through his hair, then down his back. One hand then stroked the front of his shirt, finding the skin where it was unbuttoned, while the other traced his ears, then his jaw and neck.

Sensations raced through his body and he was alive with awareness.

How could anyone kiss like this? He felt completely drunk and instantly sober. Aware of every muscle in his body, the air around him blowing over his skin, and yet his only focus was her. His will, his thoughts, disappeared. This is what it meant to be captivated by someone. For some reason it wasn't as upsetting as he thought it would be.

He'd had plenty of women throw themselves at him in the years since he started working at the resort. On occasion, when it had been too long, he'd taken them up on the offer, but more often he passed. He'd learned that quickie sex was no more satisfying that fast food. Fine in the moment, followed by hours of regret after. Not worth it.

But this? Now? Her? This was completely different.

He kept trying to remind himself she was a woman he'd just met, whose name he didn't know though she was draped over him, but the feel of her hands raking through his hair had his blood boiling and logic didn't stand a chance.

He wanted more. He moved his mouth away from hers to touch more of her, starting at her jaw and then moving toward her neck. At the hollow at the base of her throat he licked her, wanting to learn the taste of her skin, aching to know where she wanted to be touched, what excited her.

Her head fell back as he worked his way down to

23

her breasts. They overflowed in his hands, the nipples hard and responsive. He latched his mouth onto one as his fingers rolled the sensitive tip of the other and his blood surged as she moaned and pushed herself more into his mouth.

His fingers traced the sensitive skin between her breasts and he lifted one so that he could lick the skin underneath. A breeze came in and she shuddered. He could imagine how the cool air felt on her wet, heated skin, and knowing he was responsible for her pleasure was a heady feeling.

He touched her everywhere he could as her hands roamed his body, lifting his shirt out of the waistband of his shorts and sliding her fingers underneath to touch his skin. He felt as though he were on fire.

He wanted more—needed more.

As if she'd heard his thoughts, she pulled him closer and brought him onto the lounge chair with her, moving toward the center so he'd have room next to her.

He'd never known desire like this, didn't know it possible. It slammed into him with a fierceness which would have terrified him under normal circumstances, but this was about as far from normal as it could get.

He had to know how she tasted. All at once nothing else seemed as important. He put one hand behind her back and the other between her breasts and pushed gently. She stopped what she was doing to look at him, then gave him a smile that suggested she loved the way his thoughts worked. She let him guide her until she was again prone on the chair, then he removed his hand and went back to kissing her breasts, then moving his way down her stomach.

He bent and she allowed them to fall open,

exposing herself to the sun and to him. His hands traced the sensitive skin of her inner thighs. Her pussy wasn't shaved bare as so many women did and the soft coating of hair, the same beautiful light strawberry color as the hair on her head, excited him. He gently brushed his fingers through it, enjoying the texture and noticing that at the center, it was damp.

The brightness of the day made the slickness of her skin shine and he stroked a finger from her clit down to the base of her opening and to the beginning of the skin below. He was rewarded with a moan of pleasure and an increase in wetness.

Her natural and uninhibited response was as exciting as everything else about her. He breathed her in as he tasted her passion for the first time. She arched up and sighed when his tongue touched her and it was all the encouragement he needed.

She tasted of honey and salt and something that was uniquely her. Jonathan loved everything about oral sex, learning what a woman tasted like, what pleased her. It was so fucking amazing.

And this woman was one of the most responsive he'd ever been with. He wanted to devour her—and he did. While using his tongue and his fingers, he listened to her responses and intensified the things that made her moan or sigh louder.

Her orgasm was as natural and beautiful as she was. She cried out to a "Goddess" and he continued to please her with his tongue and fingers until her breathing almost returned to normal. She reached out to him and caressed his hair, his shoulders. He kissed his way up her body, loving the warmth of her skin, the taste of her lingering on his tongue.

He kissed her and she pressed herself against his length. Moving to kiss his jaw and then nip at his ear she whispered, "More."

He was on fire for her and couldn't wait to get his clothes off. His phone rang as he reached for the waistband of his shorts. Not only did the song ruin the mood, but it was Brian's ringtone. If he was calling this early, there must be something important he needed from Jonathan.

"I need to take this call, sexy," he told her, giving her a kiss. When she reached for him to pull him closer he stepped away. If she touched him again he'd be lost, and Brian could go to hell until they were done.

Done. What a ridiculous thought. He couldn't imagine ever getting enough of her.

"Just give me a minute." Less if that was possible. He intended to make this the shortest phone call in history. "What's up?" he said into the phone knowing no other preamble was needed.

"Got a security issue already. Some woman can't get into her room and she thinks her roommate is unconscious inside. Meet me as soon as you can at Room 306. I have a feeling this needs at least two people if not more to help, then to keep the stories straight. I think she's still drunk."

Damn, shit, and several other emphatic words rushed through Jonathan's mind. What he said instead was, "Okay, I'm on the beach. I'll be up there as soon as I can." He hung up and as he was putting the phone back in his pocket, he said, "Sorry to cut this short, but if you'll come to the resort with me, I'm sure we can…"

But she was gone.

* * *

As soon as his back was turned, Amina silently moved off the lounge chair and walked quickly into the ocean, transforming her legs into fins as soon as she could and swimming away from the beach. Usually she wasn't so quick to become sexual with humans, but there was something about this man that immediately touched her heart. His pain, yes, but also a desire for... She couldn't say what it was but the longing echoed something in her that she didn't want to look at too closely. Yet.

She swam to the Mediterranean because she needed a little time in the sun to rest, think and decide what to do now that Lyria was safely ensconced in some place called New Jersey. Although safe was perhaps not quite the right word given that Fiero, the sea dragon, was after both of them. She worried about her cousin and where she was staying. Unlike Amina, Lyria rarely spent time in the human world.

Amina, on the other hand, liked visiting the human resorts along the beaches and had even taken advantage of the amenities—and men—of several. It was like a buffet of fun. Easy access, lots of choices. This morning, however, she'd wanted rest and quiet. To be away from the to-do list on her desk and the restlessness of her thoughts.

And the near constant barrage of the feelings of others. She needed time to disconnect from the noise.

She liked to be free to do what she wished when she wished. Lyria was the serious one, the one good at responsibility. Amina wanted to enjoy everything she could. Her empathic abilities and the requirements of

Melusine's Band limited her life enough. She worked very hard to keep time to herself for whatever pleasure she deemed desirable at the time. This morning, the human on the beach was quite desirable.

When the man had come upon her she intended to dazzle him, an ability she and other merfolk had to make humans forget what they had seen, then slip away leaving him with the feeling of a mirage or dream. That changed when she looked into his eyes

She'd kissed many humans in her time, although generally, and unlike some merfolk, she wasn't attracted to them for any length of time. She found most of them boring and unaware of the vastness of the world they lived in. If they could have seen a fraction of what she had, they would be different. They were fun to flirt with and occasionally enjoy for pleasure, but no more than that.

But something in her was drawn to this human, and she wanted to know how his lips would feel on hers. It wasn't any hardship to kiss him.

Surprisingly, as soon as they touched something exciting and dangerous filled her with a yearning and she deepened the kiss immediately, making it clear to him that she was interested in more. She tasted his hesitation along with the salt of his skin and a hint of toothpaste, but that lasted only for a moment before he leaned forward and put his arms around her, drawing her close.

And it felt so good to surrender herself to pleasure. Along with her cousin, most of the last few months she'd been worried about Fiero, the sea dragon who was after the power in the three of Melusine's bands, and her time and efforts outside of her regular responsibilities were taken up with trying to figure out where he was and what he planned to do to acquire the bracelets and the women who wore them.

She didn't think it was abstinence that caused her to invite this man into her body. It also wasn't only because he was exactly the type of man she found attractive. What was it the human books said? Tall, dark, and handsome. He was clearly taller than her by a few inches and given that he lived on this island, the tan was no surprise. And oh was he handsome.

He was gorgeous and fit with dark hair that looked like it got in his eyes on occasion and brown eyes so dark they were almost black. The sheen of perspiration and rapid breathing from his run only made him sexier. From the stubble on his jaw, she knew he hadn't shaved yet that morning, and there was a thin scar on the center of his check about an inch below his eye. He could have lost sight in it had the cut that caused the scar been any higher. His lips were wonderfully kissable but didn't look as though they smiled much. The lines in his face were from worry, not laughter.

It was when she looked into his eyes that she was lost. Immediately she had flashes of violence and pain, both his and others followed immediately by terrible sadness and regret. She could hardly believe that a man with such intense emotions coursing through him could manage to look calm. She wondered if he knew how much pain he was in. It was the desire to alleviate his pain—not his incredibly kissable lips, honestly—which made her pull him onto the lounge chair with her.

His pain and passion hit her with the ferocity of a

hurricane, and she couldn't turn away. Usually she could control her abilities, especially around human men, but the intensity of his emotions struck her unexpectedly and quickly. All at once she could feel the ache and anger he carried around with him. As if that wasn't enough, beneath the violent emotions was a pent up hunger and need for connection she doubted he was aware of on any conscious level.

It was a need she understood profoundly, although not one she shared with anyone.

Once she touched him, all other thoughts fled and she let her body take the lead. It wasn't long before he had brought her to a breathless, crashing orgasm. She couldn't remember the last time she'd experienced pleasure like that, and she certainly had never indulged in so much with a man she'd just met. Or with a human whose name she didn't even know.

Her brazenness washed over her when he was on the phone and she was grateful he wasn't looking at her and couldn't see her blush. She may have always had a light tan, but her fair complexion made her rosy from top to tail when she was embarrassed. This was beyond casual sex. While he was focused elsewhere, she slipped off the rock and swam out to sea.

Amina put distance between herself and the beach, but she could still see him and had to admit to herself she wanted to see his reaction when he turned his attention back to her. Her eyesight was much stronger than a human's since she needed to see clearly underwater. She was more than a mile away but could read him without a problem. His body language told her he was confused, upset and then disappointed. She hated adding more negative emotions to the man's life, but it couldn't be helped. And although she was also a touch pleased at his frustration, this was the wrong time for her to be involved with anyone.

Especially a human.

She would never fall prey to the mistakes of her ancestors. Too many mermaids had lost everything due to humans. And Amina had lost her sister to the human world. Even now thoughts of Eden hurt and she still hoped one day she'd at least be able to see her sister again. But that was for another time.

For the next few hours she swam south into continually warmer waters and to the unchartered islands masked by magic off the coast of Brazil. She needed to talk to her Aunt Betta and find out if there had been any news about Fiero and what, if anything, they were doing to stop him. Not to mention if anyone had any luck finding the third band.

Amina, her cousin Lyria, and an unknown third woman were the keepers of Melusine's Bands, three heavy jeweled bracelets that, when linked together, became the most powerful piece of concentrated magic from their world. Melusine, dishonored by her husband, separated her necklace into three bracelets in order to protect her daughters. These in turn were passed down through the generations. This continued into the present day and the three oldest most direct female relations of Melusine wore the bracelets.

Somewhere in the last two or three generations, the third bracelet was lost. There were some who said this was a good thing, perhaps even what was intended from the beginning. As long as the three remained separate the power could never be used against the

31

merfolk. With one in an unknown location, they could never be rejoined. Unfortunately, when Amina was little, Aunt Betta gave the prophecy, seeing the bands either saving or destroying the Oceanide's world, depending on who controlled them, so it became imperative that the third one was found.

Melusine also created a legacy around love. Should a mermaid bond with the wrong mate, the power of the band would desert that mermaid. That was intended to keep the wearer safe from someone trying to seduce her simply for the power of the band, but it didn't always work that way. Once or twice a generation a merman tried to falsely win the heart one of Melusine's daughters in hopes of gaining access to the magic the bracelet held. It never turned out well for anyone involved. Lyria was the victim of an attempt when she was younger, and Amina had yet to completely forgive herself for how that turned out.

Of course now Lyria was falling for a human. It would be interesting to see how that turned out.

Lyria would never have met the human if it hadn't have been for the most recent threat to the bands. Fiero was determined and dangerous. He'd seriously injured Lyria in his drive to own them, which is what forced her cousin onto land. Amina knew he'd be after her at some point. It was imperative they know his whereabouts as well as track down the woman who wore the third bracelet. Amina didn't know which was the more important of the two. She supposed it didn't matter. The safety and future of their people relied on both.

Amina stepped into her home and unconsciously let out a sigh. She loved it here, surrounded by all her favorite things. Things she'd bought, found, and

32

collected as well as gifts given over the years. It was her space and it reflected all the things that were important to her. There were bookshelves in every room, most of them packed tightly, and each room also had at least one stained glass window which made colored lights dance around her home throughout the day. It also played well against the furniture and walls since almost everything in Amina's home was white. Lyria used to tease her about it when they were children.

"White is not a color," she said.

Amina would roll her eyes. "Of course it is. You heard what Mr. Empel said in science class. It's all colors. White contains all wavelengths of visible light and black the absence of visible light."

"You can't even wear it well. Your hair and skin are too fair. It washes you out."

Amina shrugged. "I don't care. I love how clear and clean it looks."

"You like that you get to say it includes all the colors. You hate making a decision and picking just one thing. It's one of the many reasons you are so slow to get dressed in the mornings."

That was true. Amina was terrible at making decisions. She could always see a reason for the other side or the other choice and if she could sense other people's feelings that only made it worse. It was particularly frustrating when she was out in a group and was one of the many reasons she preferred to be alone. Her empathy made it so she knew exactly how the people around her were reacting and how her actions were impacting them. It was a no win situation.

Amina learned ways to shield herself, but if she was tired or unprepared, groups were a disaster.

She stepped into her oversized bathroom, white of course, but currently covered with shapes of color that came through the east facing stained glass window. Yes, she'd just been swimming and was already dry, but she wanted a true shower to restart the day and help wash away the feel of her morning escapade. She needed to be composed and professional when she arrived at work. Right now she felt anything but.

When she got out she re-braided her long red hair and chose a comfortable outfit in a bold print. Lyria was right—white looked terrible on her and she never wore it. Even the jewel of her band was colored. Lyria had the clear Stone of Clarity. Amina wore the green Stone of Strength.

Amina gave herself a quick review in the mirror before leaving the sanctuary of her home and making her way to the judicial compound to see if there was any news.

Humans, she thought, would be greatly surprised, and probably disappointed, to know how much time merfolk stayed in their legged form and on land. Their bodies didn't automatically develop fins the moment their legs got wet. And they certainly didn't live underwater in castles and caves as they were portrayed in movies and stories. It was impractical. Gravity had a different influence on objects and not everything would stay put. And who would want to eat completely water-logged food?

In addition, speaking underwater was ridiculous. When she was in close approximation to other merfolk she could communicate telepathically, but beyond that it couldn't be done. Being underwater was lovely, but living there was completely impractical.

Besides, one of Amina's favorite things to do was read, and that did not mix at all with water. She would hate to lose her library or her time curled up with a book. That was one thing humans did wonderfully well—create stories, even if their ones about mermaids were far off the mark of truth.

Of course, she loved her time in the water, craved it if she wasn't able to transform because of other commitments, but it was, in some ways, the way humans loved their time in their cars. Great fun, even for long periods, but not a place to live.

Her fins were a means of transportation and freedom, a way to get to places she wanted to be and away from where she didn't. There were large underwater cave systems with air pockets that humans knew nothing about and where merfolk liked to go, although Amina preferred her island, a gift from her grandmother to her and Lyria. They both had dwellings there, far enough apart for privacy, close enough to be able to reach each other telepathically.

When Amina got to the compound she headed directly for the suite of rooms she used for her ambassadorial duties. The room was beautifully appointed in shades of blues and golds, something Amina didn't change when she took over the job from Eden, who had made no changes from how their mother had left things. Amina liked the legacy although she was trying to decide where she could add a stained glass window, something to make it personal.

As an empath her ability to not only tell truth from lie but also when someone was holding something back, when there was more to a story than someone was telling, made her invaluable to county and quadrant relations. Sometimes she checked in with her Uncle Costin, but today she wanted to be alone to focus on what needed to be done.

Her assistant was waiting for her as usual. They reviewed the day's schedule and Amina was able to get focused on what her priorities needed to be. As her assistant left, Aunt Betta came in. She kept an office of sorts in the compound where she met with friends and the wives of people Uncle Costin needed to see. She said that if she didn't have a place here, she'd never see her husband. It was close to the truth, and Amina enjoyed having her around.

They said their good mornings and exchanged pleasantries. "What can I do for you, Aunt?"

"I saw you walk by a little while ago. It looked as though you were floating."

"Floating? That would be an interesting piece of magic." Amina sensed the beginning of an uncomfortable conversation.

"You know what I mean. You were humming and seemed happier than you have been recently. You're also a little later than usual. I'm curious to know what the cause might be."

Now Amina did blush. For an empath she could be terrible at hiding her own feelings, and though she never sang anymore, she did unconsciously hum when she was happy or relaxed. "I spent some time relaxing on the beach." Her aunt said nothing. "In Jariz, you know, that little island in the Mediterranean, near Ibiza?" Still nothing. "Fine, if you must know there was a sexy man involved in my lateness and my floating."

"I had a feeling."

"That's my job," Amina said. "So what? I took a little time to enjoy some time to myself on a slow day and ended up making love with a sexy human stranger."

"That's a little more than a 'so what,' Amina. Especially with all the chaos surrounding Lyria." Her aunt smiled. "Okay, that's enough of the responsible adult talk. Tell me... was he very sexy."

Amina smiled and sighed. And then she shook her head to clear it of thoughts of her morning escapade. "Yes, but he's not important right now. He can't be." Amina didn't want to talk or think about the sexy stranger. She knew it would be hard enough to control her thoughts about him later. For now, there were more important things needing her focus. It was time for a subject change. "Is there any news about Fiero? Or our missing third cousin?"

"Nothing at all," Betta said. "And I'm at a complete loss where to look. Never before has there been a threat like this. Of course we've had our fights and feuds, some of them with kelpies and sea dragons, but this one is different. This is the one from my prophecy all those years ago. I know it.

Amina hugged her aunt. "I know you're scared. We all are, and I don't think we have much time."

Amina didn't like the sound of that. She knew her aunt still sensed things no matter how much she tried not to or medicated the feelings away. Ah, the wonders of abilities. They were almost always a blessing and a curse. "We will find him and stop him. You've given us your warnings, Lyria's in a safe place, and I am going to stay safe. I promise."

Betta left a few minute later. After lunch,

Amina's well-ordered day was thrown into chaos when a tracker naiad, on his way to report to Fiero was captured. He was brought immediately to the judicial area of the compound where Amina was called in to sense his emotions and if he was lying. Her uncle was already there.

"I know nothing," the naiad said, struggling against the rope that bound him the chair. One day, Amina would have to suggest using the human handcuffs. They were more practical, very sturdy, and didn't seem to cut into the skin the same way rope did when someone resisted.

"His fear and concern say otherwise," said Amina. "He's petrified and…" she stopped and focused. "Angry. Very angry. At you, Uncle Costin."

"I can't imagine why," Costin said sarcastically.

"No, it's not because you captured him. It's because—"

"You have *everything* when so many have nothing," the naiad interrupted. "Fiero will change that."

"Fiero wants control of the seas and doesn't care in the least for underlings like you. I would almost like to see him come to power just so you could experience how he betrays you all."

"He won't give us any specifics," Amina said. "I can sense that for you."

"Then we'll bring in something that will loosen his tongue."

Amina was shocked when one of her uncle's assistants brought in a truth potion. Compelling the truth out of someone was a serious and difficult choice, but she understood why he made it. After Lyria was attacked, it was clear Fiero was running out of patience and willing to do whatever it took to get the bracelets. Desperate times and all that.

They waited for the potion to take effect. Once it did, it was only minutes before they learned that after Lyria was injured, Fiero had someone collect the water with her blood and from it they'd created a tracking potion. It wasn't good news, obviously, but there was more. Supposedly on two recent occasions the sea dragon sensed something definitely linked to the Stone. The first time there was a feeling of panic, the second a sense of calm.

Amina knew exactly what he was talking about. She'd sensed the same thing and knew it was Lyria. She'd seen her cousin briefly after she went into hiding so she knew Lyria was safe, but the news was troublesome.

They didn't get anything else of use from the naiad. He was apparently given his instructions from someone other than Fiero so he didn't know where the dragon was staying. He was taken to the prisons and Amina didn't give him another thought, although she couldn't stop worrying about the blood-based tracking potion.

She returned to her office, but soon after decided she couldn't focus anymore and she returned to her island. She ate a light dinner, then relaxed on her couch with a book hoping that would help her fall asleep. Her mind was a jumble of thoughts. There was nothing she could do today, but she would have to talk to her cousin as soon as possible to learn if she was okay and if she needed any help.

Amina was back at work early the next day but

still having trouble concentrating. It was likely she would need to cut her day short and go to Lyria or she'd never get her thoughts to settle. Just as she read the same paragraph of a report for the fourth time there was a knock at her door. She welcomed the interruption. If it was a crisis, there wouldn't have been a knock. "Come in."

"I hope I'm not intruding, Miss. Your aunt thought you could use one of her special teas."

Amina looked up from her work and smiled. Because of the challenges of being empathic, her aunt had learned different herbal ways to help Amina relax and calm the thoughts and feelings that moved through her. Nothing to close off the abilities completely, especially not after her speech about needing to feel, but a way to soothe them and make living with the gift more manageable after particularly stressful times. "Thank you. Of course she was right."

The assistant put the tea tray down next to Amina, who took a small sip and finding the brew very hot, put it down to let it cool.

"Is there anything else I can get for you?"

"I'm good. Thank you again… I'm sorry, you must be a new member of her staff. I don't know your name."

"That's okay, Miss. In a few moments, you won't know yours either."

"What are you talking about?" But as she said the words she started to understand. Her tongue felt funny and a wave of dizziness passed through her. She reached out with her thoughts to shout a warning to Betta who was hopefully nearby and then focused on the intruder. She pulled back as though hit when she touched the woman's emotions. Hate, disgust, and a sly pleasure at Amina's discomfort.

And an image of Fiero.

A traitor in their own house.

"Is she ready yet?" asked a man from outside the room. A muscled man with blonde hair and a thin scar at his jaw line stepped into the room dressed in the clothes of a security guard. He was carrying ropes and something canvas Amina couldn't discern. The man, however and unfortunately, she knew instantly.

Wilmar.

"Almost," said the woman. "You're a little early. I don't think she drank enough. I made the tea too hot."

"Doesn't matter. As long as she's weakened I can get her into this bag." So that's what the canvas was. "Besides, you never were much in a fight were you, Amina?"

Lyria gave the scar on his jaw to him after Amina told her Wilmar didn't love her. He'd retaliated by coming after Amina. She hadn't heard about or seen him for years. Or would have thought he was anywhere near the compound.

"Why are you...?" Amina looked at the woman. She couldn't understand why someone who worked with and for the merfolk would do this.

The woman shrugged and answered, "The sea dragon has made many friends among our people. You've been too arrogant to notice the changes. There are those who don't like the disparity of wealth and power in our world."

"And you think Fiero wants to change that?" Even drugged and woozy she couldn't believe anyone would support that monster.

"I do. And he's promised Wilmar and me a substantial reward for bringing you in."

"Enough talk, Ulrike, Let's tie her up, bag her and get out of here." Well, at least now she knew the names of both.

Amina tried to move away but stumbled over her chair and couldn't right herself fast enough. In no time Wilmar picked her up and yanked her arms behind her. "I'm going to enjoy this," Wilmar said, and she knew he meant it.

She tried as best she could to struggle, adrenaline starting to take the edge off the sedative, but he doubled his efforts. She thrashed against his brutality which earned her arm another hard twist. The sound of the bone breaking was audible to all of them and she was almost instantly nauseous from the pain and knowledge of the injury.

"That's disgusting, Wilmar. Fiero better not be upset that you broke her wrist. If he lowers the reward, it's coming out of your half."

"Eh, he doesn't care about her condition as long as she is alive and his. Now help me. Hold the bag open so I can put her in."

Amina did all she could to fight against the two but in addition to being incapacitated by the drug she was given and having a broken wrist which hurt more than she'd ever imagined something could, every time they touched her she was struck with the intense emotions.

Greed. Glee. Violence.

She couldn't tell which one it was coming from, although she suspected the worst was coming from Wilmar. It was awful and more debilitating than the tea.

"This isn't working. Let's trade places," Wilmar

said. Ulrike stood behind Amina and wrapped her arms completely around her torso, caging her arms. Wilmar bent and grabbed her legs and got her feet into the bag which he started to pull up.

"Damn, this is harder than I thought. Next time Fiero needs us to get someone, we bring three people. We'd be done in no time."

Amina tried to thrash but the drug's effects were increasing and her energy was ebbing. What would Fiero do when he got her? What would her aunt, her family, and the other council members do when they discovered she'd been abducted? How could they find her? Amina tried to think of a way to leave them a clue, but nothing came to her fogged brain.

As the bag got to her waist and Amina was certain this was the way she would be leaving the compound, the doors to her suite burst open and four recognizable security guards along with her aunt stood there, blocking the exit.

Amina sagged in relief, or at least she did internally. Externally she was already sagging. The next few minutes were a hazy blur of fists flying, cursing, banging, a chair breaking and Amina screaming as though she were dying when one of the guards her Aunt Betta brought pulled her roughly out of the bag not knowing about her broken bone. Turned out the pain could get worse.

Amina was fairly certain she lost consciousness several times and she was sorry each time she came to. The combination of pain and heightened emotions in the room were overwhelming her. Finally, Ulrike and Wilmar were subdued and escorted out of the suite to the prison area. Amina was placed, gently, on a couch and her aunt checked her injuries, then carefully tasted the tea with the tip of her pinkie.

She brought the cup over to Amina. "With your permission, I'm actually going to have you drink the rest of this."

"Why? It's poison."

"No, it's a strong sedative and given that I have to call in a doctor to set your arm, you are going to want to be asleep or mostly asleep while he does this. Please, Amina, I know you're still scared. I can see your pulse in your neck, but please trust me, *patatina*. This has nothing to do with dampening your emotions. We need to help you physically."

Her aunt's pet name helped her feel calmer and she did as she was told. She sipped the tea and lay there wondering, as she always did, why her aunt chose to call her little potato.

Given the dosage already in her, it wasn't long before Amina drifted off to sleep. By the time she awoke she could tell from the shadows in the room that several hours had passed. She was still in her office, on the couch, but now her lower arm was immobile and pulsing with healing magic.

She looked around the room and saw her aunt dozing in a chair, a book on her lap. *Here we are again*, she thought, but this time the image made Amina calmer. Her aunt wouldn't be sleeping if there were something to be concerned about. She could feel the magic at work on her bones like a heated tingle.

Nothing like the ones she started yesterday with, she remembered suddenly as an image of her sexy jogger popped into her head. Well, that was a healing thought.

Amina smiled. She must be doing better if her

thoughts were willing to take her back to that island rather than stay in the moment where there were problems and concerns all around. She considered closing her eyes and allowing herself to fall back to sleep, but that would only be putting off the inevitable.

"Aunt Betta," she said and found her voice quiet and scratching. Clearly anticipating this, when Amina looked beside her there was a glass of water along with a sandwich, one of the more useful human creations, and fruit. She took a sip of the water, which felt cool and wonderful, and called out again.

Her aunt startled out of sleep. "You're awake." She looked to the window. "Sooner than I would have thought, although you never did like to take your time with anything and I was very careful about the amount I gave you." She smiled and sat at the foot of the long couch. "How are you feeling?"

Amina slid herself up to a sitting position using one arm and took stock of her body. "I think I have a few bruises, but other than that and the wrist, of course, I'd say I'm okay. I suppose I'm very lucky."

"You are, on a lot of levels, the most important being that you sent out that call of alarm so quickly. Half the council felt it."

"I'm sorry. I intended it only for you, but I suppose I wasn't being as direct as I normally would."

"No need for apologies, child. It was a good thing. Not only could we get you help, the judicial council was able to convene almost immediately and detain the two who tried to kidnap you."

"One was Wilmar."

Her aunt made a face. "The man who hurt Lyria and attacked you all those years ago?"

45

Amina nodded. "I guess he is still mad about everything. Even so, I can't believe he chose to be a traitor to his own people. They were working under Fiero's orders. They were supposed to bring me back to him."

"Yes, they told us that, or at least Ulrike did. That girl spilled everything like an overfilled pitcher until Wilmar broke away from his guards and knocked her unconscious using his own head."

Amina shuddered. She knew how strong Wilmar was, how hard he could hit. And how dirty he fought. She touched her side. Beneath her hand, under her dress was a two-inch scar. She cleared her head. Not now. Stay focused, she admonished herself. "Did she tell us anything useful?"

"Only that it's clear Fiero has more people working throughout the compound in different departments. He's collecting people, information, funds I assume, and, if he can—you."

"So what do we do? What can I do?"

"I think you need to go someplace safe. Someplace no one would think to look for you.

"Go into hiding like Lyria." She hated the thought of running.

"This attack within our own compound shows Fiero has more followers than we thought, and they can get to you when you are unprepared. Even if we are prepared. We don't know his methods. Security is creating a task force to go through as many people as possible, but there's no telling how long that will take or when it will turn up any useful information."

"So, I'm to go to a remote island and not help?"

"You could stay here under constant surveillance

to keep you safe. Round the clock guards. I know how much you'd love that, as well. Us always being in a defensive state."

Amina sighed. Her aunt was right. She'd go insane in no time. Betta continued, "I do have one recommendation."

"What's that?"

"According to your Uncle Costin, some of the best potions get their bases from a woman named Nerine. She is mermaid on her mother's side, lamia on her father's." An interesting combination. Amina tried to imagine what that was like. "The potion I take has, at its base, a potion of hers. She lives in a very isolated part of the Aegean Sea on an island she keeps very well cloaked and, in fact, rarely if ever receives visitors. She usually sends her potions out via naiads and water sprites."

"Great, how am I supposed to find her?"

"I'm going to give you a bottle she used and put a tracking spell on it. That should get you close enough to discover the island. Hopefully she'll let you on."

"What am I supposed to ask her for?"

"A potion or a charm to hide you and Lyria from Fiero. Something that can create a magical shield around you.

"So hopefully I can find her and hopefully she'll help. There are no guarantees."

Aunt Betta shook her head. "I'm afraid not."

Amina lay back against her bed, wishing Lyria were here to help heal and advise her. Her body ached and no longer in the pleasant way it did the other morning. Fortunately, that thought lead to another as images of her sexy lover drifted into her mind. She managed a small smile. At least she knew she'd be welcome where she was going. "So first, Nerine, then Lyria, and then the island of Jariz."

Not the week she expected.

* * *

"They were unsuccessful, sir."

"I can see that," Fiero roared. "Had they been successful there would be a mermaid in front of me. Preferably unconscious bound and gagged."

"Yes, sir."

"Can you explain what happened?"

"Near as I could understand, Ulrike wasn't able to get the Lady Amina to drink enough of the tea before Wilmar arrived to cart her away. She was only partially affected by the sleeping drug."

"So she fought back."

"And was able somehow to call for help."

"Amina's an empath, you idiot. It wasn't somehow. She sent out an emotional distress wave which was picked up by some other sensitive close by."

"Yes, sir."

If he heard one more "Yes, sir" from this idiot he was going to have him locked away. He felt a burst of temper building within him, and saw the sweat break out on the man's forehead. Fiero had a pretty good idea what his face must look like and what the man feared. He took a deep breath and heard his uncle's admonishing and commanding voice in his thoughts.

Just because you have the ability to use your temper and cower people to your will, doesn't mean this is the best use of your power. You cannot lead for long if you lead by fear and dread.

Years of training and discipline helped Fiero control his natural tendency to fly off the handle and get what he wanted by intimidation and force. Bullying, his uncle said, didn't make a leader.

Oh, but right now he wanted to throw all that training out the window, along with this minion. Just a few minutes of being able to lose control and rage at the situation and all the unfairness. He could break a few things—or a few people—and then then he'd be able to return to the calm focus his uncle wanted him to have.

Not being able to let his anger vent on occasion was harder for him than anyone realized. He'd made certain his Uncle Balban never realized how physically strong he really was—or how bad his anger could truly get. Fiero didn't know what would happen if others found out, but he instinctively knew this was something he needed to keep to himself.

"I... I... can try to find out more about what happened if you want."

Fiero knew the man just wanted to get out of the room with his life, and hopefully his body, intact. Taking a deep breath and willing his anger down to a simmer, he answered. "Yes, I want as much information as you can find. I am almost certain I know where the eldest cousin is, but I need to know what they are doing for Amina and how she fared after the attack. If she's weakened, we could have another chance. And I need to know what other precautions the council is putting in place because of their new awareness."

"New awareness, sir?"

Fiero ground his teeth. "If the two spies were

caught then members of the Governing Council know we have people on their staff, on the inside. They are going to be looking to find others. I need to know if there are people who must be pulled from their current positions and others who can be sent to replace them."

"Oh, of course, that makes sense. I didn't even think of that…"

"Now!" The walls shook with the force of Fiero's roar and the man in front of him went ashen.

"Yes, now. Yes." He didn't even try not to run out of the room, leaving the door open behind him through which Balban arrived moments later.

Fiero's uncle was a pure bred kelpie and even out of his water horse form, the man's strength, ability and cunning were apparent in the strong set of his jaw and the sharpness of his eyes. There was no love in this man, but Fiero had never expected any. Balban had shown him how concentration and resourcefulness could get him everything he wanted. He didn't need or want love. He wanted power.

Balban was nearly half a century older than Fiero, but like most Oceanides, he didn't age as those who lived on the land did. The man was still strong and looked to be in the prime of his life. Taller than Fiero's 6'2" by a few inches, his coloring was completely different from his nephew's—his skin was fair, his eyes blue, his hair light brown and worn tied back, as Fiero did. Fiero's father looked a lot like Balban, but Fiero had his mother's darker coloring and storm grey eyes. When he was younger, and shortly after Fiero's father died, Balban would tell him that he may have his mother's coloring, but no relative of his would have a mermaid's week disposition.

Fiero was the honed blade made in the fire of Balban's teaching.

"So we don't have the Stone of Strength," Balban said. Fiero didn't need the failure spoken out loud.

"No, but I do have a good idea from Wilmar where Lyria is so we should be able to get her in the next day or so."

Balban said nothing as he sat down on the chair behind the desk in Fiero's office immediately assuming the dominant position. Fiero sat in front of him.

"It's hard when those who serve are not as determined as you are."

Fiero nodded. "I had hopes for Wilmar, even though he is a merman."

"I know. And I agreed with your choice. His hatred of that family seemed almost as strong as ours, yet he failed."

Fiero nodded. "I am planning to get Lyria and the Stone of Clarity before the third day after the full moon." It was an important deadline. If he did not have the stone by then it would remain out of his reach, or so Lyria's uncle declared and magically sealed.

"Good. Once we have her, getting Amina to cooperate should be easy."

"And the third bracelet?" Fiero asked. "Do you know of anyone who has made progress in finding that?" The third bracelet, which held the Stone of Love, had been with an unknown mermaid for decades. Amina's family was looking for it—for her—as well.

"No, no luck there yet, but I have some thoughts on how to locate her."

"Anything you want to share?"

Balban smiled. It was worse than his frown. "Not at this time, my boy. You keep your focus on Lyria. Once that falls into place, other things will as well."

Fiero hoped so. He was exhausted from living with the constant frustration and lack of success, although he'd never tell his uncle that. Once he had the three stones and the mermaids who wore the bracelets, he and his uncle would remake Melusine's Band, then every race of Oceanide would respect them and their power over the seas. No matter how aggravating things got, remembering that always made Fiero smile.

* * *

With her wrist more healed than she would have expected, the next morning Amina packed what she needed for her trip to Jariz, taking enough for several days and plenty of money in case she needed things she hadn't brought or had to stay longer. Before leaving the compound, she exchanged the currency of her world for American dollars, which were universally accepted and valued in the human parts of the world.

She packed her bag with the kind of clothes and shoes she'd seen others wear at resorts, pleased that she already owned what she needed and reluctantly excited about a few of the pieces she might have a chance to wear. She added some earrings and was considering a necklace or two when she realized the one she always wore, with the charm given to her from Lyria's bracelet, was missing.

"Oh no," she said aloud looking around the room.

She couldn't imagine it falling off and she only took it off if she wanted to wear something else, which wasn't often. Then she remembered the struggle in her office with Wilmar and Ulrike. Damn, it probably came off then. She sent a quick telepathic message to Aunt Betta asking her to look for it and hold on to it until Amina returned. Her aunt assured Amina she would. Amina was glad to have that taken care of, but still felt rather naked without the charm. She'd had it since she was 12.

She magiced the bags into a waterproof wristlet she would wear until it was time to interact with humans, then she took a last walk through her home, trying to think of anything she'd forgotten. She was dawdling, of course, but she needed the time to regroup and get focused. When she couldn't delay and further, she headed out to find Nerine's island.

Her first indication that she was getting close was a dramatic change in the water temperature from warm to cold. She stopped for a moment, shivered, and allowed herself to sense the currents, as any mermaid could, so that she could follow the chill and hope it would lead her where she needed to go. As she continued a few miles in she thought she saw an island in the distance but if she turned her head the wrong way it would shimmer out of her sight. Assuming this was part of the cloaking mechanism Nerine used, she continued on following until she finally came within about a half-mile of the location at which point the island came clearly into view.

The look of the island alone was probably a huge deterrent to most people who found the place. No sandy beaches, no welcoming paths, no flora of any kind. Instead there were rocks and darkness and gloom, almost the cliché version of an old gothic island home. All it needed was someone leaping in despair from a cliff.

Once in the shallow water, Amina shifted to legs and then magiced herself dry and wore a simple dress of dark blue. Somehow wearing anything bright or floral seemed wrong. She walked around the edge of the island looking for a way in and eventually found a path, not particularly distinct, but enough to start.

As she walked further in, not only did it get darker, but the path, although now more visible, was laid with sharp broken shells, very difficult to walk on and something that would have been painful under bare feet, which is how most Oceanides walked. Some instinct had told Amina to put slippers on her feet before she started into the island, and she was grateful she had. It was definitely arranged to deter intruders. As she walked on, Amira reminded herself she wasn't an intruder.

Okay, she didn't exactly have an appointment, and she wasn't expected, but she had to hope that once Nerine heard the situation and how they were all in danger the other mermaid would be willing to help.

Finally, at the top of a hill she saw Nerine's home and couldn't help but smile. It looked like a cross between the houses on the Addams Family and the Munsters and for the first time since thinking about meeting Nerine, Amina thought she might like the woman. The building looked like nothing an Oceanide would create. She had to wonder if Nerine, like Amina, had watched those funny old human television shows.

It was the sort of house humans would expect to find hidden deep in a forest, except merfolk didn't like to be in enclosed areas so the house stood in the open. As she got closer, it looked as though no one took care of the place. If she didn't know better Amira would have assumed it was abandoned. This too might have sent visitors back to the water.

Nothing was going to stop Amina.

She got to the front door and knocked. Immediately a harsh wind blew in without warning nearly knocking her on her feet and chilling her to the bone. She was grateful she was completely dry or it would have felt even colder. The Oceanides whose skin was almost always damp, would be at a distinct disadvantage. Amina waited for the wind to pass before knocking again.

This time Amina heard buzzing. It was distant at first, then got closer and louder. Before she could decide what was making the sound, she turned and found herself fighting off dozens of honey bees. The animals of Earth interacted with all the other beings— humans and Oceanides alike. The flowers on her island drew all sorts of insects so she was familiar with bees, but these were loud and large.

And coming right at her.

Amina knew it was another illusion, but the sound and the closeness of the tiny furry insects unnerved her terribly. She did her best to stand her ground and the number doubled. Not knowing what else to do, Amina bent down and covered her head, nearly turning herself into a ball, trying to be as tiny as possible. She didn't move until the noise was gone.

As her heart rate returned to normal she had to

admit, it was a good trick, and if it indicated the strength of the magic Nerine had at her command instead of making Amina want to leave, it deepened her commitment to meet this mermaid. Clearly she had a great deal of power and if Amina could convince her to help, then whatever Nerine came up with could help keep Amina and Lyria safe. That was worth any illusion or threat Nerine offered.

In fact, it was time to stop dealing with these distractions and move things along.

"I am not going away no matter how many things you send to scare me," Amina called. She couldn't be certain Nerine was close enough to hear her, but it was a good bet the woman was nearby to make certain her tricks worked.

"I was beginning to get that sense," said a voice on the other side of the door. "Very well."

The door opened and Amina got her first look at Nerine.

She almost gasped.

Merfolk are generally considered beautiful by Oceanide standards, and even more beautiful by human standards. It was one of the things that lead to the legends of men being seduced to their deaths in the sea.

Nerine was breathtaking by any standard.

Full red lips that Amina couldn't help but envy, and the darkest hair and eyes she'd ever seen on an Oceanide, although at second glance she thought she detected purple in Nerine's eye color. She had pale skin, high cheekbones and, since her hair was pulled back, Amina saw ears that tipped in the tiniest of points making certain Nerine couldn't easily blend with humans. The only visual reference Amina could think of was a human one, one made more interesting by the house itself. Nerine looked like an exotically dark, sexy mix of Morticia Addams and Snow White. She was dressed in a simple shift of dark rose and had a shawl around her arms which she pulled close. Amina didn't know if she'd ever met a more beautiful creature.

It was mesmerizing.

And even a little disconcerting.

"Yes, my looks are a 'gift' from my father. Lamias are excellent predators and, generally speaking, all predators are beautiful." she said clearly noticing Amina's stare. "I use glamour when I must. Do I need one now?"

Amina shook her head. "No, of course not. I'm sorry. I don't know what I was expecting."

"A snake, perhaps. I can shift to that form if need be, but, as you know, legs are much more practical for getting around on land."

"Yes, they are." She sounded like an idiot. This was not helping her cause. "Let me try this again. I'm Amira," she said. "You must be Nerine."

"I must. I'd say welcome but you know that I don't really mean it."

"May I come in?"

Nerine took a step back and Amina crossed the threshold. The moment she did, the gothic home disappeared along with the dark clouds and cold temperature, revealing weather much more appropriate for summer in the Aegean Sea and a dwelling much more suited to an Oceanide.

Gone was the heavy exterior, dark woods and stone. In its place was sprawling white stucco home with blue shutters and windows every few feet. It was large and beautiful.

"I appreciate you being willing to see me."

"I think willing would be an overstatement, don't you?" Nerine shrugged and in that moment Amina got a flash of emotion. Sadness? Loneliness? Resignation? It was hard to tell because it came and went so quickly. Amina tried reaching out with her gifts, but Nerine put a hand up.

Nerine led her to a large living area with overstuffed couches in light and dark blues. She smiled to herself thinking her dress was going to blend in. Still, it was much more comfortable and welcoming than Amina would have expected after her initial view. It seemed in contrast to the young woman in front of her who kept her arms crossed and avoided a lot of eye contact. Nerine motioned for her to sit and said, "Don't try to read me, Counselor."

"You know who I am."

"Who and what. And what you wear," she said, nodding at the bracelet.

"Then I hope you'll call me Amina. Do you know why I am here?"

"Neither prophesy nor telepathy is my gift."

"Have you heard about the unrest and the new power rising in my Quadrant and elsewhere?"

"Heard, no. Sensed, yes. All, or nearly all, of the Oceanides have. There is a great deal of fear in the ocean."

"Fiero, the sea dragon, is making a bid for power. He wants the three bracelets held by Melusine's daughters." Nerine stiffened. "He intends to find a way to unite them and rule the Oceans by force. He attacked and injured my cousin Lyria a few days ago sending her into hiding. And I was nearly abducted from where I work yesterday afternoon."

"Why are you telling me this?"

"It is said your potions are the best for helping an Oceanide with what they need. In the past years your magic has helped my aunt manage, well actually, control her gift of prophecy."

"Ah, yes I heard about this. A potion of mine is mixed with something to give her this relief."

"Yes. Well now Lyria and I need your help. Fiero has spies, and because of the recent attack, he also has some of Lyria's blood which he is using to track us. I need something that will hide Lyria and me from him." Nerine said nothing. "Please."

Nerine sat silently considering, Amina hoped, her request. No matter what she did, she couldn't pick up any distinct emotions.

"I am well protected from you, empath. Stop pushing."

"You can feel that?"

"I don't have to. It's your nature to seek feelings in others. I wonder how you would manage without your gift. Would you be so comfortable around others if they were closed and unknown to you?"

Amina drew back. Nerine's words worried her. "Are you telling me the price for your assistance? You want to take my abilities?"

Nerine gave a sharp laugh. "Have you not noticed I live alone? What would I do with the ability to read others' emotions?"

"Then what is your price?"

Nerine didn't respond. Her face revealed nothing

although Amina thought she saw something sad pass across the other woman's face.

Finally, she said, "I know something that will shield you from Fiero and others who are looking for you."

"What is the cost?"

"No cost, but there is a catch. A side effect so to speak which will make you understand my comment about your ability."

"Which is?" A list of challenges ran through Amina's mind from the inability to shift from fins to legs to being temporary blind or deaf.

"Your gift will be dampened, unusable. Lyria won't be able to heal anyone. You won't sense emotions from others. There's a possibility of you sensing intense emotions from someone else, but it will likely be barely noticeable. If I shield you, this part of you gets shielded as well."

Now it was Amina's turn to be silent. She'd never been without her gifts, even before the arrival of the Stone of Strength. And she didn't know what Lyria would think. Of course, Lyria could decide for herself if she wanted to take the potion. Offering her the opportunity was not the same as making her drink.

Amina could say yes to receiving the potions and then decide later whether to drink it or not.

No, that was silly. If she accepted it, she was drinking it.

She searched her feelings and thought about the situation as a whole. She would be away from work and family, the people who needed her gift. No one knew her where she was going. There was no reason to think she'd need her empathy.

"Will the potion affect anything else? Like finning?"

"No."

"How long does the effect last?"

"I couldn't say." Amina raised an eyebrow so Nerine continued. "I'm not being deliberately evasive. I truly don't know. I need to strengthen an existing potion which is a general blocker. For that, the effect is short term, lasting about a day or two. You need something stronger because you are trying to block your full existence from others who are actively trying to sense you.

"Is that what you use to keep hidden?"

Nerine gave a short laugh. "Have you ever seen a Lamia?"

"No."

"Ever sensed one?"

"No," Amina said, never having thought of this before.

"My father's heritage comes with more advantages then pretty looks. Being able to conceal ourselves is one of them. I need no additional magic to keep myself removed from the awareness of merfolk, or most Oceanides. Not that many want to find me in the first place."

Something in Nerine's tone made Amina wonder if the woman's isolation was entirely desired.

Amina took a deep breath. She couldn't allow herself to be distracted by worrying about things she could not help. Perhaps when the threat passed she'd reach out to Nerine and try to get to know her.

For now, a decision.

"I can accept the side effects. I don't know if

61

Lyria will, but I want to be able to offer this to her too."

"Very well." Nerine stood. "This will take me about an hour. You are welcome to explore the house. There is a library down the east wing if you care to read and relax in there. Help yourself to anything in the kitchen."

Nerine held her shawl tight around her as she left Amina alone.

More surprises, Amina thought. Being trusted alone in Nerine's home. Of course, much of this visit was not what Amina had expected. She found a sweet fruit drink in the refrigerator, poured herself a glass and headed to find the library.

She was sitting in a cozy chair flipping through a book on American film when Nerine came in with two tear-shaped bottles.

"It's ready." She handed the bottles to Amina.

"It's warm."

"And the potion is active as long as it is. Once the bottle feels cold, the power is gone and it becomes nothing more than a sour liquid."

"You still haven't told me your price?"

"There is no cost to you or your cousin for this. The threat is imminent. I will do my part to help."

"Thank you, that is very generous." Nerine was a mystery Amina hoped to solve in the future.

"Do what you must to keep the bracelets from the one who wants to claim the power. That will be thanks enough."

Amina nodded, opened the bottle and drank the contents. It was sour, but not unbearable. She handed the empty container back to Nerine. When there were no obvious physical side effects, Amina said, "Thank you for your help. Oh, I'm going to be staying on the island of Jariz at a place called the Suadela Resort. It's actually not far from here."

"Why are you telling me this? Hoping I'll visit?"

"Of course I am. We can go bar hopping together. Maybe get our hair and nails done." Nerine's reaction was worth the saucy comment, and Amina laughed. "I've always found it to be good practice for at least one person to know where you are at all times. I know where Lyria is. My family knows I came to see you. Now you'll know where I'll be if they come and ask."

"Great, your family will be visiting too."

"Hopefully not, of course."

"Of course." Nerine lead her to an easier way off the island. Here was the beautiful beach, the soft sand. Much more appropriate.

Amina walked into the water, magiced off her clothes and finned. As the other woman turned to leave, she called out, "May I ask if you would do one more thing?"

Nerine turned back. "If it will get you to leave sooner."

"We don't know who wears the third band. Years ago my Aunt Betta's prophecy said that all three would be needed to end this threat. If you hear about anyone who knows where the Stone of Love is, please let me know."

"If I hear."

Amina dove into the waves and headed to see Lyria in New Jersey and arranged for them to meet off the coast.

The meeting with her cousin left Amina with

more questions than answers. As she left the Atlantic she wasn't certain what confused her more—the fact that Lyria had unexpectedly tapped into a deeper power of connection with the Stone of Clarity or that she was falling in love with a human. It was the power linking which she'd sensed those two times and assumed Fiero had as well.

Amina could see how much Lyria cared for the human she was staying with, although she knew the potion was working when she couldn't feel her cousin's emotions in any way. It had been both disconcerting and a relief. It may be risky to be without her gifts, but it was more important she not be found.

Lyria wasn't certain about taking the potion, but Amina couldn't linger. She said her goodbyes and was off to the Mediterranean turning her thoughts to the sexy man unknowingly waiting for her.

Chapter Two

"Sir, there is no need to scare your wife and children anymore. Let them go." Jonathan was exhausted. They had been at this for over two hours. The number of people outside the brownstone was growing by the minute. He and David Chase been involved in breaking up domestic disturbances in the past four years of their partnership, but never had one come to this. "At least put down the gun. We can talk."

"Talk? I know there's no talking. There's a ton of cops waiting outside my door to shoot me and neighbors and so-called friends waiting to video tape it and get it out on social media the minute that happens. My life is over, why shouldn't her's be over too? This is her fault," the man gestured to his wife with the gun. "My kids don't need to be raised by some slut and her new boyfriend."

"It's not true, none of it," she tried to calm her husband. Jonathan knew that was the worst thing. The man needed to feel in control, that he was right. "Please, honey, Peter, listen to the officers. Put down the gun. This isn't what you want."

"Oh, and now you think you know what I want. You've never known. You've never understood me."

"Sir, we're here to listen and to help. We want this to end as well as possible for everyone," said David. He was a good cop and trained in handling domestic situations. "Let us get your kids out, 'cause I know you don't wanna frighten them anymore. Please." The man was worn down. Jonathan could see it in his eyes. This is not what he expected or intended when the cops arrived after being called in by the neighbors to break up a fight. There was no telling how this was going to end, but at this point, it wasn't looking good.

"Kids, come here." Keeping the gun trained on his wife, the man hugged his son and daughter to him, kissed the top of their heads and pushed them toward David.

"Officer Bartlett, would you take Jenna and Christopher out."

"Are you sure, David, maybe you should do it." His partner had three kids of his own. He was better with them than Jonathan was.

"It will be fine. You take them. I'm sure there's an aunt or grandmother outside waiting to care for them."

Jonathan took the kids by the hands and walked them out and down the front stoop of the Brooklyn brownstone. As someone from Child Services came and rushed the children off to someplace safe, he took a deep breath of fresh air and prepared to go back.

That was when the shots rang out.

Three shots.

First two, then a brief pause, then a third.

With the sound of the third shot, Jonathan woke up yelling, "David, no!"

Tangled in the sheets and covered in sweat, he turned, put his feet on the floor and his head in his hands. It had been over two years and still the nightmare came. His heart was still racing and even though he was awake, in his mind he saw the images that greeted him when he ran back into the house.

It should have been you, David's widow told him at the funeral.

He couldn't disagree.

No one would have missed him. Sure, a few friends and fellow officers would have come to his funeral, had some drinks and toasted his short life afterwards, but no one would have really missed him. Only child, absent dad, drunk mom. Maybe his final and best foster mom and her son, Brian, would have been sad.

He didn't mind his life. He expected he'd have a family of his own someday and that would be enough, but David already had a family and now, like Jonathan, his children would grow up without their father.

The sun wasn't up yet, but Jonathan knew there was no way he was going to fall back to sleep. He wasn't even going to try. As usual when this happened, he decided to go into work. That was the advantage of managing security for a place that was open around the clock, every day of the year.

He went to the bathroom, threw some water over his face to clear out the last of the nightmare and looked in the mirror to see if he needed a shave or if he could get by a little longer without one. He decided he could wait.

Shit, he looked like hell. Tired. Old. Older than 31, that was for certain. He didn't think anyone at the resort cared about how he looked—most guests looked through the employees—but if he was going to keep on living, which it seemed as though he was for the foreseeable future, he really should think about trying not to act as though he were already dead.

Like finding more women on the beach?

Whoever she was, she definitely made him feel alive the other morning. Maybe he should think about having a social life. It had been a long time since he'd considered mingling with people outside of work. Maybe that was part of the problem. He could start going out with Brian and some of Brian's friends on the island. He was always asking Jonathan to join him, even though Jonathan always said no. Brian was a good friend. They'd known each other since high school. Brian went to college; Jonathan went onto the force, but they'd stayed in touch and got together when Brian was in the city.

Maybe he was ready to return to the land of the living, or at least the interacting.

With those thoughts still in his head, Jonathan got dressed, grabbed his helmet, jumped on his motorcycle and drove the mile to the resort.

"Hey everyone, surprise inspection. Boss man, don't you trust us to do our jobs?" said one of the night security staff.

Jonathan smiled. "What can I say? I love my job, and I have to make sure to keep you guys honest."

None of his staff knew what woke him when he suddenly showed up at work during the overnight shift, but he did it with enough regularity that it was a running gag. Better do your job, they all said. There was no telling when Jonathan would drop in.

"Anything I need to know about?"

"Mostly quiet. The bachelor and bachelorette parties got a little out of hand, but we were able to avoid bloodshed," said Mateo who headed up the overnight. "Quite frankly, I don't think either of them should be getting married, but hey, who am I to judge. I had my first ex-wife by the time I was 24."

"Let's put them down for a late check-out tomorrow, send a note to the front desk and let them know why, and hope they all sleep in and sleep it off before heading back to the mainland."

The island of Jariz was close enough to the coast of both Spain and Italy that they had groups of friends coming for one final pre-wedding bash on a regular basis. Jonathan had learned a lot of Spanish that hadn't been in his high school course since starting this job, and he was considering picking up an audio course on Italian so that he didn't need to rely on others to translate for him. Fortunately, most people spoke English, even when they were drunk. He'd gotten very good at speaking slurred English in his time there.

"No other excitement?" As he said it, his thoughts went once again to the woman he met on the beach the other day. Of course, "met" was a bit of an overstatement. He didn't even know her name before she disappeared. He'd asked around as discretely as he could try to find out if anyone had seen her and had looked closely at every redhead in the resort, but no luck. It was as if she'd vanished into the ocean.

Still, she'd left a lovely memory behind. He wished he dreamed about her, although his waking thoughts did drift toward her quite a bit. Her lips, her taste, the sound of her voice as she cried out her orgasm.

69

In his day dreams—and several fantasies—his phone didn't ring and she didn't disappear. He took her there on the beach, not caring who might catch them and then took her again after they'd rested.

His jeans were getting uncomfortable. He needed to change the direction of this thoughts and, perhaps, get away from others for a little bit.

"All the paper work filled out on the wedding parties?" he asked.

"Absolutely, boss," said Mateo. "They may not remember signing the pages, but since that room has video surveillance, we can prove it to them if they balk. Fortunately, there was no property or serious bodily damage."

"There was a little," said one of the younger, newer guards, "I hope the bride has some good make-up. She's gonna have some scrapes and bruises from the fight she got into with one of her friends."

"She was fighting with another woman?" Jonathan said.

"Yeah, I guess a friend said the bride should be careful what she ate or she'd gain back all the weight she'd lost for the event. Ah, drunken truths."

"They can get you into trouble, that's for sure," Mateo said.

"More good reasons not to over indulge. Okay, if anyone needs me, I'll be in my office getting some work done—or napping on my couch."

"I'd recommend the nap, boss."

"You're probably right."

He grabbed a cup of coffee from the employee cafeteria on his way to his office. Being that it wasn't a place guests went—when there were security issues, there was a room on the first floor off the main lobby where people were taken—his office was in the basement, where most of the inner workings of the hotel took place. It was a good-sized room with a round table with chairs in addition to his desk and the couch. He occasionally held meetings with his shift advisors in here. Mostly, it was a place to regroup, review paperwork and enjoy the silence. Four cinderblock walls tended to be very quiet.

He liked working security, liked contributing to a community again, even if most of the people in it changed regularly. In the nearly two years he'd been here, he'd gotten to know most of the staff, although they seemed to turn over fairly regularly as well.

His thoughts returned to the idea of getting out again. It didn't make his heart race or his stomach turn. That had to be a good sign.

Along with the fact that he was still semi-erect from his thoughts of his beach beauty. He could fix that by reviewing some of the resort statistics—end of month reports, upcoming guest numbers—or he could give in and take some time to fantasize about her again.

Pleasure won.

He thought about searching on his phone for sexy videos from pornhub, since there was always something there to catch his interest, but today he didn't need anything but thoughts of the luscious redhead with the sweetest kisses, succulent breasts, and a pussy he could lick for hours.

As he sat on his couch and undid his pants, he thought for a moment how amazing it was that a woman whose name he didn't know could be so completely unforgettable. But she was. He wanted her fiercely and he still hoped he'd find her again.

His cock remembered as vividly as his mind. He was completely hard as he wrapped his fingers around his shaft and held himself loosely. He touched himself lightly at first, not wanting to move to quickly to the end. His shaft was sensitive, but not as sensitive as the underside of the crown at the head of his cock.

He wasn't a very hairy man. His chest was covered midway and a dark line of hair went to his crotch. And there, for comfort because of the heat and because he liked it, he kept himself trimmed.

If he found her, would she like what she saw? Would she hunger and want him the way he did when she pulled him to her on the beach?

What would it feel like to her have her hands on him?

His cock bobbed up at the thought.

He traced the head letting himself enjoy every slow, soft sensation. Her fingers. Her tongue. The slippery feel as she lapped at him, then sucked him into her warm mouth.

He was so hard now. He turned to stretch out and leaned further back into the couch one leg in front of him, one on the floor. Spread.

God, he'd love to be spread like this before her. Letting her see him as he'd seen her. He wanted to feel her hands on his chest, her hair brushing his inner thighs.

He'd want her hair unbound when she was between his legs. He could imagine running his fingers through the softness. It would fall over her face, shielding her from him, but he'd pull it back so he could see her, see his cock sliding in and out of her mouth. Her lips wrapped around him. Her tongue making circles around him and she sucked deeply and heightened his pleasure.

He could hear her moan as he pulled a little at her hair, letting her know he was excited, that he wanted more. She'd move her hands to his balls cupping and caressing them as she continued to lick and suck him. Her nails would tease, rake over the skin, maybe along his inner thighs finding more places to touch him, finding more ways to create pleasure.

He imagined sitting forward a bit as she sucked, reaching forward to touch her breasts, squeeze them and pinch her nipples. She'd squeal and he'd feel her reaction in the vibrations against his cock.

Or he'd turn her.

Yes, he'd grab her and put her on top of him. Pull her legs to him on either side of his head, open her, spread her and dive into her pussy as she continued to lick his cock. He'd breathe her in and every time he licked her in the way she liked, she'd suck harder on his cock, take more of him deep.

He'd slide a finger and then two into her wetness and be able to see her stretch for him, get wet for him. He'd find that spot a few inches in, curl his finger, see how it would make her gush for him while he lifted up his hips under her slight weight and pushed himself wholly into her mouth until he could feel the back of her throat.

The images and need combined with the harder and faster stroking of his hand brought Jonathan close to his climax faster than he expected. His strokes increased. He tightened his grip, while running his index finger over the tip, lubricating himself with his pre-come.

He wanted her so completely. He wanted to please her and be pleased by her. He wanted her in his bed for hours, days. Until they were exhausted but still not sated.

He pictured her riding him.

He pictured her on her knees before him.

Every image was more exciting than the one before and he came hard, arching off the couch, yelling, completely lost in thoughts of her.

As his hand relaxed and his heart rate slowly returned to normal, his thoughts began to clear as well.

That day on the beach could have easily been her last at the hotel. She might have checked out only hours later.

She could have been visiting with someone and wanted one anonymous fling with a stranger to complete her hedonistic vacation wish list.

So many unknowns other than her name.

But the taste of her, the image of her was burned into his brain. He had felt empty and disconnected, angry and closed off for so long. Those moments on the beach changed that. There was magic in those moments with her, and he wanted to have it again. He needed to believe, at least for a little while longer, that she was still on the island and he could still find her.

Still have her again.

He sat there exposed for a minute more, then stood, cleaned himself up and looked at the clock. Plenty of time to have breakfast, work with the change of shift staff and have another nice, normal day.

He was going to do a lot of walking today. He would check every pool, club and beach. He either needed to find her or know if it was time to give up.

* * *

For her first few hours at the Suadela, Amina hid in her room. She sat on the beautiful, large king size bed with her arms around her legs and did nothing.

She was disconnected from the world and she didn't know what to do.

It was almost like it didn't exist at all, no matter that she could see, hear and feel it.

Amina didn't know how many times over the course of her life—and especially since she bonded with the Stone of Strength—she had wished she weren't empathic, wondered what it would be like to be normal.

Well she'd gotten her wish and for the moment it was terrifying.

She was alright at first, but as she checked in to the resort, things became more difficult. She'd registered under the last name Brookes and told anyone who asked she was a therapist taking a vacation, since it wasn't far from the truth. She stood in front of the very polite front desk person and… felt nothing. It was as if there was a thick, clear wall between her and the woman in front of her. She knew she couldn't reach out, and it wasn't as if she wanted to or needed to, but the fact that there was nothing there was odd.

And somewhat terrifying.

Amina's heart rate picked up. She wasn't exactly panicking. She knew what was going on, but it was such a strange sensation that she was uncomfortable. It must be what waking up blind or deaf must be like. As the bellman came up and offered to help her with her bags and as other guests smiled at her anxiety increased. They were just bodies. She sensed nothing, felt nothing but her own growing alarm.

By the time she got to her room, she knew she needed time to adjust and relax or she might stay behind a locked door for the next several days.

Was this how the rest of the world experienced other people? All the time?

Outside were all these people, having fun and interacting with each other and Amina was sitting in her room practically wrapped in a ball.

She was so scared, so off balance.

She wished she had one of her aunt's soothing teas. She could order some tea. Room service would bring it. But it wouldn't be her aunt's. And it probably wouldn't help. Because the only thing that would help would be to feel normal again and she couldn't feel normal again until she had her empathy back and that couldn't happen until she knew she was safe from Fiero and his minions who could trace her if she weren't being magically masked. Who knew when someone was going to tell her it was safe, and no one, not even Nerine, knew how long this potion and its side effects were going to last.

Her head hurt.

What did people do for that?

Deep breath.

She lay back on the bed and stare at the ceiling. How could she deal with feeling so cut off?

Feeling. She was completely aware of *her* feelings. No one else's. Even at the end of most days when she was alone, the emotions—traumas, anxieties, joys—of the people she interacted with stayed with her. But what she was experiencing in this moment? These were her feelings.

This was new.

And yes, it was scary, but as she took a minute to think about it, focus on herself, she realized that it was also completely wonderful! She could sense her own concerns, her hopefulness, even her desire to relax.

Her abilities were wonderful and most of the time she was grateful for what she was able to do because of them, but now she had a gift to give herself— knowing what she was feeling. Wanting. Needing.

Her stomach growled.

That one was easy.

And she was not going to order room service. The book on the desk about the resort listed several restaurants. She was going to put on something fun to wear, go out and enjoy herself.

Not just enjoy—delight herself.

She chose a simple A-line dress in greens and blues and a favorite pair of high-heeled strappy silver sandals.

It took a little while, and a few wrong turns but she found a place for a quick bite, then she picked up a book from one of the hotel shops and went to sit by the pool. The resort had a wonderful energy and the guests were clearly there to have a good time, nothing more serious.

When she mingled with humans she usually chose to go to resorts that specialized in singles. Twice she had spent time at ones with both single and couples—and twice she'd nearly ended the relationships of the men who were attracted to her.

There was some truth to the siren legends told by

humans. Oceanides' natural state was compelling and alluring to humans, males and females. She knew many mermen who enjoyed playing with human females. Not being ready to make a long-term commitment, to this point in her life Amina tended to stay away from relationships with her own kind. Besides she enjoyed so much of what humans created—music, fashion, and especially movies.

Lyria thought she was crazy, especially when it came to shoes, particularly high heels, but Amina thought they were fun.

She was also completely enthralled by the Internet. Her Uncle Costin had found a way to bring the Internet to the Governing Compound after she'd taken him to a human library and showed him all the information available through this technology. Not many merfolk or Oceanides used it, but Amina was glad to have the access. She used this to book herself a room for two weeks at the resort, which was another good reason to go to a singles resort. No one would wonder at a woman alone for that amount of time. If she needed to, she'd extend her stay, but she believed two weeks would be long enough to find out who the traitors were and get rid of them. Amina didn't always love the responsibilities of being Counselor and Head Ambassador for her Quadrant, but she also didn't like being away for too long. Hopefully Aunt Betta would send word sooner rather than later that it was safe to come home.

Now that she was making the adjustment, there was nothing to distract her from enjoying the Suadela, not even the emotions of the crowds around her since she couldn't sense them. It was a vacation within a vacation.

The resort was as beautiful inside as the arrangement on the beach promised. There were four pools, many clothing optional areas, clubs, restaurant and plenty of stores. It was a self-contained piece of paradise.

Later in the afternoon she took a quick swim, heading out far enough so she could fin for a little while before coming back and sitting on the shaded lounge chairs. She left the beds to the couples—and her memory.

That was the only downside. She hadn't yet seen her beach lover. She knew from the phone call he was an employee but their paths hadn't crossed yet.

As the sun began to shift lower in the sky, she thought she'd have an early dinner and then check out some of the evening activities around the resort. There was always dancing and other things going on and she wanted to join in. She liked dancing.

The front desk clerk recommended a restaurant on the second floor when she told him she didn't know exactly what she wanted, but hoped for a lot of different choices. Amina thanked him for his help and headed to the stairs.

She was almost to the top when a commotion came from down one of the halls. As it got louder, Amina knew whatever was happening was coming toward her, but instead of moving, she froze.

Suddenly a child, not much higher than her waist, came barreling around the corner and nearly banged into her as a hotel employee yelled, "Stop! Thief! Stop!"

Amina made very brief eye contact with the wide frightened eyes of the young boy who couldn't have been more than ten. The only emotion she got off of him was fear, but that was only from his facial expression and body language. Still, something about him touched her.

He needed help.

As he ran off, she did the only thing she could. She let go of the rail, intentionally missed the next step and fell down the flight of stairs.

"Jonathan, we need your help in the main lobby. Copy."

* * *

The voice on walkie-talkie was a welcome interruption. It's not that Jonathan wanted there to be a problem, but filling out reports and looking at numbers on his computer screen was rapidly driving him insane and if he drank any more coffee to try to stay awake, his eyes would fall out of their sockets.

"Got it. What's the problem?"

"We have an injured mermaid."

Jonathan sat there a moment, certain he'd heard wrong. "One more time, Carlos?"

There was a laugh and then, "Okay, she has two legs, but seriously, wait until you see her. You'll swear she's a mermaid. One of the island kids ran past her, and she fell down the second floor lobby stairs."

"I'm on my way." As he finished the sentence he was writing, Jonathan grabbed the walkie-talkie, his phone, and a clipboard which had blank incident reports. He sighed thinking about the additional paperwork this would mean.

As he made his way from his office to the lobby, he thought about the problems the island kids caused.

They were an issue not only at the resort but all the tourist attractions on Jariz. They ran around without supervision, begging, and, more often, stealing from visitors. They used to stick to the center of town and visitors were encouraged to stay at their resort and, if they left, to stay vigilant or travel in groups. Unfortunately, tourists not leaving the hotel meant local businesses suffered, which added to the problem.

However, in the last few months Jonathan received emails from several of the resorts reporting problems and violence on their sites. Since the opportunities to steal from the tourists had diminished, they were finding new methods to get to the money. Desperation was occasionally the mother of invention.

In addition, to improve their results the kids had organized into at least two gangs with young adult or adult leaders encouraging them to try new ways to thieve alone and in pairs or trios. Like Fagin's boys from *Oliver Twist*. Jonathan thought he'd left gang struggles behind when he moved from New York City, but clearly it was a problem in other locations as well. Where there was something of value to be taken, there were gangs to "help" the process.

He worked his way through the groups of people walking to different parts of the resort. Most were clearly headed to the beach or one of the pools, the most popular parts of the resort during the day. The clubs and special party rooms got attention at night.

There was no one at the bottom of the stairs, but a small crowd was surrounding a woman sitting on a chair in the lobby, a crowd of all men. As he got close he said, "Security, let me through," and they parted so he could see the injured guest.

"You," he said, spotting the woman from his morning encounter two days ago. His body tightened and he had to hope that seeing her didn't give him an instant—and visible—erection.

Seeing her sitting in his hotel was a surprise and a relief. And he could see why Carlos called her a mermaid. Her hair fell in loose strawberry blonde waves around her face. Her dress was a long cotton confection with blue and green swirls. Today she wore a little make-up which made her eyes stand out and her lips shiny. God, he wanted to kiss her right then and there.

She looked up at him with her deep green eyes and smiled. "You," she echoed.

"I didn't think you were still here."

"I wondered if I'd run into you."

They laughed as they talked over each other.

"Let's try this one at a time," he said. "I'm Jonathan Bartlett. Can you tell me what happened?"

"It was one of the street kids," said Carlos. "He ran right into her and knocked her down."

"That's not true. I missed the top step," she insisted. "Yes, he banged into me, but he'd already left when I went for the top step. I was watching him run away, foolishly not looking at where I was going and in these shoes, one slip was all it took." She held up her leg showing off a strappy silver sandal with what had to be four-inch heels. He would have commented on the shoe except the movement caused the slit in her dress to fall open to the top of her thigh and none of the men could manage a sentence or a thought.

It took him a several seconds to stop staring before he asked, "Are you hurt? Did you twist an ankle?"

"Amazingly, no," she said. "It's my wrist that got hurt.

Only then did he notice her cradling her hand, her left, not the one with the unique bracelet he'd noticed on the beach. "Do you think it's broken?"

"It only feels sore, or sprained. I'm not sure which."

"There's a doctor on staff. I think we should call her and ask her to take a look."

"I don't think that will be necessary," she said.

"I got this, boss," Carlos said, and stepped away to contact the doctor.

"Boss?" she asked.

"I'm the head of security here. That's why I was called first when you fell. Usually when someone gets injured or has an issue, they want to speak with someone in authority. I'm the first call most of the employees make."

"I see. It's not a problem, just a little tender and hard to move. I don't think I need any medical assistance."

"Doc will be here in a minute. She wasn't with anyone."

"I guess that decides that," Jonathan said. "Assistance is on the way. Do you need anything in the meantime?"

She stared at him without answering and he had the distinct impression that he *was* the answer she was thinking of. He certainly was feeling a growing need for her.

"I think I'm good for now," she said.

He heard a world of meaning in her "for now."

"By the way, I'm Amina Brookes." She held out her hand.

He shook it, feeling odd to be reminded that he had licked her to orgasm on the beach, but they never exchanged names. His tan covered up any blush that might have shown, although his naturally dark skin, a gift of his Cuban mother, usually helped with that. "Nice to meet you."

"And I'm Dr. Barofsky. Now that we know each other, everyone other than Jonathan can go back to what they were doing."

Jonathan liked the resort doctor. She was efficient, helpful and nothing threw her off her game, which was good because most of the injuries he brought to her were caused by drinking too much, which lead to some bizarre results on many nights.

"It's your wrist? Let me take a look."

Amina winced at times as the doctor palpated her wrist, but nothing seemed broken, which Dr. Barofsky confirmed a moment later. "Ice and ibuprofen should do the trick in this case along with a brace for your wrist, which I'll have sent to your room. And no more falling down stairs."

"Wasn't planning on it the first time, so I'll definitely work to avoid a repeat," Amina said.

"Smart woman."

"I think we should upgrade this smart woman to a villa," said a new voice.

"Amina, this is Edward Vickers, our general manager," said Jonathan.

"Pleased to meet you," she said shaking his outstretched hand.

"I'm sorry you were hurt. We've had an ongoing issue with the island children running amok through the resort. I know it's an inconvenience for our guests."

"Well, as I told Jonathan, that really wasn't the cause. It was my own foolishness."

"Nevertheless, we'd like you to be as comfortable as possible for the rest of your visit. I checked with our front desk already and saw you were in a regular king room. We have one of our detached villas available and I'd like you to enjoy that with my compliments for the rest of your visit."

Amina smiled at Edward and Jonathan felt of pinch of jealousy. "Thank you so much, Mr. Vickers. That's very kind of you."

"You're welcome, and please call me Edward. We'll have someone from guest services pack up the things in your room and move them to Villa Four. Jonathan, will you oversee this?"

"Absolutely." It was security's job in this situation to make certain everything made it from one room to the other, but he was pleased it gave him an excuse to check in on her later.

"For now, feel free to relax either by the pool or at one of the restaurants, again, my compliments, while we make this change for you."

Edward took Amina's hand again and helped her to stand. "Where would you like to go?"

"The restaurant. That's where I was heading before my less than graceful collapse down your stairs."

Jonathan held back the growl as the two walked off, and he was rewarded with Amina turning to look at him. When she winked, his blood heated.

Employees were not encouraged to fraternize with the guests, but it happened and as long as no one complained, management didn't interfere. Jonathan had rarely been tempted, but Amina gave new meaning to the concept of temptation.

He couldn't wait to be alone with her again.

* * *

As she sat at the restaurant and enjoyed a beautiful meal of sashimi, various dipping sauces, vegetables and rice, Amina thought about Jonathan. Now she had a name to go with the sexy man she'd enjoyed on the beach. She'd wanted to see him again and was glad to be right about him being employed here.

She loved the surprised, then delighted, look on his face when he saw her again. Holding his gaze, tinging her words with innuendo was so much fun, especially when neither of them could do anything about it. And she found she enjoyed not knowing exactly what he was feeling. She needed to read his facial expressions and body language like everyone else.

Yes, spending a few days here was going to be lovely in many ways. She continued to enjoy her food and people watch.

"Ms. Brookes, I am Hugo. The front desk sent me to bring you the key to your new room. The villa is ready, if you will follow me."

"I need to sign for my meal."

"It's taken care of," Jonathan said appearing out of nowhere and taking the key card from the bellman. "I will escort Ms. Brookes to her villa. Thank you, Hugo, we're all set."

Hugo gave a small bow and left.

"Here is the brace Dr. Barofsky recommended for your wrist. If you hold out your hand, I'll help you put it on." It wasn't as bulky as she thought it would be. Instead it was made of a flexible material that held her wrist tightly. She decided to try to bring it back with her. Lyria might appreciate seeing it and trying to recreate it. Jonathan offered her his arm and said, "Are you ready to see the villa?"

"As I'll ever be," she said and she wondered if he knew she meant for him. "Is it okay if I go barefoot?" She held holding up the silver sandals. One fall was enough, even an intentional one. The wrist sprain was a little too real since she landed on the one Wilmar had broken.

"Absolutely. There are very few rules here."

"Except for nudity on the beach."

He smiled and gave a small laugh. "Except for that, yes. The license is in process and," he changed his voice to sound deep and serious, "any infractions could jeopardize its acceptance."

She laughed. "From what I have seen so far, most people walk around nearly nude already."

"Yes, and they can be as nude as they want indoors, but outside the key word is 'nearly.' Then the areas are designated, although at this point I'm not sure why. The beach, however, even though the resort holds the lease on it, is still under the laws of the island, and until we get a special permit you have to wear at least something that could be considered clothes when you are there."

"Does that make it less popular?"

"Not that I've noticed."

"And yet you have those wonderful big beds out there. How can people not want to… indulge?"

"Oh, they want to, but public acts of sex are also not permitted—anywhere."

"How many rules are you going to break, Mr. Head of Security?"

"With you? I have a feeling there are a few more that are going to go by the wayside if I'm not careful."

"And are you planning to be careful?"

"Honestly, for the first time in a long time, no, I'm not."

"That is good to know," she said. He was so much fun. And it was particularly interesting to be near a man whose emotions she couldn't read. To not be getting impressions from anyone was unusual, unnerving and generally quite nice. Being close to someone was always so challenging for her since she was able to pick up on their emotions, sometimes even before they knew them. It made intimate relationships very difficult for her, and she'd taken very few lovers over the years because of it.

Of course, Jonathan's body language was pretty clear. He was walking very close to her, so close she was surprised he didn't put his arm around her waist rather than keeping it properly looped with hers.

It was enticing to be with a man she'd already enjoyed sex with and play the opening moves of getting to know him.

"This is you. Number four," he said.

"I am going to get completely lost when I try to come back here on my own. I wasn't paying attention to where we were going or to any turns we took."

"It's not difficult to get to the main building when you leave," he turned around and pointed, "since you can see it from here. And when you need to come back to your room, any of the staff can help you."

"Any you recommend in particular?"

"As a matter of fact, yes. But I'll let you guess who," he said with a wink. Before she could say anything in response, he inserted the card key in to the slot on the door and opened it with a flourish. "My lady, your new home away from home."

She smiled and stepped in. He didn't know how right he was about that. There was no returning home until she was called back so this was where she would stay until told otherwise.

Of course, that was not going to be a hardship at all. Her room in the main hotel was lovely. Simply furnished with everything she needed and clearly designed with the knowledge that most guests were going to be playing in the resort not staying cooped up in their rooms.

The villa, on the other hand, was a destination in and of itself. She stepped into a lavishly decorated living room with furniture in soft yellows and blues. There was a bar in one corner, an entertainment system in another and double doors leading out to a beautiful deck area. There was even a bookcase with novels on the shelves. Amina could tell from the names and colors on the covers a few of them were romances. She almost squealed with delight. If she didn't want to see anyone she could easily stay in here for the remainder of her visit.

It would be even easier if Jonathan could stay with her. He was one person she wouldn't mind seeing more of.

"What do you think," he asked.

"It's beautiful. It's too much, really."

"Well, Mr. Vickers wants you to be comfortable and since the doctor insists you wear that brace for the next few days, this should help with comfort. Through this door is the bathroom," he said and led her into a room almost as big as the original room she was assigned.

It was easily the biggest bathroom she'd ever seen and she thought the one she had built in her home was quite large. One wall was entirely mirrored with two sinks in front of it. On each side of the counter there were piles of towels. She ran her hands over them enjoying their soft fluffiness. She could dry herself magically, but there was something lovely about towels.

The shower had its own stall and the tub was big enough for several people. She looked into and was pleased to see it had jets along the sides. Both she and Lyria loved the pleasure of long hot baths. She was definitely going to indulge in this luxury. As traced the edge of the tub, Jonathan continued his tour.

"So, one door leads to the living room, and the other connects to the bedroom."

He gestured to the other room. They stood there in silence looking at each other, then Amina peered around his shoulder to look at the bedroom. All she could see from where she stood was a giant bed. *That's all it really needs,* she thought.

"Are you going to take me on a tour of that room as well?"

"In a moment. If I don't kiss you right now I'm going to lose my mind."

"Well, we wouldn't want that."

He leaned forward and captured her mouth with his. The feel of him, the taste of him, was exactly as she remembered, as she desired, and she immediately put her arms around his neck to bring him closer. He was a wonderful kisser and the moment she opened her mouth, his tongue found hers.

She couldn't stop the sigh or the desire to melt into him. Even more enjoyable, was knowing only her own feelings. On the beach she'd sensed his sadness and his need, now, she could only feel her own need and being able to concentrate on that without any other focus was quite a new—and pleasurable—experience.

She wanted more. Just as she hoped he would take the kiss further, however, the doorbell rang. "Hold that thought. All of them."

She stepped from the bathroom to the living room. "Who is it?" she called.

"Room service," said a voice on the other side.

"I didn't order room service," she called back.

"Compliments of the management."

To Jonathan she said, "If the management wanted to compliment me, they'd leave us alone."

He laughed as he went to get the door. "I completely agree."

A young woman who must have been in her late teens, but looked even younger, wheeled in a table filled with sandwiches, fruits and desserts, a pitcher of lemonade and champagne in an ice bucket. "I just ate. I am going to be 20 pounds heavier before I leave here.

"I promise to help you burn it off," he said. He leaned to kiss her again but they were interrupted by the squawk of his walkie-talkie.

"This is getting to be a habit with us," she said.

"It better not." He took the offending piece of equipment off his belt. "Barrett, here," he answered.

He walked away to have some privacy while he listened to the problem.

The young girl from room service was taking things off the cart, placing them on the table near the back door and putting other things in the refrigerator. "I wish they would stop doing things for me. The move to this villa was enough."

"I think Mr. Vickers feels bad because he believes the island child was responsible for your injury," she said.

"I told him that wasn't the case."

"He seems to think you're covering for the boy."

"I'm not. I'm a bit clumsy when it comes to heels and stairs." Okay, that wasn't true at all. Amina was natural graceful, but the fall was intentional and all this attention was making her a little uncomfortable. "Well, thank you for helping…" She looked at the girl's name tag, "Sofia. Oh, what a pretty name. I'm Amina."

"Nice to meet you, Miss." Amina didn't need her gifts to see Sofia wasn't used to being spoken to by guests. Most probably ignored the young girl, but there was something about her that made Amina want to reach out.

"Well, duty calls," said Jonathan coming back. He didn't look worried so much as annoyed. She could understand that. She was aching to spend more time with him. "I need to take care of things, but I was thinking I'd check back later this evening if the place doesn't get too busy, and see how you are doing. Unless you're planning to go out."

"I'm staying in. I've had enough excitement for one day. I'd love it if you came back."

"Good, so would I. Here is my direct line in case, for any reason, you need me sooner." She liked the sound of that. He gave her a quick kiss, nodded to Sofia, and left.

Amina was thinking of how much fun they were going to have when he returned when the girl interrupted the images flitting through her head.

"Is there anything else I can get for you?"

Amina blinked. She was thinking things she shouldn't be thinking of in front of such a young person. She looked at the array of food on the table. "Someone to help me eat all of this. This is much more than I need." Going with her instinct she said, "Can you take some of this with you? Take it home, if you want?"

Sofia's posture straightened and her eyebrows went up a little at the offer. She looked at the abundance of food with interest. Then her face resumed its calm, detached appearance. "No, Miss. If they find us with food, we are fired. We get our meals for free during our shifts and that is enough."

Amina nodded. She assumed the answer would be something like that, but she wanted to try. "I understand." She thought for a second and asked, "How old are you, Sofia?"

"I'm 20."

"You're lying." Sofia took a step back as though she'd been hit. Amina didn't know how she knew. She couldn't sense a lie, but there was no way this girl was that old.

"That is what it says on my application and that is what they believe here."

"Will you tell me the truth?"

93

The girl looked at Amina with such sadness. However old she was, she'd seen too much in her short life. "I am 17," she whispered. Then added, "I'm almost 17."

She walked over and took Sofia's hand in hers. "Thank you for trusting me. I won't tell a soul. I promise." There was almost nothing she could do for the girl so she went to her bag, found the wallet she brought and placed a $20 bill in the girl's hand. The American money would go far, she hoped. "Take this. Don't argue."

Sofia looked down and again the look of surprised delight crossed her features. This time, it didn't disappear. "Thank you."

As the girl left the room, Amina missed her gift of empathy. She wanted to know what the girl was thinking, what was worrying her, because it was clear there was a problem or, more likely, a set of problems, and the child needed help. She sat on a chair and looked at the array of food which was more than one person could or should eat. The fact that some were given in abundance what others needed always seemed unfair to her.

She furiously blinked back the tears that came to her eyes. She could not solve every problem, as Lyria often told her. Even now that she couldn't immediately tap into the hurt and concerns of others, she still felt the desire to help and the guilt that came with not knowing what to do, or if there was anything she could do.

At least, in this case, she hadn't hurt anyone.

Revealing the feelings of one person often hurt the feelings of another. One of the first things that happened after Amina's bonding ceremony was her destroying Lyria's relationship.

Because the bracelet had come to her suddenly, and because she was past the age of 18 at the time, it had been necessary for her to bond with the power of the bracelet as quickly as possible. The bracelet and its bearer were vulnerable until the bonding happened. The ceremony was scheduled only a few days after the bracelet arrived.

When Lyria and Eden had their joint ceremony, three weeks after the death of their mothers, it was tinged with the grief of loss, but Aunt Betta and Uncle Costin worked to make it special. They succeeded. There were more joyous moments than sad. Zia and Zan were honored, but the future was celebrated as well. Musicians and dancers were hired and a huge party was held after the ceremony.

It would have been impossible for Amina to create such a big event, but Aunt Betta did her best to pull together a special dinner and invite as many friends as possible on such short notice. She even managed to bring in some musicians, which truly touched Amina since everyone in her family knew she loved music.

She was sitting watching the others when Lyria came over, breathless from a dance with her boyfriend, Wilmar. Amina hadn't seen them together often, but she knew they'd been involved for quite a while. "I hope you are having fun," she said to Amina.

"I am. I wish I could talk to Eden just one more time, but I am holding in my heart that she is happy with her decision and her life."

Lyria hugged her close. "I like those thoughts. I will keep them for her as well."

A moment later Wilmar came over with a tray and gave a drink to Lyria and Amina while keeping one for himself. "All the best to you on this occasion and for the future, Amina," he said and lifted his glass to her.

Amina was hit with such an intense swell of emotion she'd dropped her glass. Before she could register the action and without thinking she said, "How dare you pretend to care about my cousin, you slimy piece of algae?"

Lyria stared. "What are you talking about, Amina.

Amina couldn't take her eyes off of Wilmar. "He is with you because of your power and the respect he has been shown by being involved with a member of the High Court and the wearer of the Stone of Clarity. He doesn't care about you at all."

"That's not true," Lyria said but her voice quivered. "Wilmar loves me."

"He doesn't care about you. He doesn't love you. In fact, he feels you are haughty and aloof. No wonder I've almost never seen the two of you together. You knew I'd figure it out." Amina didn't realize how loudly she'd been speaking until she heard the slight echo of her last words. The room had become silent.

"How dare you," Wilmar said. He put his arm around Lyria who stiffened at his touch. His eyes were so cold but Amina didn't flinch. "Everyone knows I love Lyria. We've been together over a year."

"Everyone knows that because you've made certain they only saw that." She swiveled looking at others in the room. She didn't know what she was searching for until her eyes met those of another mermaid. She stopped and pointed. "She is the one you care for. And it would seem, lucky for you, that she returns the feelings.

The other mermaid squealed as the attention focused on her and ran out of the room.

"I think that is even clearer than Amina's declaration," Lyria said. Her voice was calm but Amina could feel the storm brewing in her cousin. Lyria removed Wilmar's arm from her shoulder and took a step to stand by Amina. "I think you should leave."

"Lyria, you know me. She's lying. She's wrong."

"Amina's been known to hide the truth when we were children, but when it comes to emotions, she's never wrong. Leave, Wilmar."

Now the focus was on him. Amina could feel his anger and she was grateful for the crowd in the room. Her older cousins, Uncle Costin's sons, came forward. One stood behind her and Lyria, the other walked over to Wilmar.

"You heard her. It's time for you to go."

Lyria left the party a few minutes later and didn't speak to Amina for days as she grieved the loss of the man she loved and who she thought had loved her in return. Lyria was so upset, and tired of people trying to help her she left the area without telling anyone where she was going.

Amina knew it wasn't her fault, and she wanted to believe Lyria would have figured out the truth sooner rather than later, but, oh, how it hurt. She missed her cousin every day Lyria didn't speak to her.

The day after Lyria left, Wilmar found his way back into the Government Compound and cornered Amina at knifepoint.

"You'll tell her you were wrong, or so help me I will slit your throat, little witch."

Amina was petrified, not only by his actions but the feelings of loathing rolling off of him like a bad aroma. "You know I can't do that. She wouldn't believe me. And besides, it's not true. I wasn't wrong. You don't care about her. You don't like any of us."

"Stop doing that," he roared.

"I cannot control what I sense any more than you can control your hatred. I know only the truth. If you had cared for her, you would never have lost her."

"You are the reason I lost her. Lost everything. And you are going to pay."

"What is going on? What are you doing?" One of the building's sentries was nearby and heard Wilmar's raised voice.

"It's nothing," he said, pressing his body against Amina so she was against the wall. Making it look as though the display was affectionate he said, "The lady and I were planning a little get together later.

"It's not true," Amina yelled. "Get help. Don't let him leave."

The sentry ran off immediately. "You stupid krill!" Wilmar said. "You've cost me everything so I will take everything in return."

He pulled his knife back as a larger group of sentries made their presence known. Frantic and furious he stabbed out at her, dragging his knife into her side and pulling down. Amina screamed and slid down the wall. The last thing she saw before losing consciousness was three sentries bringing Wilmar down to the floor.

She was in and out of consciousness for the next

several days. There was no healer strong enough to help her in Lyria's absence. Finally, as she turned a corner and began to improve, Lyria returned. Her cousin had never looked so wretched. Amina could hardly stand the overwhelming feelings of guilt and worry pouring from her.

"It's not your fault," Lyria said over and over. "Do you blame me for telling you the truth about Wilmar?"

"No, of course not."

"Are you sorry I did?"

"I'm sorry that my feelings were hurt. I'm sorry that I fell for him, but no, I'm not sorry for knowing."

"Then you can't be sorry for not being here. Our gifts aren't perfect. There are downsides."

"That's not how I feel," Lyria said.

"I know."

And she did. Their gifts were wonderful most of the time and she loved what she was able to do and how she could help people, but there were costs.

Amina appreciated and accepted the challenge of being an empath, but since becoming the Lead Counselor, every time her gift put her in a situation to offer knowledge someone didn't want to hear she was right back to that first night when she'd accidently broken Lyria's heart.

Wilmar had never been seen again until the attack on her the other day.

A lot had happened since he was asked to leave.

A lot had happened in the last two days.

For now, Amina didn't want to think. Especially since there was little she could do with any of the thoughts or ideas she had. She found a romance novel she hadn't read yet in the bookshelves, poured herself a large glass of lemonade and headed out to her terrace to read and relax.

* * *

It didn't take long for Sofia to hear people talking about the beautiful woman who fell in the lobby and who was wearing a bracelet that must be worth a fortune.

"I'll bet you could buy a car with that bracelet."

"A car? More like a house."

"Do you really think it's worth that much?"

"Do you think she ever takes it off?"

"If it were me, I'd sleep with it."

"If it were me, I'd never bring it to an island like Jariz."

The employees were buzzing about the piece of jewelry and the fact that the woman was not only here alone, but now she was staying in a villa, isolated from other guests.

Sofia was worried about the kind woman. Amina. She'd introduced herself, offered Sofia food and then given her the largest tip she'd received in months. Most guests figured that all-inclusive meant they didn't need to tip, which was technically true, but it was greatly appreciated.

"You brought her a cart from the manager, didn't you?"

One of the other room service waiters asked her. "Yes," she said and tried to busy herself with preparing tables for the upcoming dinner rush."

"What was she like?"

Sofia didn't want to tell anyone about Amina. They would already be vying to take any future orders to her villa. Sofia wished there were a way she could warn or protect her.

The waiter, Owen, older and bigger than she was stepped in front of her, blocking her ability to work. She knew he reported to Elias, one of the gang leaders and he scared her. "I said, what was she like?

"Like all of them. Busy, distracted, and arrogant." She didn't like lying, but she liked them talking about Amina less. She wanted them to forget about the beautiful lady who looked like a princess and acted like a sister or a mom.

Sofia shook her head. She was being foolish. Had she experienced so little kindness recently that when one person showed her a little attention, a little warmth her thoughts went crazy? Perhaps, but Amina was a tourist. Here today, gone tomorrow. No problems, no worries, no cares.

"Well, as long as she's not someone who stays in her room. Judging from her looks, I'd say she's going to be very popular with the other guests. Judging from her jewels, I'd say she's going to be popular with the gangs."

"Mr. Barrett has taken a personal interest in her. He was in her room when I made my delivery. I saw him give her his direct number." And she thought given his attention to Ms. Brookes that she might have interrupted something more intimate going on between them.

"Fuck, that sucks," he said and walked off.

Sofia breathed a quiet sigh of relief glad to remember seeing the head of security with Amina when she arrived. Hopefully that would spare the woman unwanted attention from greedy employees.

Of course, it wasn't the employees who were the worst threat to valuables of guests. There were the sticky fingered children who wandered the streets of Jariz, begging in the streets and pickpocketing in pairs or trios who were a much bigger threat. Sofia did everything she could to keep her little brother, Raul, away from these gangs, but the older he got and the more things he wanted which she couldn't provide, the more they intrigued him and the more she feared he would join.

And tonight was one of the nights she wouldn't be able to watch him. She'd accepted a double shift. At her dinner break she'd run home, make certain he had what he needed for food and something to keep him occupied for the evening before rushing back to work. She thought of the treats Amina offered to her and wished she'd been able to say yes. She would have loved to bring something special to Raul.

Truthfully, she would have loved them herself. Sweets were one of her biggest weaknesses. Seeing the buffets laid out for guests or the desserts they ordered that went less than half finished always made her stomach clench. She snuck some here and there when she could. Everyone did, although it still made her feel guilty and poor. She wasn't a thief, but why should something go to waste when someone else—namely her—could enjoy it.

Shift change was at 3:00 and Sofia worked through it, helping the process from day to night go smoothly. She liked the room service department. There was just enough interaction with the guests to keep it interesting and plenty of behind the scenes work to keep her safe. She always made certain to keep the door open when she brought an order to a guest. Once she had forgotten and the guest, already a little drunk, had become too friendly. Never again. She would not allow herself to be treated like meat.

She took the earliest dinner shift and was home a little after 5:00, bringing her dinner home with her for Raul. There were always snacks and leftovers from events to eat at the hotel. It was important that he get enough. She spent a few minutes with him, hugged him goodbye—he told her on his birthday he was too old for kisses—and headed back for the rest of her shift which wouldn't end until 11:00 that night.

Then tomorrow, it all started again.

She was trapped in an endless loop and she couldn't see a way out. Was it any wonder Raul looked at the kids who were part of the gangs as heroes? She certainly wasn't anyone's hero.

Chapter Three

I found her, Jonathan thought. Or she had found him. It didn't matter. She was here. Actually, when he checked her records, now that he knew her name, it stated she'd come back, not still been here, because her check in date was only the day before. No matter. She was here now.

He'd been so concerned when he discovered she was the woman who'd been injured. She could have insisted on leaving immediately. Although he wouldn't have wanted her to get hurt, the move from the main hotel to one of the villas was perfect. It was isolated enough that he wouldn't be seen coming or going.

As an added bonus, they wouldn't be bothering any neighbors when she called out his name when she came, because, damn, he intended to please her until she screamed.

He flew through the rest of his responsibilities for the day and realized there was no reason he couldn't be done early. Not only was he the boss, but he'd been on site since 5:00 that morning. The nightmare that woke him and brought him to work early seemed far away.

And Amina was close. Very, very close.

Her name was as beautiful as she was. He'd never heard it before, but then again he'd never met anyone like her. She sat there in the lobby with people falling over themselves to help her and not once did she seem egotistical or entitled as so many of their guests did. Room service arrived and she was flattered. She didn't expect or want the extra attention at all.

Of course, that had nothing to do with the extra attention she was going to get from him. That they seemed to both want.

He winced. Oh my God, he was thinking and acting like a horny teen. If he didn't get it under control he was going to make a fool of himself when he went back to see her.

But damn, the woman could kiss. When his lips met hers, something in him ignited. And it was more than just the pleasure of the kiss. It was the relief. The knowing that she was back in his arms and wanted him again.

He hadn't dreamed her or her desire for him.

Shutting down his computer and knowing he wouldn't be in early the next day, he let the night staff know he was off the clock and then headed to one of the stores on the property that catered to supporting the guests' various sexual indulgences. He wasn't looking for toys or anything to enhance the experience. Amina was enough for that, but he did need condoms since it wasn't something he automatically carried with him, although it was a running joke that they should be left out in bowls at the bar like peanuts.

It had been a while since he'd been in this store. They had quite an inventory. Lubricants of all types and flavors, massage oils—he decided to make note of that for later—and a condom selection that could almost be called a buffet. Jonathan didn't know they made so many types. Ribbed and lubricated yes. Tingling, studded and edible were new to him. And *why* anyone would want an edible condom was beyond him.

He finally found a familiar brand, bought a box, accepted a wink from the sales girl and headed to Villa Four. He knocked but there was no answer, nor when he rang the bell. Thinking she may have decided to use the tub which she'd looked at longingly, he used his key card and let himself in.

"Amina?" he called. He didn't want to upset or frighten her. She did expect him to come back.

Right?

He growled at himself and told the teenager who clearly still lived in his head to shut up.

He was about to check the bathroom when he heard humming. The same humming he'd heard when he found her on the beach. He followed the sound out to the terrace where he discovered her reading and sipping lemonade. She was the picture of beauty and serenity. He almost didn't want to disturb her.

This time she was dressed. For now.

"Knock, knock," he said.

She startled only a little, then looked up at him with a huge smile. "Hello there, Jonathan. Welcome back." She put the drink and the book down, stood and wrapped herself around him. He tasted the tartness of the lemons and the sweetness of her and was completely lost. He was never going to get over how her kisses set him on fire.

"Did you have a good rest of your day?" she asked as she broke the kiss.

"I did. No more ladies tumbling down stairs."

"Oh good, I would hate to think you had to go check on someone else this evening."

"No, only you."

She gave him a knowing look and then kissed him again, moving from his lips to his jaw, standing on tiptoe to kiss his ears, which were quite sensitive, and then to his neck and the open space of his shirt.

"We are going to make for quite a spectacle if we stay on the terrace," he said.

"It doesn't look like anyone can see us, there are all these bushes. And just a few days ago we were quite out in the open."

"Yes, and if you remember, I told you then that public acts of sex were not permitted."

"And if you remember, we broke that rule a few minutes later."

He laughed. "That is true. Still, I think I'd like to know that I'm truly alone with you and that we can't be interrupted."

"Is your phone off?"

"It is," he said.

"No walkie-talkie?"

"Nope, turned it in for the day."

"Then I think we finally have a chance."

"Best news I've had all day," he said. He kissed her again and didn't stop as he walked her back into the villa. He stopped for a moment to make certain the back door was locked—couldn't turn off years of police training—and then continued kissing her as he unbuttoned and took off his shirt and started undoing his belt.

"So many pieces to what you're wearing. For me

107

it's easy." And she pulled up the hem of her dress, then pulled the whole thing over her head. She was naked in an instant. "See? All done."

God, he wanted to devour her. Instead, he did the next best thing. He grabbed her by the hips, picked her up and brought her directly to the bedroom where he deposited her in the center of the bed.

He kicked off his shoes and she undid the button and then the zipper on his pants. As soon as he was naked he joined her on the bed.

Finally.

Finally, he was naked with her. Finally, he was next to her. The only thing he wanted more was to be in her. Was it possible for a man to die of desire? He thanked God for a healthy heart and steady blood pressure.

Then he stopped being capable of reasonable thought as she once again stopped kissing his lips to kiss her way down his body. Her hands were everywhere. His chest, his arms, his thighs and then, just a whisper, over his cock.

He moaned.

Fuck it, he was going to die here and he didn't care at all.

* * *

Amina loved the feel of him. He was all muscles and heat, strong hands and tan skin from the sun. Tan lines on his arms and legs because he worked. She kissed and licked at him, getting to know more of how he felt, how he tasted.

Of course there was one way in particular she

wanted to know how he tasted and as she worked her way lower down his chest, she stopped him as he sat up. "Lay back, Jonathan. Let me please you as you did for me."

The look on his face was exciting. His longing, his hunger.

She kissed and licked her way down his body, feeling him tense when she touched some spots, sighing at others. And when she wrapped her hand around his cock, his moan bathed over her, thrilling her.

Never before had she had an opportunity like this, never had she enjoyed sex with another person without sensing their emotions. They either mixed with hers or conflicted with hers, and neither made the experience as pleasurable as she wanted. Once she'd tried a stronger dampening tea, but it dulled everything and neither she nor her partner enjoyed anything that evening.

Tonight, and Jonathan, were magical. For as long as Nerine's potion lasted she had only her feelings in her mind and body and she could focus on something other than those. She could focus on her partner. On him, this man who had brought her such unquestioning pleasure the other morning.

Now she could do the same, she hoped, for him.

Her mouth joined her hands on his cock and she listened as his moans got louder. She ran her tongue around the tip and was rewarded with a drop of liquid. She licked and got her first true taste of him. Salty, smooth. Indefinable and unique to him.

She opened her lips and took more of him into her mouth, letting her tongue continue to swirl around the crown of his cock, while her hand stroked the base, where she let her fingers caress his balls and the sensitive skin beneath them. His hands reached out and ran through her hair, stroked her jaw, feeling what she was doing to him. It sent tingles through her body. She loved being connected by touch.

Each time she did something he particularly enjoyed, he moaned or lifted his hips so she knew how to please him more.

He hardened more as she continued to lick and suck. She thought he was getting close to his climax when he reached out and touched her shoulders.

"Don't, don't make me come like this. I want to be in you. I want to look into your eyes."

She reluctantly stopped what she was doing and kissed her way up his body. "You are lucky that sounds so appealing. I will finish what I started that way some day."

"Someday I won't stop you, but for now, come here."

She smiled and lay on top of him, kissing him deeply. "I'm here."

"And I am so very grateful."

He rolled her to the side then reached over her to the floor to find his pants. He brought out a box of condoms and took one out. She'd seen them before. She smiled at his thoughtfulness. She couldn't tell him she was not fertile at this time and since she wasn't human there was no way to pass anything between them. He wanted to protect her. There was something wonderful about that.

He took out the small circle from the package and she took it from him.

"I'll do that," she said and she placed the condom on the sensitive tip of his cock and then rolled it down slowly. Very slowly.

"You're trying to kill me."

"No, I'm not. That would have a terrible impact on what's going to happen next."

"Very true," he said and he reached between them, between her legs and traced the opening of pussy. "You are so wet."

"I want you as much as you want me, and pleasing you was very exciting."

He continued to touch her, making her wetter, making her want. Deciding two could play at that game, she ran her hands around and beneath his balls.

"I can't wait any longer. Please tell me you can't either."

She didn't answer. Words seemed unnecessary. Instead she pulled him on top of her and let her legs fall apart.

He kissed her deeply, his hands stroking her sides, caressing her breasts. She wrapped one leg around him, reached down and guided the tip of his cock to her opening, then teased them both by running the tip of him against her folds. She shivered. No, she didn't want to wait.

She released him and he slid into her, slowly at first then completely.

By the Goddess he felt good. She arched to take more of him, all of him.

"Yes, Amina, yes," he said then called out to his own deity. His head fell forward and he kissed her breasts, sucked deeply at her nipples. She squealed. "Sensitive there, are you?"

"Very," she said.

"Shall I be gentle then, or a little rougher?"

"Rougher." And he did as she asked, sucking hard on one nipple while pinching the other. The shivers it sent through her were indescribable and she felt her pussy contract then bathe his cock. In response he increased the speed of his thrusts. She loved how aware he was of her, of what pleased her.

She was so hungry to touch and be touched. Not having extra emotions interfere with her pleasure was more exciting than she ever imagined. She touched him everywhere she could reach running her hand down his face and chest, mimicking some of the things he did by teasing the tip of his hardened nipples with her finger.

"Amina," he said and kissed her before continuing, "I hope this will be the first of many times together especially since tonight I am so turned on, so fucking hungry for you, I don't think I can make this last."

She smiled liking the addition of the human curse. She understood what he meant. "I think this pace is just perfect for tonight."

He returned to kissing her but this time he slid a hand between them and found her hardened clitoris. She gasped against his mouth as he continued to stimulate her. "You don't want me to last either," she said. She liked how breathless she sounded.

"I figured if I was going to go over the top, we ought to go together."

"Yes, let's."

And they did. Her climax built quickly as he continued to use her wetness to create slick circles against her clit. "Oh yes," she cried as her orgasm built. "Move your hand."

He did as she asked, and she wrapped both legs around him, pulling him as close and as deep as she could. Raising her hips to meet his thrusts. Taking all of him into her.

"Amina, I can't stop."

"Don't," was all she managed before her climax hit her and she called out his name as she raked her nails down his back.

"God, yes," he yelled and his climax followed shortly after, her name on his lips.

They continued moving together for a few minutes more then he eased himself out of her and to the side and brought her close, kissing her, stroking her shoulders and down her arms. She shivered. Every part of her was sensitive.

Alive.

And she relished it all.

"Give me a moment, beauty," he said and kissed her as he got out of bed. She wondered what he was doing until she heard the water running in the bathroom. When he came back, he was carrying something.

"What's that?"

"For you. To make you more comfortable."

She gasped then sighed as he pressed a warm washcloth to her pussy. "That feels wonderful."

"You've never had a partner do that?"

"No," she said but she would be certain they did going forward.

"Just a little something my foster brother, Brian, told me when he taught me about women. The basics of sex and not getting a woman pregnant I learned from whichever adult was willing to talk about it, but it was Brian who gave me the information I really needed. Including how to care for a woman after sex."

"Are you two still close?"

"Yes, as a matter of fact we are. He works here. He got me my job here."

"Well then please thank him for me the next time you talk."

Jonathan laughed. "I will and I'm not just saying that because I think he'll get a kick out of knowing I was listening." When he was done, he put the washcloth on the nightstand.

The breeze from the room's overhead fan touched her skin, now wet in spots and she shivered, "Shall we get under the covers," he asked.

"I think so."

She put her head just below his shoulder, above his heart. "I'm so glad I came back," she said.

"That's an understatement for me. I've been looking for you since that morning."

"Well, here I am."

"Why did you come back? Not enough vacation the first time?"

"Something like that. It was necessary to cut my visit short, but I also needed the rest of my vacation." It was only a little lie.

Amina couldn't remember the last time she felt so relaxed. And satisfied.

They lay there for a while, not talking, just enjoying each other's nearness. When she yawned he asked, "Do you want me to go? I could stop by tomorrow and see how you're doing."

He continued to be so considerate. She didn't need her gift to know what he wanted. It was the same as what she wanted. "Stay," she said.

And he did.

* * *

Amina!

It was after midnight when Amina heard Lyria's call.

That's not possible, she thought, but as soon as the thought completed, she heard Lyria's voice again.

Where are you? It was definitely Lyria's voice. Something must be wrong. *Can you hear me?*

I can, Amina thought, not understanding how it was possible.

Are you safe?

She looked at Jonathan, sleeping soundly, and the bracelet on her wrist where it belonged. *Yes, I'm fine, but how are you doing this? I am too far away and took Nerine's potion. This shouldn't be possible.*

You would be amazed at what I have discovered is possible. The Stone of Clarity has given me a gift. Fiero claimed he captured you. He had your necklace.

Bastard. She should have known. *Wilmar took it. It was lost when I was almost abducted. The Stone gave you a gift?*

I will explain at another time, just know that I am safe and have nothing to fear from the sea dragon any more. Stay where you are and let me know if you need me.

I will. Be well.

And you.

115

The connection was broken. Lyria was gone, but Amina knew her cousin was safe. It was a huge relief and she relaxed in a way she hadn't been able to in weeks. She curled under the covers, got closer to Jonathan and fell back to sleep.

* * *

He had woken up with a goddess in his arms. Sometime in the night he remembered to get up and close the blinds to the bedroom so that the sunrise wouldn't wake them too early and he was grateful he'd thought of it. Although he could see the sun peeking around the edges, the room was still mostly dark. And he was in bed with the most exciting woman he had ever met.

Last night with Amina was everything he had fantasized about and so much more. He'd had enough experiences in his life where the reality was not even as remotely good as the fantasy. To have reality be better was wonderful and more than a little amazing.

After taking care of his waking needs, and turning on his phone just in case, he got back into bed with her. He could happily stay in this bed forever, but unfortunately he looked at the time on the clock and whispered, "Damn." Clocks should be banned from bedrooms, he thought. He might mention that to Brian.

"Is that how you usually say good morning or are you talking in your sleep?"

"Oh, I'm awake," he said. "I hope I didn't disturb you."

"No, I tend to be an early riser, but I'm so comfortable I decided not to say or do anything." She gave him a soft kiss. "Why did you say damn?"

"The time. I'm due for my shift in less than an hour, and I really should get back home to shower and change. Chances are someone will notice sooner or later than I'm spending a lot of time with you and in your room, but I'd like to delay that for as long as possible."

"You could shower here," she said. "And I could join you." Instead of answering her, he grabbed her hand pulled her out of the bed and brought her straight to the bathroom. She laughed. "Well I guess that answers the question nicely."

He started the water so it would get hot, then left her for a moment so she could take care of her needs while he got coffee going. When he came back she was already in the shower.

"Hey, no fair starting without me."

"My hair is much longer than yours, in case you hadn't noticed. I think I deserve a head start."

"You deserve whatever you want my sweet, and I promise to do my best to give it to you."

"I like that promise. Will you help me with my hair?"

"With pleasure."

Her hair came almost to the center of her back and it took the entire little bottle of shampoo to create enough lather. He made a mental note to have a bigger bottle sent to her. He massaged the bubbles into her scalp and she moaned with pleasure. The sound made him hard.

It was going to be a long day away from her.

Standing on her tiptoes, she did the same for his hair and he understood the moan. Her fingers sent tingles through his entire body.

He rinsed the suds from them both and then looked at her in wonder as she smiled at him. "I need another good morning kiss." He needed more than that, but the condoms were in the other room and if he started something he wasn't going to leave.

She wrapped her arms around him and tilted her head back as his mouth came down on hers. He was so hungry for her. His tongue danced with hers as his hands found her breasts. He teased her hard nipples and enjoyed hearing and feeling her moan this time.

"We're never getting out of here if we keep this up. And you're going to be very late."

"I think it's time for another damn."

"Probably."

They reluctantly separated and finished. He couldn't resist drying her when they got out, touching her everywhere, nipping at her shoulders and teasing her pussy. "You don't play fair," she said.

"Can't seem to find a good reason to."

He couldn't remember the last time he felt this at ease and playful with a woman, especially after a first night. Nothing with Amina was normal, and he had no complaints.

Quickly slipping back into his clothes he poured them both a cup of coffee. "Is there any milk and sweetener?" she asked.

He found some in the refrigerator. "If you call room service for breakfast, you should have them bring you their coffee bar as well. It has flavored creamers, sugar, cinnamon and a few other things as well."

"Sounds wonderful. I will do that."

His phone pinged. "Okay, no more time to

waste," he said and drained his cup. "I'm usually done between 5:00 and 6:00. I'll come by after that."

"Sounds wonderful. I think I'll head to the clothing optional pool today."

"You're killing me."

"Just giving you incentive."

He came over, took her face in his hands and kissed her. She tasted of coffee and something he was coming to recognize as her. "None needed, but I appreciate the image."

"Anytime," she said with a wink.

He kissed her again. Fuck it, he could be late once in a while.

Chapter Four

He was wonderful. In bed, out of bed, she'd never met a human like Jonathan. If this is how Drew treated Lyria and made her feel, it was no wonder her cousin was falling for him.

Not that Amina thought she was falling for Jonathan. They'd only spent a few hours together. A few amazing hours, and there were more to come, but still. She would enjoy their time together, their limited time together, and remember how he made her feel, how he treated her so that when she was ready for a serious relationship, she could look for and repeat some of what he had shown her.

That was all there was to it.

Alone, she magically dried herself and ordered breakfast along with the coffee bar he had suggested. The description in the menu book sounded wonderful, especially as it included hot chocolate and whipped cream. Chocolate… one of the world's great gifts.

She was dressed and reading when there was a knock. "Room service."

Her stomach growled in response and she laughed. She couldn't believe how happy and light she felt. Given all that was happening only a short swim away, it seemed wrong, but Amina couldn't stop smiling.

She opened the door to see a familiar waiting with her table. "Good morning, Sofia. Come on in."

"Good morning, Miss." The girl wheeled the table in and efficiently began setting up the table for Amina's breakfast.

"I can't believe you're working again so early."

"Double shift most days, Miss."

Again with this girl, Amina wished for her gift back. She wanted to know how worried Sofia was, and what else was going on for her emotionally. "That's a lot of work for a young girl."

"It's okay. I don't mind. It's worth it. My working keeps my brother, Raul, safe and cared for."

"There's an adult who helps?" Sofia looked panicked. Clearly she had revealed more than she intended. "I told you, secrets are safe with me. I know what it's like to be responsible for others."

Sofia swallowed and Amira could see it was an effort. The girl looked as though she might cry. "Thank you, Miss."

"Guests don't often talk to you, do they?"

Sofia finished what she was doing and looked at Amina. She looked tired for such a young girl. "Guests don't often see me, let alone talk to me. It's that way with all of the employees. Except some of the older ones who the guests think are sexy."

Amina thought there was probably a blush under Sofia's tan after admitting that. "Well, that is unfortunate and wrong. I liking talking to you when you're here and I'd like you to please call me Amina."

Sofia offered a smile.

Amina waited.

"Yes, Amina," she finally said. "Is there anything else I can do or get for you?"

Amina looked at the beautiful laid out table and her stomach grumbled again. "I think I'm fine. After all you brought me yesterday you must be surprised I'm hungry again."

"You sent quite a bit back."

"That's true. But don't worry. I'm not going to starve."

"Well that's a relief, Mi... Amina. If there's nothing else, I'll wish you a good day."

"You too, Sofia," and she gave the girl another $20. Whatever the money could buy her was nothing compared to the good it could do Sofia and her brother. "I hope to see you again."

Sofia nodded and left.

* * *

Sofia had barely walked back into the room service area when she was grabbed by Owen. Dragging her by the upper arm to a corner he said, "You were at Villa Four again. Did you see the bracelet?"

She wanted to lie, to protect Amina, but there was no way to do that. "Yes, the two times I've seen her she's always wearing it."

"What a fool, but I suppose her stupidity and ignorance will be our benefit."

"What are you going to do?"

"What do you think, little girl? What we always do. We're going to separate the pretty tourist from her pretty trinket. I'm sure whoever bought it for her will be happy to replace it after the insurance money comes in. Everyone will get what they want."

As he walked away, Sofia shuddered. She had a very bad feeling about this. As soon as she had a break she was going to try to sneak back to Amina's villa and warn her somehow. She needed Amina to understand how dangerous it was to wear the bracelet in public. It needed to be put in the hotel safe or she wouldn't be safe.

By the time she got her chance, there was no answer at Amina's villa.

* * *

It had only been a little over a day since her arrival, but by the afternoon Amina was feeling restless and wanted to get out of the resort for a while. Lying out naked by the pool was wonderful, but she hated that she couldn't simply go to the ocean's edge, change from legs to fins and swim for miles. Her short swim yesterday had been nice, but not enough. Not knowing where Fiero's minions could be, it was too great a risk. Learning that Lyria was safe only calmed one set of fears.

Amina was used to having the vastness of the Ocean as her playground. She would swim miles on any given day and still be at the compound when she was needed. At times when she was working to solve more difficult challenges between two groups of Oceanides, she made certain to schedule long meal breaks which would allow the participants—and her—to have some distance from each other and the situation. Frequently, those breaks lead to a break through and the obstacles were solved much quicker.

Most mermaids had some form of wanderlust, but Amina's was pronounced, and she was used to being able to find ways of indulging it. Being confined to the island and the resort was making her uncomfortable.

She'd heard other guests say that leaving the resort could be dangerous. There were gangs and other thieves about and they targeted the tourists, even though the outside money was badly needed. Guests were encouraged to shop at the resort stores which catered to every indulgence. However, in town there were supposedly some wonderful and unique shops and restaurants. Amina loved shopping in the human world. She decided to go exploring.

Choosing a comfortable dress, flat shoes and a small bag containing money, she headed into town. It wasn't often she chose to walk long distances, and she decided to enjoy a slower pace, since when she swam she was quite fast.

She had walked less than a half a mile from the hotel when the site and the sights around her changed. It was as if she was in another world. The part of the hotel which faced the ocean showed an island that was beautiful and lush. This part was much less so. She stuck to the main road but when she looked down side streets she saw tiny homes built close together and in poor condition. There were old women on stoops watching children in tattered clothes. They sounded like any other children the world over, but she knew their lives were filled with challenges she couldn't begin to understand.

Soon she reached the center of town and the shopping area known as the Stall Market. Immediately she was bombarded with goods being pushed toward her and offers of a lift to anywhere she wanted to go on the island. She didn't need empathy to know she was surrounded by feelings of both hope and resentment. The island natives were desperate for the money only the tourists brought, which made the outsiders reviled and desired in equal measure. Not wanting to buy anything immediately, she joined a group going on a tour of the local castle, former home of the monarchy who once ruled Jariz.

The castle, while in need of renovation, was beautiful. It reminded her of the central building in the governor's compound with its large rooms and endless hallways although that structure had been built for utility, not luxury. Amina wondered what it had been like for the island and islanders during the monarchy. Clearly they thought it was difficult and unfair or they wouldn't have exiled the ruling family. According to their tour guide, Jariz was now part of an autonomous community that united several islands under one government. From the explanation, it was similar to what Uncle Costin had done for their quadrant.

It made Amina wonder if there was an underclass among the Oceanides, like the one here, she wasn't aware of. She thought of the naiad they had questioned the day before her attack. He'd hinted that there were many who didn't like the status quo and wanted a change, even one as potentially dangerous as Fiero. Ulrike had suggested something similar. When she went home she would look into it.

When she returned to the market after the tour she was hungry and thrilled to see she had so many choices from the food vendors. Since she wanted to keep walking and exploring, she chose food easy to eat and hold including a savory chicken and vegetable dish pierced with a stick and for dessert a roasted spear of pineapple. She'd never had fruit cooked before and she marveled at the intense sweetness that was brought out in the process. It was something she might try to replicate.

Finding a fountain with children playing in it and people sitting around the edge, she dipped her hands in the water to wash the stickiness from them before she returned to do a little shopping. She'd seen some sparkly trinkets and beautiful scarves she was interested in purchasing. She was watching the play of the sun on the water when she was interrupted.

"Excuse me, can you help me, Miss?"

She turned to see a young boy who couldn't have been more than ten standing next to her with his hand out. He was small, darkly tanned and while she didn't understand why, she thought there was something familiar about him.

"What kind of help do you need," she asked. She assumed he was begging for money, but something about the boy tugged at her.

"I need money, Miss. My sister and I, our parents are gone and there's no one to take care of us. She works all day at the resort, and I don't want to her to have to work so hard. I want to help too."

That was it. It was his eyes that were familiar. "Sofia is your sister, isn't she? You're Raul. I met her. She told me about you. You two definitely look like family. Aren't you supposed to be in school?" The boy went from looking hopeful to looking petrified. He turned to bolt but Amina grabbed his hand. "Don't go, please. I'd like to help you if I can. I didn't bring much money with me, but I do have some."

"You can't tell her," he said in a panicked voice. "She can't know that I'm peddling instead of sitting in school, which is totally boring and unhelpful anyway. Nothing we learn there is useful. Please, promise me you won't tell her."

"So she doesn't know you're out here." Amina wasn't the least bit surprised but she wanted to try to get Raul to stay and tell her what he might really need to change his situation.

"No, Miss. And you shouldn't be out here either." He looked at her and motioned her to come closer. In a quiet voice he said, "They are watching you."

"Who is?"

"Elias and his gang. His lieutenants work up at the resort and they let him know to be on the lookout for different guests. He mentioned the woman with the valuable bracelet and offered a reward for anyone giving him information about her. Even more money if they find a way to bring the bracelet to him. You've been watched since you got here. You shouldn't wear it in public. You should put it in the safe."

"I'm afraid that's not an option. See, it can't come off." She showed him the bracelet and the fact that it had no clasp. No way of taking it off.

"Miss, that is not good. You shouldn't let anyone see it. Find a way to keep it covered. And don't leave the Suadela again. Stay there. You'll be much safer."

Something struck her. "Raul, if so many are interested in this bracelet and there's a reward for getting it to Elias, how is it that no one has approached me sooner, at least not individually."

"I told you. They are watching. Making plans. I was picked to talk to you. I'm young and the tourists

127

usually feel really guilty when I ask for money so they give it to me." He looked proud for a moment then horrified. "Oh no, you *are* going to tell Sofia about me, aren't you?"

"No, Raul, I will do my best not to let her know what you are doing, but just as you want me to be safe, I want you to be safe as well. Are you part of Elias' gang?" He shook his head. "Do you want to be? Or do they want you to be?" This time there was no answer. That was answer enough. He was either being groomed or tested or both. It was not a good situation, no matter what. And if Sofia knew she'd be miserable.

He was so scared and small. It broke her heart. He and Sofia were too young to have to be dealing with problems like these. Sofia worked long hours to make sure they had the basics and couldn't hire someone to watch Raul. Because she couldn't be around, her brother was vulnerable to being brought into one of the violent street gangs. Amina needed to talk to Sofia and possibly find a way to help them that would have a longer term benefit. For now, she gave Raul a few of the dollars she had in her purse.

"Thank you, Miss," he said. "And remember what I said. Go back to the resort and stay there."

"You're welcome. And I appreciate your warning."

After he scampered off, Amina didn't feel like staying in the market any longer. His words had worried her on several levels and she decided that, as difficult as it was, wandering away from the hotel could not be a part of her days.

Limits. She would never like them.

She started her walk back, thinking mostly about the castle and the possibility of enjoying a long hot soak in the huge tub after she got to her room, but minutes after leaving the town center she sensed she was being watched.

It wasn't the same sort of sensing when her empathic gift was in use, just the knowledge any creature has when they are being staked as prey. She sped up her steps gradually so as not to alert the predator and seem scared. She searched for a place she could step into for safety, but saw nothing. Looking to the side she let out a small squeal when she turned back and a large man unexpectedly stepped in front of her.

"What's your rush, pretty thing?" Amina didn't think his choice of words was an accident. She was certain to him she had no value beyond what she could give him. "A sweet lady like you shouldn't be out alone. Haven't you heard the rumors about the dangerous crime levels in this area?"

She tried to turn around and go back to the town only to find that there were two more men standing behind her. They laughed. It wasn't a pleasant sound. "The rumors are true," said one who was brandishing a knife he seemed very comfortable with.

"Let me pass," Amina said with more confidence than she felt. "I am going back to the resort. I'm expected there." It was sort of true.

"Not until you give us the jewelry you're wearing. Your earrings and necklace don't look like they would be worth much, but that bracelet everyone is talking about," he grabbed her hand and pulled her forward bringing her wrist close to his face and her body too close to his. "This is worth a fortune. Give it to us and we'll let you go. Fight, and this won't go well for you."

One of the men behind her reached around and grabbed her breasts making certain she understood the threat. "It's not going to go well no matter what, princess," he said. "Unless you like it rough. And in groups."

Amina's head was spinning with thoughts and fears. She tried to think of a magic she could use to stop them from trying to get the bracelet off of her, which was impossible, and then raping her, which was very possible. Transforming to fins would be no use, and most everything else she could do was practical, everyday things—dry herself instantly, keep the salt of the ocean from clinging to her skin, and shrinking her own possessions so they could be easily carried and transported. Useless. Offensive spells required potions and charms. She had neither.

There was the option of screaming, but somehow she knew that wouldn't help. Even if someone did hear her, chances were slim anyone in the area would go against these men in order to assist her. They ruled by fear and backed up by brutality.

"So, what's it going to be?" asked the thug in front of her as he twisted her right wrist to make his point. She couldn't help but cry out. The pain would have been worse in her left, but this was strong enough to make her eyes water.

As her fear built she sensed a warmth in her wrist. At first she thought it was because the man had started to break her bone but then she noticed a faint glow coming from the Stone of Strength. Before anything more could happen a familiar voice interrupted.

"Let her go."

Amina turned and saw Jonathan holding a helmet

and sitting astride a motorized bicycle. No, a motorcycle. She remembered reading a book where the hero had been a biker.

"Move along, *desconocido*, this is none of your concern."

"Yeah, we've got no problem with you."

"Well, I'm so glad to hear that, because I don't want to have any problems with you either. Or the local police." He took out his phone and hit two buttons. "Captain Givas, this is Jonathan Bartlett, head of security at the Suadela Resort. Yeah, I was headed in to work when I passed three men threatening one of my guests with a knife and not letting her pass." He paused and listened as he kept an eye on her would-be attackers. "Describe them? Oh, I can do better than that. Let me snap a picture and send it to you."

In that moment things moved very quickly. The man in front of her dropped her wrist and took off running. The men behind her cursed and did the same thing. And Jonathan moved to Amina as she nearly collapsed on the sidewalk.

"I've got you," he said. "You're safe now." He went back to his phone call, but didn't let her go. "Thanks, Captain, they're gone now. What a surprise. They ran surprisingly fast for men of their size. I'll let you know if the lady wants to try to have them found." He hung up the phone. "It's over."

She looked at him and couldn't form words for a moment. "Thank you," she finally managed. "I don't want to think about what was going to happen if you didn't come by when you did." Her body gave an involuntary shudder.

"Well, I did come by, and you don't have to think

131

about it. Let's get you back to the resort. Ever ridden on a motorcycle?"

"Can't say that I have." She didn't think she was capable of saying much in the moment.

"Then here, put this helmet on, sit side saddle, and let me take you back to the resort." She stared at the seat of the motorcycle not understanding what he meant by side saddle until he picked her up and put her down with both legs on one side, accommodating her dress. "Now, if you can just trust me for a few more minutes, wrap your arms around my waist and we'll head out of here."

She did as he asked, and he kept a very slow pace back to the hotel. Part of her wanted him to go as fast as possible, but the more sensible part of her understood why he was being so deliberate. She wasn't used to feeling helpless. Breakable.

Even when Wilmar and Ulrike tried to drug and kidnap her she hadn't been as frightened. There she knew help would be on the way and she could reach out if she needed. Today, she was completely isolated and if whatever fates hadn't sent Jonathan on that road at that moment she wouldn't have escaped.

She shuddered again.

Jonathan must have felt it because he called over his shoulder. "Stay with me, beautiful, we're almost there."

He must have called ahead without her noticing because when they arrived the General Manager was out front waiting for them.

"I'm so sorry to have caused problems and concerns again, Mr. Vickers."

"Not at all, Ms. Brookes. I'm sorry you had to

experience that part of our island. If you would accompany me, I will help you place that bracelet in the hotel safe so you do not have to worry about it for the rest of your stay."

"Thank you, that's very kind, but as you can see—it's not possible for it to come off. Where it goes, I go."

The manager gave her a very worried look. "That's troubling. I'm not certain you will be safe with such a valuable piece visible." He paused and thought for a moment. "Jonathan, you need to stay with her."

"Of course, I'll walk her back to her villa."

"At all times. Ms. Brookes needs a bodyguard. You are the most trusted member of our security staff and she already knows you. I'm sure you can work it out with the rest of your staff to manage without your leadership for the remainder of her stay. You won't be far, and you'll be on site so you can check in with them as you feel necessary, as long as you don't leave her side."

Amina looked at Jonathan. At the moment, she would really have liked to have the gift of mind-reading to know what he was thinking.

Chapter Five

I am the luckiest son of a bitch on the planet, Jonathan thought as he stared at Amina, who looked so pale he was concerned she might faint. He'd been wondering how to make excuses to stop by and see her and now he was being ordered to stay with her at all times. He hated the way this came about, but he couldn't argue with the result.

"Yes, sir," he said trying to sound professional and not like he wanted to do a fist pump. "I will see to it that Ms. Brookes stays safe. I think we should start by heading back to your villa so you can rest. Could you call room service and ask them to send something… soothing?" *Preferably alcoholic,* he thought. He didn't normally encourage anyone to drink, but she looked as though rum might help. "Are you okay to do a little more walking or should we take one of the carts?" When she looked at him and didn't answer, he asked the doorman to ring for one of the modified golf carts which were used to help staff and guests reach the different parts of the resort.

Minutes later he was opening her door with his master key to let them into the villa. "What can I get for you?" he asked, brushing her hair back from her face. At least she didn't startle at his touch. That was a good sign. "What do you need? Talk to me, Amina, let me help, please."

"A shower. I'd really like a hot shower. I can still feel those men against me, grabbing me. They were going to—"

"Yes, I know what they threatened, but you're safe now. A shower sounds like a good idea. Should I help or do you think you can manage?"

"I can manage."

She walked to the bathroom and shut the door. Moments later, he heard the water running and once it was, he opened the door a little so that he could hear if she was in trouble. He hoped to hear her humming, but he didn't expect it.

The next few hours were crucial for dealing with what had happened. After his partner had been shot there were days of meetings and paperwork and it was a while before anyone remembered Jonathan probably needed the help of a counselor. By that time, he'd been living in his thoughts for so long it was impossible to unravel the pain and guilt.

He was still struggling.

Bringing his thoughts back to Amina, he wondered how he could help her. He'd had one actual rape victim and several near attacks when he was working in New York and that had been more than enough. It was something he trained his staff here to watch for. Drinking did terrible things to people's inhibitions and compromised their ability to consent. His staff knew to look for the signs of someone being coerced into something they either didn't want or couldn't completely agree to.

135

While he was waiting for her to finish bathing, room service arrived with an array of blended, frozen fruit juices with two bottles on the side, vodka and rum. There were also some sandwiches and fruit tarts. Simple, satisfying. This would work perfectly if she were interested in eating.

She came out of the bathroom wrapped in a hotel robe, her skin red from the high heat of the shower. He wasn't surprised she wanted to feel clean of the touch of those men. She jumped when she saw him. "Sorry, I forgot you were here."

"That's okay, you're entitled to be a little skittish given all that happened."

She nodded. "I'd rather not think about it all."

"Come sit on the couch with me. Are you thirsty? Hungry?"

"Thirsty," she said as she sat down. She moved as though in a trance.

"We have our famous papaya mango slush and I can mix it with a little rum if that sounds good."

"Not too much rum, please."

He mixed them both a drink, his without the alcohol. He handed her a glass, watched as she took a sip, and sat near her but not exactly next to her on the couch. Space could be very important at a time like this. "I'm so sorry about what happened. I can't imagine how frightened you must have been."

"I don't really want to talk about it either," she said, staring into her glass.

"So no calling the police and reporting it." She shook her head. "I can understand that. There's probably not a lot they could or would do, but please trust me when I tell you that it will be much easier for

136

you going forward if you talk about it. I'm here to listen, nothing more."

"So you're a security guard and a therapist?"

He didn't mind the touch of anger in her voice. It was a good sign—honest emotion. "Well, not long ago I was a New York City cop, but when my partner was shot and his wife told me that I should have been the one to get killed, it derailed my career and I ended up here. And before I got here, there were months of seeing a therapist—correction, therapists—so I have a feel for the process even if I don't know what I'm doing."

She looked at him. "I'm sorry about your partner. I had no idea. That must have been awful."

"Thank you. It was, and truthfully I'm still not over it." He explained why it took so long for him to get help. "Between that, and having worked with attack victims, I know how important it is for you to express what you're thinking and what you're feeling or your thoughts and feelings will get worse."

She laughed. "This is so ironic."

"It is?"

"I'm *am* a therapist. Well, a counselor."

"Really? Okay, now it's my turn to apologize. I must be making a total mess of things."

"Actually, you've got it right, and I know I need to talk about what happened, except at the moment that's the last thing I want to do." She downed more of her drink. He wondered how soon the rum would start to hit her.

"Understandable. How about just a little for now."

"I was in the Stall Market and a boy came up to

137

me to ask for money. We talked for a little bit, and he told me that word about my bracelet had been passed among the street thieves and that I should put the band in the hotel safe. I showed him, like I showed Mr. Vickers, that the bracelet has no beginning and no end. He told me I should get back to the resort and stay there. So, I did. Only I was foolish and didn't think to look for a cab or a way to get back with a group. I walked there so I started walking back. Which is when those men stopped me."

"You weren't foolish."

"I made a foolish decision."

"There's a difference in those two sayings."

She smiled at him. "If you ever want to give up the security business, you should consider becoming a therapist. You're good at this."

"I'll take that as a compliment, but I don't think it's really my style. I'm better at saving damsels in distress and whisking them away on my trusty steed. Well, motorcycle."

"I really was one of those, wasn't I? How cliché."

"Well, clichés exist for a reason."

"Why were you driving by? Did it really take you that long to get to work this morning?"

"No, I took a late lunch and thought… Oh, I hope you're going to laugh at this. I thought that since there was a possibility I might stay with you tonight again, I should probably bring a change of clothes with me, which I didn't think of as I left this morning."

She smiled and it was wonderful to see. "You're going to need more than one change of clothes now."

"Apparently. Other than the terrible end, did you enjoy your trip into town?"

"Yes. I visited the castle which was lovely and tried roasted pineapple."

"Two local favorites."

"I wish I hadn't tried the walk back."

"Of course you do," he said.

"If you hadn't come by when you did I don't know what would have happened. Actually, I do know what would have happened and…"

"Stop right there. I know your mind is going to go there, probably more than you'd like, and many times over the next several days, but the truth is I did come by and nothing did happen. You have to do what you can to steer your thoughts to how well it turned out in the end. Call it fate, divine intervention or a guardian angel. You weren't hurt and you're here and safe now."

"I like the idea of you as a guardian angel."

He smiled but said nothing. He was no one's guardian angel and he was sorry he'd brought it up. David wouldn't be dead if there was angelic intervention.

"Can I ask you something?"

"Of course," he said.

"How do you feel about crying women?"

He stared at her for a moment. He decided on complete honesty. "Well, I'm not a huge fan of seeing anyone cry, and I hate it more when I'm the cause, but overall I understand the need and how crying can help."

"Oh good, because right now I need to really let all of these emotions out and I'll probably cry and wail and maybe even hit the couch a few times."

"Sounds good and healthy to me." He took her

drink from her and pulled some of the decorative pillows out from behind their backs. He put one in her lap and gave her a napkin as well. "It's better than a tissue," he said. "What can I do? Do you need me to leave the room? I could go into the bedroom."

"No, I'd actually like you to be close, please, and if I reach out, will you hold me?"

"Absolutely." He liked that she knew and asked for what she needed.

She nodded and he saw the tears well up in her eyes. She started to say thank you but the dam of emotions she'd be holding in for the last hour broke—no shattered—and emotions wracked her body making her shake.

He'd never seen a woman fall apart like this. She moved from tears to sobs, from sobs to deep moans and from the moans to yelling and hitting the pillow. Normally he'd run around trying to fix the situation, do something—anything—to make her stop, but there was something about Amina's tears that didn't frighten him. In fact, he found them astounding.

He'd experienced her sexual passion. This was emotional passion.

She wasn't faking or trying to get him to do something. She was honestly feeling, letting go of her fear and angry and grief. It was actually... quite beautiful and there was a part of him that wished he could have experienced something like this when David had died. Maybe the nightmares would be gone by now if he had.

She put the pillow in front of her face and screamed. He was grateful she'd muffled herself. He couldn't imagine what people would think if they heard.

Still he did nothing to interfere. Part of him wanted to help, of course, but she told him what she needed and he was going to respect her wishes.

As she put the pillow down, she turned to him, red-eyed, puffy-lipped, and fell over into his arms. He held her close, her body warm from the turmoil it had just gone through. As the hysteria abated her body slowly relaxed. He kissed the stop of her head and she took her first deep breath since he'd put her on the back of his motorcycle. When her arms came around him, he knew she was almost completely on the other side of the storm.

A few more minutes passed before he heard her say, "Thank you."

"You're welcome. It was an honor."

She looked up. "An honor?"

He kissed her softly. "When someone gives you something so precious, or shows you a part of themselves which is that vulnerable, it's an honor to receive it."

Her eyes welled up. He understood why and didn't say anything, just put his hand on her head and pressed her back against his chest.

"I'm exhausted," she said.

"I'm not surprised."

"It's too early for bed, and too late for a nap."

"We're on island time. It's never too late for nap. Let's get you to bed. I'll set an alarm to wake you in, say, two hours."

"That sounds good."

Jonathan walked her to the bedroom and when she leaned against him, he put his arm around her. She seemed so small and frail in this moment. He needed to keep his thoughts from straying to the possibilities of what could have happened to her as much as she did. Turning down the covers, he let her slide into the bed.

"May I ask another favor of you?"

"Absolutely," he said.

"Would you stay with me? Hold me."

"Definitely." He walked to the other side of the bed, moved a pillow close to hers and let her put her head on his shoulder as he put his arm around her. He stayed above the covers. She may have wanted him close, but he knew that had limits in this moment. He didn't want to give himself any temptation that would be hard to fight off. Besides, he was her bodyguard now. There would be time enough to return to the fun they'd previously had.

"Thank you. This feels just right."

And as she fell asleep against him, Jonathan had to agree.

* * *

When Amina woke the room was nearly dark. Jonathan was by her side, also asleep, and the bedside lamp next to him was on. She stretched and her movement woke him. "Hello there, kitten."

"Kitten?" She'd been called many things in her life but never compared to a tiny feline.

"Yes, you were sort of purring in your sleep."

"Purring?"

"It could have been a light snore."

"I do not snore," she said. Did she? She actually had no idea. She'd spent the night with very few partners and none had mentioned it before.

"After crying I think most people do. Also, whatever you were dreaming about made you dig your nails into me a few times."

He showed her left over marks of the half-moons on his arm.

"I'm so sorry." She was a little horrified.

He laughed. "It's fine, although if you are going to dig your claws into me, I'd rather it was in the throes of passion rather than a bad dream." He wiggled his eyebrows at her.

Now it was her turn to laugh. "Thank you for being so understanding. And thank you again for earlier, for being there as I cried." She rolled her head in a circle to loosen the muscles. Crying like that always left her a little stiff, but she had to admit that otherwise, she felt rather good.

"I was happy to help, truly," he said and putting a hand under her chin, he tilted her face up to him and gave her a soft kiss.

Just right. "So, any ideas of how we can pass the rest of the evening? And hold off on the wiggling eyebrows until later."

"Very well," he said but made an exaggerated pout face. "There is always a lot going on in the resort, but I have a feeling groups of people are the last thing you need and want right now. I noticed the way you rolled your head a moment ago. How about we see if we can schedule you for a massage?"

She'd never had one, but they appeared in the romance novels on occasion and sounded quite lovely. With her gift dormant, it could be exactly what she needed. "Do you think there will be one available?"

"A phone call or two should tell me." He was as

good as his word and a few minutes later he said, "Let's go. We have side by side massages on the beach scheduled in 20 minutes."

"That was fast," she said.

"I know people."

"And you decided to join me?"

"Yeah, I wasn't even thinking of that, but Lacy, who was doing appointments at the spa said there were two available. I decided to treat myself."

She kissed him. "Perhaps I'll treat you later."

"Can I wiggle my eyebrows now?"

He led them to the edge of the property, where the sand started and there was a line of canvas tents with massage tables beneath them. Under one, there were two tables and two waiting personnel, one man, one woman.

"Good evening, Mr. Barrett. We're all set," said the woman who was so petite Amina wondered if she was strong enough to knead sore muscles.

"Thank you. This is Amina and she's had a hell of a day. She could really use to feel relaxed and pampered."

"Don't worry, Mr. Barrett, we'll take good care of you both."

The man stepped up to Amina and held out his hand, then brought her to what she saw was the lower of the two tables. "I am Samuel, and I will be taking care of you tonight," he said in a deep accented voice.

"Oh, but I thought she…" Amina pointed to the other woman.

"No, Miss. Paola will be taking care of Mr. Barrett. We work not only with the body's muscles but its energy too. As long as you don't mind, we find it is helpful when we care for the opposite gender, especially during a side by side session. It helps the... how do you say it?"

Paola answered, "The yin and yang. By mixing the two, a more powerful flow and force is created. Will you be comfortable with that, Miss?"

"Yes," Amina said, "That will be fine."

"Wonderful," Samuel said. "Then I invite you to get as undressed as you wish, the more of you I have access to the better, and slide under the sheet when you are ready."

Amina didn't hesitate to take off her dress, hang it on a hook and go back to the table. The sheets were cool and soft against her skin. She noticed Jonathan standing there. "Is something wrong?"

"I don't usually get undressed in front of other staff members."

Paola laughed. "You are not the first of our employees I have helped. Would you like to know where Mr. Vickers has a scar?"

Jonathan held his hand up and looked a little horrified. "No, thank you. I'm good. I'll just leave everything on the chair." Amina watched as he stripped to his underwear, then hurried under the sheet. He was so sexy, even when he was silly.

Either Paola or Samuel put on some soft music and the massages began.

"Relax, Miss," Samuel said shortly after putting oil on her back and starting to work on the muscles at the top. "I promise I will not go harder than you wish."

That wasn't the reason why she tensed. When people touched her, she always got a clearer read on their emotions. It took her thoughts a moment to

145

remember that this wasn't an issue. Even though she hadn't been receiving emotions for a few days, being touched by a stranger automatically triggered that response.

Amina sighed, both at what Samuel was doing, which was wonderful, and feeling sad that her reaction to others was so negative. Maybe when she returned home and to work she'd try to accept touch no matter what her gift's response might be.

Whatever Samuel was doing continued to be wonderful, and she let her mind drift into nothing allowing her to only be aware of how talented his hands were and how happy her body was feeling.

"Hey, cut that out over there," said Jonathan in a muffled voice.

She turned to look at him and saw his face down in the circle at the top of the massage table. "Is there a problem?"

"Yes, you keep moaning and sighing and I am not the one touching you."

Everyone laughed. "I'm sorry, but Samuel has a gift and it needs to be acknowledged every now and then. I'm sure Paola is making you feel equally wonderful."

"She is, but you don't hear me calling out do you?"

"Then maybe I should push your muscles a little deeper," Paola said.

"Holy hell," Jonathan called out a moment later.

"Now what?"

"Oh nothing, she just found a knot between my shoulders that has probably been there for years and it just undid."

"You're welcome," Paola said just as Amina said, "Good job."

She smiled and settled back into the table. This really was what she needed.

She turned onto her back when Samuel asked and noticed how much looser her muscles felt. It was heavenly. A few minutes later she sensed Samuel's hand hovering over the scar that Wilmar had given her years ago. He wasn't massaging it, but the heat from his body was reaching hers, warming her skin. "May I ask what you are doing?"

"I am pulling out some of the charge from this past injury."

"Charge?"

"It is hard to explain, Miss, but I will try." He spoke slowly as he continued to work on her. "Most of our scars are, of course, on the inside. Times we've been hurt. Sad or angry. Those scars are important, but harder to reach. When I sense them, I use something called Reiki, a special form of healing where I, and others who are trained, can channel energy into our clients through touch. It is intended to help the emotional as well as the physical healing process. You hold a great deal of worry in your body, Miss, so in addition to the work of massage I am adding some of this healing energy. When I reached your scar, I sensed something particularly strong there. Not just the pain of the injury, but pain from why it happened. I wanted to pull out some of that pain, through Reiki, so you could experience greater healing, greater happiness."

Amina was glad she wasn't required to respond. Her throat had closed and quiet tears slid down her face.

147

She had worked through many of those feelings when the incident happened and again when Lyria returned to discover Amina had almost died, and she hadn't thought about it again in the years since.

Samuel, however, was right. There was still an emotional pain connected with that time, not just the injury but the intense grief of hurting Lyria. It was the first time, but hardly the last, her gift had brought someone information, truth, they didn't want to know or hear. She was grateful she never again hurt another family member or someone she loved the way she did Lyria, but she had also, if she were to be honest, never completely forgiven herself. She was not sorry Lyria was free of Wilmar, but she was sorry for what Lyria had to go through to have that freedom, as well as the role she had played.

As Samuel moved his attention to another part of her body, Amina focused on the scar and remembered the scene with Wilmar. For the first time, nothing inside of her clenched with sorrow or grief.

It was a welcome and unexpected surprise. She was going to have to learn more about Reiki and see if she or other merfolk could learn to practice it. It was an amazing combination of what Lyria did with healing and her work with emotions. The potential for lasting change was truly astounding. What an unexpected gift.

When Samuel finished a few minutes later, Amina wrapped the sheet around herself and gave him a huge hug. He was confused at first, then returned the embrace. "Thank you," she said quietly, "for your knowing and your helping."

"Please continue to take care of yourself, Miss. You have much going on inside you. "

She was going to say "You have no idea," but looking into his eyes she had the impression he just might.

"I hope," he continued, "I was able to help in some small way."

"Yes, thank you. I think you have."

He gave a small bow and left. Not long after, Paola finished with Jonathan and left as well.

Still wrapped in his sheet, Jonathan came over and wrapped his arms around her. "I could ask if you enjoyed that, but I could hear that you did."

"Sorry to tease you so much."

"No, you're not."

"No, I'm not." She kissed him softly. "Now what?"

"How about some night swimming."

"Pool or ocean?" she asked knowing what she hoped he'd say.

"Ocean."

"Do we need to go back to get our swimsuits?"

"Well, we should, but I know a private grotto where no one will disturb us, so being naked won't be a problem."

"Sounds perfect," she said. They got dressed, Jonathan grabbed some towels from the massage area, and they headed to the beach.

It was early evening and there were still plenty of people out, a few swimming, some relaxing on Amina's favorite lounge chair beds, and most on the chairs around fire pits. She could see them drinking, laughing and eating.

All at once Amina was struck by their happiness and her own situation. Not one of them knew that the

Ocean was in danger and that if Fiero got what he wanted, even humans could be in danger. She didn't think Fiero would care if they knew about magic and merfolk as long as he ruled. They had no idea her life and the lives of those she loved were being threatened.

No idea there was a mermaid walking by.

"Are you okay," Jonathan asked.

"I'm fine, why?"

"You stopped walking and were just staring out at the ocean."

"I'm sorry. Have you ever just suddenly been pulled out of your vacation or where you were having a good time to think about reality and what you had to face when you got back?"

"It's been longer than I care to admit since I've had a vacation, but yes, I know what you mean. Thinking about home?"

"Yes."

"Want to talk about?"

She took a deep breath. "No, I want to see that grotto."

"Alright, but if it ever comes invading again, talk to me, okay?"

"Okay." They started walking again but he stopped suddenly "What?"

"You don't have a boyfriend or fiancé or something waiting back there for you, do you?"

She kissed him deeply. "Definitely not."

"That's a relief. Come, not much further."

They walked a little longer down the beach to where the sand became barely a strip in front of an outcropping of rocks, then they reached an inlet where there was a little beach, a lot of rocks and total privacy.

"Believe it or not, the water is very deep there," he said. "We assume it's some sort of crater from a meteorite landing. It made the hole, and kicked up these rocks. It's actually one of the reasons we don't use this for guests. It's too hard to monitor and too easy to get injured, but if you trust me, I think we'll enjoy it."

"I trust you," she said and it warmed her heart to know how true that was.

* * *

He'd been joking that he was jealous of hearing her moan at the hands of another man, especially since he knew Samuel was madly in love with his wife, but the sounds of her pleasure had affected him.

He'd had to think of as many non-sexy things as possible when he was on his back while Paola worked on him or he risked tenting the sheet. Every time she moaned he thought about how awful dogs smelled when they got wet or the look on a guest's face just before he or she got sick. Or his mother. It wouldn't, he assumed, be the first time Paola had seen that reaction from men while she worked, but still, as a fellow employee it was important to keep some boundaries. It was also why he'd chosen to keep his boxer briefs on during the massage.

Boundaries.

Now, however, he stripped, put his clothes on a rock, and climbed to a slightly higher point that bordered the water. "Join me," he said and he dove in.

The water was warm at first, then he swam a little deeper to where it cooled. There he continued a bit further, then turned and swam for the top, breaking the surface with a gasp. He loved that feeling. Going as down as far as he could, for as long then reaching air just as his lungs were beginning to burst.

He looked around. He was alone. "Amina?"

Just as he was about to worry, she bobbed up next to him and wrapped herself around him. Warm water. Hot woman. "Hello there," she said.

The moon was a little past full and lit them well. She was so damn beautiful. But it was more than that. When she smiled he felt as though he were being drawn in, taken in. It was incredible.

"Kiss me again," he said.

And she did, her hands in his hair, her legs around his waist.

"It really is beautiful here. Thank you for bringing me."

"You're welcome. Getting a massage is great, but I always feel a bit oily afterwards. A swim in the ocean always seems to fix that."

"It offers lots of gifts," she said.

Jonathan looked at her. It was an odd thing to say, but he didn't know what to ask to clarify what she meant. Before he could think of something, she'd slipped out of his arms and gone underwater again.

He dove after her searching with his hands to try and find her since beneath the water it was too dark to see. It wasn't a large inlet, but he couldn't catch her. He came back to the surface. She wasn't there.

And then she was.

"You must be part dolphin."

"I love swimming."

"Do you live by the ocean?"

"I do."

"I just realized, I never asked or looked to find where you are from. You have no accent so I can't tell from that."

She paused. Maybe it was too personal. Maybe she didn't want him to know. "I live on the coast of Brazil."

"Practically the other side of the world."

"Only from here," she said with a smile. "And I'm here now. That's what matters."

"Very true."

They swam for a little longer, kissed and touched playfully, then wrapped themselves in the towels he'd taken and headed back to the villa. "How are you feeling?"

"Much better than I imagined I would, or could, a few hours ago."

"I'm glad to hear that."

"Thank you again. For everything," she said.

"You're very welcome." He was relieved. She probably still wasn't out of the woods completely. There could be some bounce back, nightmares. He knew what that was like, but he was hopeful.

When they got back they both headed straight for the food that was still on the table. She hadn't eaten since the afternoon and he had a feeling he'd skipped lunch. As they devoured the sandwiches and vegetable platter he decided to ask her about the bracelet, hoping she'd tell him and it wouldn't upset her.

"What do you want to know?"

"Well first, how is it that it doesn't have a clasp?"

"Oh, yes, that is unusual. It's been passed down in my family for many generations. Mother to

153

daughter, or aunt to niece if a woman had no daughters. When the time comes, some of the links on the bracelet are cut, then they are soldered together on the wrist of the new wearer."

"That's amazing."

"It's meant as a sign that the power of the bracelet is unbreakable."

"Power?"

"You don't think something that has been handed down for so long is without power, do you?" she said. "My family believes each woman who wears this bracelet, which is one of three that are passed down, is destined for great things. To help many. The green stone in the center of mine is known as the Stone of Strength. When I'm working, counseling people, I sometimes think of the women who wore it before me and hope I can draw on their wisdom and experience."

"Did you get it from your mother or your aunt?"

She paused before answering. "My mother."

"Are you close?"

"Were."

He could see the sorrow. "I'm sorry. I shouldn't have pressed."

"It's okay, really. You're my bodyguard because of this bracelet. It's understandable you'd have questions."

"It's almost hard to see the stone with all the charms and stones hanging from it."

"Those are added by previous wearers. Each woman adds things that have meaning to her, which she thinks will enhance the bracelet."

"Have you added any?"

"Not yet," she said. "I'm sure I'll find ones I

think are right at some point." A yawn hit her and she apologized.

"No need to be sorry. This has been a long and unexpected day, and even though you slept for a while before, I think heading to bed early is a good idea." They got up and walked toward the bedroom, but a thought hit him and he stopped.

"Is something wrong?"

"Amina, I'm going to stay with you no matter what and keep you safe, but I don't want you to feel pressured to have me stay in bed with you. Now, don't get me wrong, that is definitely where I want to be, but just because circumstances…"

She silenced him with a kiss. "You are such a gentleman and I appreciate your gallantry. Now, get into that bed and hold me all night."

It was an order he was happy to follow.

* * *

Nothing was working. Fiero couldn't remember a time when he'd been this mad and frustrated. For years he'd gotten what he wanted and now he and his uncle were finally going after what was most important—they were being met with failure after failure.

It was beyond irritating.

And he was starting to doubt himself.

His attack on Lyria had produced no results and, in fact, something happened between her and the Stone of Clarity that made him think it could be permanently out of his reach. She bonded with it in a way he didn't know could happen and she used some sort of magic from the stone to violently repel him.

Rachel Kenley

At least he'd been able to kill her precious human.

But not before she'd given him some sort of warning:

Be very careful. There are those close to you who would betray you for their own desires.

His uncle couldn't be who she referred to. Balban was the one who supported Fiero, helped him work through the plans, modify them as necessary, find support throughout the Oceanide community. There was no one else, close to him. Since the death of his brother, Yacopo, 16 years ago, he'd learned to harden his heart and stand on his own.

Unfortunately, that clearly did not help him get either the Stones or the mermaids who wore them into his possession.

There was a knock on the door and he barked, "Yes?"

His assistant, a strange looking naiad-selkie mix entered. Most of those who worked for and with him and his uncle were of mixed Oceanide blood, as he was. Those not mixed, like his uncle, supported them because of how the ruling merfolk treated those they saw as beneath them, not as good.

"Not as good." Those were words he heard from his father often enough.

"Sir," she said nervously. "Your uncle wishes to see you."

"Thank you," he said and waved her out of the room.

He went immediately to his uncle's quarters knowing without asking that the summons meant immediately. It always did.

When he arrived, Balban was finishing a meeting and Fiero waited in the sitting area just outside the office. He barked when he was done, "Come in, Fiero."

Fiero entered the sparsely furnished room and sat, waiting for the yelling to begin. Braced was more like it. He knew what was coming and it made him tense and restless. This was going to be a miserable experience. His only hope was it might get over quickly. Failure wasn't something Balban tolerated.

"So, she claims that the Stone of Clarity can never be yours."

"Yes, uncle."

"That it is both bonded to her and shielded from you or anyone else."

"Yes."

"Tell me again what you saw."

Fiero tried not to sigh as he repeated the story of how they located Lyria and used Amina's necklace, which had been stolen in the botched kidnapping attempt, as a way to make Lyria believe her cousin was in danger. He'd gotten her alone, the human didn't count, but when he attempted to harm her and take her with him the Stone had produced a power that he didn't expect, didn't know was even possible. It had protected her and repelled him. His magic did no good, in fact when she forced his spell back at him, he was nearly injured. He managed to barely get out of the way in time.

His uncle waited before saying anything. Fiero ached to pace, but he knew that would only show his frustration, which Balban saw as a weakness. "So Lyria is out of your reach along with the Stone she

157

wears. Amina is in hiding somewhere and knows that we intend to capture her."

"Yes, and the whereabouts of the third stone and its wearer are still unknown."

"Then there is only one other option. We must create a way for the Stone of Clarity and Stone of Strength to come to us. Once we have them, we'll find a way to use them to locate the Stone of Love."

"Come to us? That's not possible? They appear to the rightful wearer on her right wrist after the death of the current wearer or if given through a special ceremony as a bequest."

"Exactly. Lyria and Amina have no offspring."

"They do not." Fiero didn't know where his uncle was going with this, but something about the statement made his blood feel cold.

"Costin's sons have no daughters yet, correct?"

"Yes. I think only the older one is even mated."

"Then should something suddenly happen to Lyria or Amina, no one knows to whom the bracelets will go next," Balban said.

"Not as far as I know."

"Then that is who we must find."

Fiero still didn't see where Balban was going with this. "Who?"

"Whoever is next in line, of course. The next generation of mermaids who are, at this time, the heirs of the bracelets and the Stones." Fiero said nothing and waited for his uncle to continue. "If we capture and imprison those two—or better yet three—mermaids and kill Lyria and Amina, the bracelets will automatically appear on the wrists of the females we are holding captive. The bracelets and the mermaids are ours."

"You want to kidnap two—or three—mermaid children?" This was beyond anything he could have imagined or thought his uncle could ever conceive of.

"No, I want to capture the power the next generation will hold if we do nothing so that it can be ours to use. We cannot have the bands as long as they are with the current mermaids. Therefore, all we need to do is find the next bearers and make sure that when they get the bracelets, they are under our control."

Fiero thought about this. What his uncle was suggesting, while true, was more horrible than anything they had done so far. It was one thing to hold and try to claim an adult. It was quite another to take a child away from her mother, her family, and everything she knew.

That's what had been done to him when his father had come for him. Yes, his mother had been sick and she wanted to spare him watching her die, but the memories of being forcibly taken from his home had never left him. Sadly, it was one of the only childhood memories he had. After he came to live with his father, his memories of where he grew up vanished like they had never been. He assumed it was some magic performed by his father so he'd never think to leave. It isolated him in his grief.

Now Balban was suggesting they do something similar to at least two children who had no reason or desire to leave their homes. The thought made Fiero nauseous, but he couldn't let his uncle know. This was not something he was willing to do. How could he even think about being an effective and powerful ruler, something his uncle continually told him he must be, if he was willing to hurt the innocent?

"You really think this is what we should do? That it will work?"

"Absolutely. Why worry about dealing with the adults, trying to make them compliant when we can control children whose fears will be so great they will do exactly what we ask?"

"But taking them from their families? Do you really think that is a good idea?"

His uncle said nothing for a moment and Fiero wondered what was coming next. "You're right." Not what he was expecting. "The last thing we need is two brats crying for their mommies. We'll abduct the families as well. It's brilliant. It will give us more leverage over the girls because we can threaten the parent or younger siblings if they don't do as they are told."

Fiero was grateful for all the years of training which enabled him to keep his emotions off of his face. Somehow a bad situation had become worse.

But he could see from the gleam in Balban's eyes that there was no way to change the older man's mind. Balban was going to move forward on this horrible plan. Fiero needed to come up with a way to get Lyria and Amina into custody before Balban destroyed the lives of two innocent children.

Chapter Six

Amina had no idea what time it was when she woke, and she didn't care. She'd slept better than she expected and although that was probably due to the massage coupled with emotional and physical exhaustion, it was also because of the man in bed with her. Is this what Lyria was feeling? This connection?

With a human?

Amina didn't make commitments or form attachments with many people. Because of her gift, she was wary of getting close and finding out too much about a person, or worse, hurting them with knowledge they didn't want to receive. Lyria was only the first person badly affected by her empathy. Amina had lost more female friends than she kept over the years and by this point most mermen were wary of getting close, let alone involved. It was one of the reasons she found Nerine intriguing and hoped to visit the woman again. Nerine didn't seem bothered at all by who Amina was or what she could do.

Of course, Nerine was protected by some potion or her heritage, but Amina didn't mind that. Without any assistance or input from her gift, she genuinely liked her. The only question was would Nerine open the door again if Amina went to see her?

That was an issue for another day. For now, she would be staying on Jariz, and with Jonathan, at least for a few more days.

And then what?

Return home. Face Fiero. End the threat.

Go back to work. Help her people.

Be alone.

Because even with family and the few friends she had, since spending so much time with Jonathan, and even talking with Sofia, Amina couldn't deny her life was her work, family and family at work. And not much more. Most of her time was spent with Lyria and Aunt Betta. Or disappearing into books about romance she never experienced.

Undistracted by the emotions and needs of others, Amina had no choice but to honestly look at her own and see that she didn't experience much.

Yes, she took time for herself. She traveled around the world, came on land to shop, go into movies and find new books. None of those things offered connection. Material needs fleeting and unfulfilling.

What she most wanted was to love someone and be loved in return.

Her mother, Zan, had not been lucky in this area. Eden and Amina were born early in her parent's marriage and then her father had disappeared. The marriage was officially ended when Amina was only two years old. She'd never seen her father again. Another cost of her "gift." At least that was her assumption. When her father was spoken of, it was often said he couldn't handle living in a house with three empaths, with Zan being one of the strongest and most gifted of her generation, as Amina was now. Amina believed she was one of the reasons he'd left. If she'd been a son, at least there would have been someone he could connect with.

But she didn't know the truth. She'd been so young when her mother died, and she'd never thought to ask. Did Eden know? And is this one of the reasons, among others, she denied her family and heritage? For years Amina had wondered about Eden and if her sister was happy. At the time Eden turned her back on her birthright, Amina was told it wasn't for love, but that was years ago. How was Eden today?

She'd been told that because of the decision she could never contact Eden. Now she wondered who made that rule and why? Would Amina be cast out if she found and spoke to Eden? She thought not.

After everything was done and the threat of Fiero was ended, Amina was determined to at least find her sister. She may not be able to connect with her, and Eden may not want to see her, but she was going to try.

She was starting to see that for all she'd done in the last six years, there was still so much she didn't know, rumors she'd accepted as truth.

And what about love?

Could she truly feel it for another? Could she receive it? Or did sensing the emotions of others make it impossible for her to know her own or trust theirs? Did she avoid opportunities for connection, because the emotions of others overwhelmed her or because she didn't want to have to offer any of her own?

In different ways, she'd been abandoned by both parents.

She'd hurt the cousin she was closest to.

Emotions may be her livelihood, but they certainly hadn't brought her much joy.

Until now.

Now that she had only her own to feel and focus on she was truly enjoying them. Yes, yesterday had been terrifying and she wouldn't want to go through anything like that again, but it was also so real. Those were her fears and her relief. She felt nothing from her attackers and when Jonathan rescued her she could simply fall apart and not have to worry about the consequences to anyone else.

He'd been so strong. She'd cried once with a man she was seeing after a series of negotiations fell apart. When she went to reach for a tissue after she was done, she'd found herself alone. Yet another piece of "proof" that she would never be loved.

Not that Jonathan had mentioned love. Nor had she, but oh, she was feeling all of those things she'd dreamed of and read about. Connection, excitement, wonder. Each time she took a risk with him, he proved himself worthy of her trust.

How could she ever go back to a life without that?

Without him, a voice said.

Amina gave a soft sigh and closed her eyes. She didn't have an answer yet and it wasn't going to come to her lying in bed.

She got up, took a robe from the closet, even though it was just as easy—and more pleasant—to be naked, and went to the living room to call room service for breakfast. She was hungry again and she wanted to try some of the things that arrived as part of the coffee bar yesterday. She ordered a variety of dishes, not knowing what Jonathan wanted and sat on the couch reading. Reading would keep her mind on something other than her own life.

It wasn't long before there was a double rap on the door followed by the now familiar "Room Service."

Rather than calling out and risk waking Jonathan, Amina opened the door. "Sofia," she said to the familiar face. "It's so good to see you! Although I hate that you work such long hours. You do sleep, don't you?"

"It's okay, Mi—Amina. We do what we have to for family. And yes, I do get some sleep."

"Don't I know it," she said. It was part of what was on her mind. She was glad for the distraction. "Well, come in. And could you set up on the table outside this morning."

Sofia brought the cart in and, with her usual efficiency, set up the dining space. "Shall I get the pieces from the coffee bar?"

"Please, except for the whipped cream. That doesn't really sound good on coffee or first thing in the morning."

Sofia put the creams and sugars on a platter and then added that to the table. "Anything else?"

"You could stop for a moment and tell me about how you're doing. And Raul?"

The girl's hesitation told Amina so much. She ached to help, especially after seeing Raul in town yesterday, and what made it worse was that she knew there was likely nothing she could do. She couldn't give Sofia enough money to make a difference in the long run or she'd risk making the girl the target of thieves. Amina wished she could take the two of them away.

"He's doing okay. He hates school and not being able to help because he's too young. I try to tell him it will all be worth it, but at his age, all he can see is what he's not allowed to do."

"You're not much older," Amina said.

"No, but I am old enough to get a job and take care of us."

"You should be in school, too."

"There's nothing there for me to learn and school won't keep a roof over our heads or put food on the table." She took a breath. "Amina, thank you for asking and your concern. I do appreciate it, but you and I both know there is nothing to be done for my situation. I will do what is needed so perhaps Raul can have a better life, but mine is decided."

Amina's eyes welled with tears and she blinked them back. She understood too well what Sofia was going through. Not the poverty or the fear for a sibling, but living a life already decided. Amina knew not only that she was going to continue as Lead Counselor for as long as she could, but that any and all relationships in her life would be affected—tainted—by her position and her gift.

"Don't feel sorry for me," Sofia said with a touch of anger and defiance in her voice.

"That is not what I'm feeling," Amina said. It was interesting to have to explain herself to this girl. "Yes, I am sorry your situation is so challenging, but I am sad because, believe it or not, our situations are similar. My life was decided for me too. Trust me when I tell you that having money does not necessarily equal freedom."

"It allows for some. And more opportunities."

"Yes, but there are other things that curb choice." Like a sea dragon who wants to imprison you.

"Good morning, Ladies," Jonathan came in wearing only shorts and looking adorably sleepy. He made a beeline for the coffee, poured himself a cup and without adding anything, drank it. "Ah, much better." Amina made a face.

"I like it strong and bitter. One thing this island does extremely well is dark coffee. So, one more time, good morning," he said and this time he leaned over and kissed her."

"Good morning. Mmm… Coffee kisses, strong and dark."

"Good morning, Sofia. You won't mind if I don't kiss you."

"Of course not, sir!" The girl was completely startled and bewildered. "That would be, I mean, that wouldn't be." She stopped. "Will there be anything else?"

Amina was determined to find a way to talk to the girl again later. "Yes, thank you. I think we're all set for now."

Sofia gave a small bow, then took her cart and left.

"You completely unnerved her with that kiss comment," Amina said when they were alone again.

"I'm sorry. Before a full cup of coffee my brain and mouth are not in sync. I'll apologize to her later." He drank some more coffee. "Let's eat before things get cold, then I'll jump in the shower and be fully human."

167

Amina ate until she was full, trying some of everything she'd ordered and particularly liking the Greek omelet and the potato casserole side dish which had cheese and bacon in it.

As they were finishing Jonathan asked, "Is there anything you'd like to do today?"

"Other than stay safe?"

He took her hand and gave it a squeeze. "You are safe. I promise."

He didn't know quite how wrong he was, but since it was true for now—and she couldn't exactly tell him about the other danger she was in—she smiled. "You know this place better than I do. What ideas do you have?"

"Well, I need to get some clothes from my apartment, so I thought we'd take a ride there and then I'd show you some of places on the island that are off the beaten track. I promise, no crowds, no gangs."

"Sounds like a good plan."

"Were you okay on the motorcycle or shall I borrow one of the hotel cars?"

"I have to admit I don't remember much about that ride, but it does seem like fun."

"Well, I promise not to drive too fast and we'll grab an extra helmet to be safe."

Less than an hour later they were on their way to his home with her wearing his helmet again and a box lunch packed into the storage on his bike.

* * *

Sofia had herself under control by the time she got back to the kitchen with her room service cart. Each time she spoke with Amina part of her wanted to reach out and ask to be held and another part of her wanted to run. Never before had her heart wanted to connect with a guest, or anyone for that matter since her mother had disappeared. She was good at keeping a distance from everyone, guest and fellow employees. She wasn't willing to trust anyone to get close or they might find out her actual age and take Raul away.

But Amina was so different. It never occurred to Sofia that someone who looked like Amina, who was as kind and thoughtful, could also be living a life that was difficult and lacked options. When Amina first began to cry, Sofia was so angry. She didn't want pity. Didn't need it. She was healthy and capable and making the best of her life. Then Amina shared the reason for her tears, a wall inside of Sofia started to fall. Someone who understood. Someone else who struggled, but kept going.

Sofia couldn't help it. If she could have one wish, it would be for Amina to stay on Jariz, and they could find a way to help each other.

"You served her again." Owen was waiting for Sofia after the cart was back in place.

So much for wishing. "Yes, that's my job."

"Don't get smart with me." She said nothing knowing he'd get to his point. "Was she wearing the bracelet?"

"Yes, of course, but didn't you hear? Everyone's been talking about it. She can't take it off. Mr. Vickers asked her to put it in the safe, and she told him it wasn't possible. Now Mr. Barrett is staying with her all the time as a bodyguard."

169

"I know. I heard. Did you think I was out of the loop?" She shook her head. She got away with one dig. Two wouldn't be tolerated. "His being there is going to make it more difficult, but not impossible. There are all sorts of ways we can separate the two of them so that we can separate her from the jewelry."

Sofia didn't like the way he said that last part. "What are you going to do," she asked before she could stop herself.

"Not sure yet, but I don't expect you'll know one way or the other when I do. Unless you think you want to help." Sofia shook her head not trusting her voice. "Didn't think so. Get back to work."

Her mind racing, Sofia did as she was told wondering if there was any way she was going to be able to help Amina before or when they tried to hurt her.

* * *

They pulled up in front of the house where he lived, and Jonathan helped her off of the bike.

"It's lovely," Amina said looking at the house.

"It is, isn't it? But that's not where I live." He pointed at the garage. "I live there, in the apartment on the second floor. This is Brian's house."

"Brian?"

"That's right, one of the few employees you haven't met yet. Brian was a friend of mine back in high school. He's the assistant head of the Rooms Division and got me this job when I needed to get out of New York. Come on. I'll show you the place."

They walked up the stairs on the side of the

detached building. He unlocked the door and opened it with a flourish. "Ta da!" She stepped in and looked around. "Yes, I know what you're thinking. It's not much and it's smaller than your villa."

"Yes, that's exactly what I was thinking."

"Well I don't deserve much, so this is perfect."

"What do you mean 'don't deserve much?'"

Jonathan looked at her. "Is that was I said?" Holy shit, he couldn't believe his own words. "Guess I didn't have enough coffee this morning. I meant that I don't *need* much. Seriously, I'm only here a few hours a day and that's mainly to sleep. I mostly eat at the resort since I'm there long hours, so as long as I have my coffee pot, a shower, a bed and a place to keep my clothes, I'm all set." He looked around. "Which is about all this place has."

She stared at him as if she wanted to ask or say something more, but didn't. Thank God. There was nothing he wanted to say on the subject. She walked in to the living room. "Oh, books," she said happily. "You have so many books."

"I do. I go to the movies on occasion, or catch one at the resort, but you need to have dish television to watch anything good and I prefer books, anyway. Thank goodness Amazon mails everywhere, although the shipping costs are sometimes almost as much as the books."

"You could get one of the eBook readers that are available," she suggested.

"I have one, but most days I stick to good old fashioned paper."

"Me too."

"You enjoy reading?"

"Very much," and for the next few minutes they talked about books and exchanged the names of favorite titles and authors.

Jonathan was glad for the distraction of an easy topic. He was still reeling a bit from his "deserve" comment. He couldn't believe that had slipped out.

He came to Jariz just over a year after David's death. After the shooting he'd been assigned desk duty for three to six months as a standard operating procedure. After the six months was up he couldn't bring himself to go back onto the streets. He didn't want a new partner. He didn't want any partner. Up until that point he'd been very good at his job, so his sergeant offered him some options and he considered them half-heartedly.

He moved through life like a ghost. He broke up with the woman he'd been dating—actually—she broke up with him since he couldn't muster any enthusiasm for being with her, and stopped seeing friends. He barely ate, lost weight and muscle. Therapy helped a little but didn't change anything. He never filled the prescription for the depression meds he was given. He didn't actually want to feel better, but also didn't turn to drinking as so many cops did when the job or a situation got to be too much.

Then Brian called. He would have thought it was out of the blue but his foster mother heard what happened and called Brian. Jonathan would have been annoyed at her interference, but when Brian invited him to come out to Jariz as his guest for two weeks and see what he thought of the place since he was looking to fill the Head of Security position, Jonathan said yes for the first time since the shooting.

He updated his passport, packed two bags and left as soon as he was ready.

Nearly 4,000 miles from home, Jonathan finally thought he might be able to start over. He liked the work and the people he worked with. Problems were temporary and easily solved. He started using the gym and jogging on the beach, getting stronger and, if not happy, feeling content.

It had been over two years since he arrived and as he looked around his apartment, he saw visual proof that he hadn't let go of the grief and loss. The place was Spartan. No pictures, no color, nothing personal.

But did he really feel he didn't deserve more?

He didn't have an answer. What he did have, however, was a beautiful, thoughtful charming woman to protect, and he would rather concentrate on her than think about his past.

"Ready to see more of the island?"

"I am," she said.

They got on his bike, with her wearing his backpack of clothes that wouldn't fit in the bike's small storage area, and hit the road with her arms around his waist.

Away from the main area and other hotels, the island was beautiful. There were farms, forests and trails. He drove them to the top of cliff that looked out over the sea, a place he'd found a few weeks after he started his job when Brian noticed Jonathan hadn't taken a day off since he'd started.

"Rent a convertible, see the sites," Brian told him. "If you don't spend at least one day a week out of the hotel… I'm telling your mother."

As threats went—it was pretty good.

But he'd bought the motorcycle instead of the car. The weather was usually sunny and even when it wasn't, his drive to the hotel could hardly be called a commute. And although they both wore them today, on backloads helmets weren't required.

He parked the bike, put down the kickstand, and lifted Amina off. She was so light. He kissed her before putting her on the ground and took her hand as they walked close to the edge. They could hear the ocean breaking against the rocks below.

Jonathan took a deep breath. This was paradise. "I come up here to get away from it all. It's an ideal place to be alone."

"You don't mind not being alone now, do you?"

"Not in the least. I've never wanted to share it with anyone before, but this morning it was the first place I thought of taking you."

"Is it illegal to have sex here?"

He turned and looked at her. "Excuse me?"

"Do you really need me to repeat it?"

"Just making sure I heard what I thought I heard. And yes, it's illegal to have sex in public anywhere on the island. But we did say we'd think about breaking some more laws while we were together, so why don't we start with that one."

He took out a blanket from one of the storage compartments on his bike and spread it out for them. When he looked up, she was naked.

"How is it you're always getting undressed so quickly?"

"Most of the wardrobe I brought was one piece." Today, her pants and the halter top, in shades of orange, were all one. And now rested in a small pile at her feet. "And generally speaking, I don't wear underwear."

"A very good policy." He made quick work of his own clothes, making certain to keep his shorts—and the condoms—nearby. As soon as he was undressed he took her hand and pulled her to him, slanting his mouth against hers and letting the taste and smell of her encompass him. She, in turn, wrapped one arm around him as another raked through his hair.

Moments later they both sank to their knees and continued kissing and touching. His hands covered her breasts and stroked her nipples into hard peaks before covering one, than the other with his mouth, pulling, licking and sucking. Amina continued to touch him everywhere she could. His chest, back, ass and finally his cock, which swelled in her hand.

God, he was ready for her in no time. It was a heady experience.

Even more so when he reached between the soft lips of her pussy and found her already wet for him. He aroused her with first one then two fingers, sliding them into her, stretching her. Exciting her more. She moaned, sighed. Her body responded by getting wetter, the lips more swollen under his touch.

"Where are the condoms?" she asked.

He kissed her, reached for the pocket of his shorts, and took one out of his wallet. She took it from him and in three quick moves, covered his cock. Then pushing him onto his back, she straddled him. She held his cock by the base, moving it so it lightly touched her opening, driving them both insane. He was about to tell her she was killing him when she slid her body down on him, sheathing him inside of her.

Jonathan moaned and arched his hips up to be as deep inside of her as he could. Amina leaned back and put her hands on his thighs. Her breasts jutted out, her hair hung back, teasing his crotch. He'd never seen anyone so beautiful.

He reached up to touch her, to rake his nails down her torso, to tease her nipples again as she rode him into a frenzy of need.

He grabbed her hips. "Kiss me," he demanded.

She bent forward, doing as he asked, curtaining them with her hair as it cascaded forward. He was surrounded by her and there was nothing he wanted more. She alternated between lifting her hips to take him more fully into her and then grinding and swiveling against him in circular movements that felt sexier than they looked.

Which was saying something.

He'd never felt as excited or free as he did with her, and although part of him knew he should be concerned about being out in the open, since he'd never had anyone come across him in all the time he'd been visiting this spot, he surrendered to the joy and pleasure of being with her, being in her.

"Amina, I'm close. Come with me." This position allowed him to reach her clit each time she moved her hips up. The bud was slick and engorged and his touch made her gasp and call out his name. He kept his focus there to give her the greatest pleasure he could and when he felt her pussy tighten around him followed by a rush of wetness he let his own orgasm rush through him.

She collapsed on top of him, kissing him then putting her head over his heart. Neither one of them said anything and the comfortable silence told him so much about how special this woman was quickly becoming to him.

* * *

Balban had never been to a part of the Ocean darker or colder. Although it was what he expected when he went to see the Angler Witch, he could not have imagined how truly unnerving her realm would be.

The messenger he'd sent to ask for this audience came back changed and scarred from the experience. The man was no longer of any use to anyone, and Balban was surprised he came back at all. Fortunately, not only did he return, but he returned with an acceptance, a chart for where to go, and a light which Balban now used to guide him to the meeting place.

No one knew what combination of Oceanides created the Angler Witch only that she controlled more magic and power than any other sentient creature in the seas. Balban couldn't imagine why someone with so much power chose to live in such an isolated and desolate place, but that wasn't his concern. He needed her to help him if his plan to rule the Ocean was to succeed, and he was willing to do whatever that would take.

His body, older than he would ever admit but fit and strong, felt as though he'd been swimming for days instead of hours. The colder the water, the more of the drain on his energy. Part of him wondered if he would have the strength to leave when the time came.

That is far enough, said a female voice. He immediately knew who it was, but not where she was.

177

He stopped swimming, wondering what would happen next. He didn't have to wait long.

A sudden current came from behind him and pushed him forward with a force that was like the engines he saw in human automobiles and boats. He couldn't have fought if it he tried. He wasn't a man who was unnerved or frightened often—he would say ever—but being out of control like this was alarming. At least it required no energy from him.

He didn't know how long it lasted or how far the current took him but when it stopped he was at the opening of a cave. It glowed dimly with power, and he could see that beyond the entrance there was no water.

Come forward.

Balban steeled himself and went through the barrier. Magic pricked his skin almost as though it were checking him, testing him. He changed from his water horse form and walked deeper into the cave on two legs. There was only one way to go so he followed the hallway noting the bioluminescent lights on the walls which were inlaid with gems and crystals he knew were likely worth a fortune. She left them in a wall as decoration. He would have to see about relieving her of some of this wealth after he came to power.

It wasn't long before he turned a bend and stepped into a room which was clearly a receiving area. The witch didn't sit on a throne, exactly, but that was the impression he got as he came into the room.

He didn't know what to expect of the Angler Witch, but he was surprised to see that she was young and smaller than he would have expected.

"I am neither," she said. "This is the form I chose for today. I am Sulimene."

A thought-reader. Not what he wanted for this meeting, but it could be very useful in the future if she would consider becoming an ally. He did his best to maintain his thoughts and his heartbeat now that he knew she could read one and likely sense the other.

"The note given to me by your messenger claimed that with my help you believe you could put an end to the reign of merfolk. Tell me, why do you think I would want that?"

That was direct, not something he expected from a woman. Clearly there would be no chance for him to charm her first. "They speak of you as a monster. You are given no lands of your own, no voice in how you are governed."

"I have taken what I want and have what I need."

"This is only because you have not had the opportunity for more. I can offer you that. I will rid the seas of the Merfolk rule and give a chance to those who have been left out. Not just my people, but all people and those of mixed races too."

He knew this is what those who were on the fringes wanted. Someone who understood what they were going through, someone who would take their side. They needed a champion, a leader, who could change their lives and give them what they hungered for. And who would destroy their enemies in the process.

Or at least someone who seemed to.

There were few Oceanides who would benefit from Balban's rule, he knew that. But as long as they did what he wanted, as long as he had the power, he would make it seem that they were getting what they wanted. Once they crossed or questioned him? That was another matter entirely.

"Help me and I will free you."

"Do I seem trapped to you?"

He said nothing for a moment. She had a way of twisting his words. If she didn't have access to such powerful magic, he would have been happy to let her stay here in her frozen isolation. But he needed her help and he was determined to win her favor.

"Sulimene, please. You can tell me everything that is right with your world and show me all the power you wield, but just as there was a reason for me reaching out to you, there was a reason you allowed me to come."

Now she was silent. Good.

"Let me hear your plan and my place in it."

He told her of his desire to create a new rule of the Oceans, one that was more inclusive, and accepted all Oceanides regardless of their history or heritage. However, those currently in power would not be easily removed. So far all of his efforts through Fiero had failed. He was convinced she was the only one who could help him reach his goal.

"I want to unite Melusine's Band. Bring together the three stones and use that power to change the governing of the seas. However, I cannot get them from the three who wear them now. I need to know who the three heirs are."

He kept his plan in the front of his mind, thinking it over and over as she stared at him. He knew she was getting the details from his thoughts so he pictured the world his followers wanted, all the benefits he spoke of, as he waited.

"You need magic to find the mermaids who will wear the bands next."

"Exactly."

"This will allow you to dispose of the three who wear them now and have the bands in your control." He nodded. She took a deep breath. "You were right when you said there was a reason I granted you an audience. As you have guessed, I too have things that I want to see come to pass which would benefit me and my future. I have no love for the way the seas are run. I am neither invited nor welcome in their circles. There are times when it is good to be feared, but it is better to be powerful. My remoteness limits my power."

"I completely understand."

"Yes, I think you do."

"I don't know what your price will be, but I can assure you the rewards will be great for everyone."

She returned her silent thoughts. Balban did everything he could to keep his thoughts calm and hopeful. "Very well. I will help you," she said. "You need will need a combination of magics. No one thing will work. First, there must be a spell that will identify the girls. Then charm that will lead you to them, and, finally, soothing potion for capturing them."

"Soothing?"

"Those who are compliant are easier to capture."

"Of course," he said. This he understood completely.

"You will have these in the morning."

He was stunned. And thrilled. "You can do that so quickly?"

"Didn't you come to me for my abilities? Because you heard I could get you what you needed."

"I'm sorry, of course. I had heard of your power but I didn't know how strong, how capable you were."

181

"Do not doubt me again."

"No, never."

"And your price?"

"Your nephew," she said.

"Fiero?"

"Yes. You must give up his life in exchange for the three you will receive."

Balban barely hesitated. "As you wish."

"Then it will be done.

"Thank you. I know that this is the beginning of a spectacular change for us both. I am very grateful for your assistance."

Balban bowed and left the receiving room a moment later, more excited and hopeful than he had been in months. He knew as soon as he thought of it that capturing the heirs to the Stones he was on to something.

He gave his nephew a brief thought, then brushed it aside. Fiero had become more of a liability since his failed attempt at capturing Lyria, and Balban could see the boy had doubts about this new plan. It didn't matter. Fiero had always been easily manipulated and had no idea Balban never intended to let him rule. Truly, it wasn't a lot to give up to have what he most wanted.

* * *

The Angler Witch was alone again, and happy for the solitude. She got rid of the glamour she used in front of Balban and once again became the woman she now was. Older by far than most, though it didn't show. And wise from those years. No one would ever guess that Melusine was still alive, and for now she intended to keep it that way.

She banished the cold from the room where she met with Balban and let the warmth sink into her body. Let him believe what he wanted. That was so much easier and fit with her plans.

What a wretched creature. He reminded her of her wretched husband, now long dead. She'd never much liked the few Kelpies she met, but she had nothing against the race as a whole. Balban was not a good example of his people and hopefully after this was over she could help find a way to mend that bridge so in the future kelpies and sea dragons were not vilified or ostracized because of the foolish actions of one male. After this threat passed, there was much healing that would need to be done.

She had no doubt every promise he made, every pretty picture he painted, was false. Balban would destroy anyone he thought was as powerful or, worse, more powerful than he. She would be on the top of the list of creatures to terminate as soon as the Band was his. The fact he was so willing to sacrifice his nephew told her much. Poor boy. He had no idea he was being used—or sacrificed. Ah well, there was better in store for him.

The potion and the magic were not going to work. There were ways to make him think that things were going the way he planned and hoped, but ultimately it would backfire on him and then the mermaids would have a chance to defeat him. If they came together in time.

There was no way she would ever allow someone as shallow and power hungry as Balban to rule the

Oceans. There was no way she would ever allow him to hurt her daughters.

Melusine looked into a reflecting pool and with a wave of her hand created three circles of sight. There they were her precious daughters, united by the magic stones.

Lyria was safe for now, but she and her new love had one more battle ahead of them. Amina was going to be drawn out when Balban tried to use the potion he was given. Melusine hoped in her heart Amina would tap into the strength that was her birthright.

She gazed at her remaining daughter, so troubled, so unsure and so kind, although no one knew the last. She had no idea how powerful the Stone of Love was going to be in her life. In the coming days, she would not be able to deny its influence. Melusine smiled. She would fight the pull of love, but she would succumb. And it would make her stronger.

Soon her daughters would come together to destroy Balban once and for all. That was not for her to do, although she enjoyed the opportunity to help. She wasn't certain if she would reveal to them that she still lived, still did what she could to protect them, but there was time to decide.

For now, she would watch from a distance.

And hope.

Chapter Seven

As they ate dinner in the villa, delivered as always by Sofia, Jonathan asked, "So what do you want to do this evening? There's a lot to choose from." He picked up the piece of paper that was slid under the door each morning and posted throughout the resort which listed all the activities available. "We have dance clubs, fire pits at the pool, swim up movies, bands playing."

"Swim up movies?"

"Yes, you get a flotation device from for the pool and lay on the water and watch the movie on a big screen. It's sort of a variation on the drive-in movie."

"Different, but sounds fun. I love movies."

"It's pretty popular, especially if it's one of the clothing optional pools." He checked the page to see what else was happening. "Oh, tonight's special event is a BDSM club in the Pallas room."

"BDSM," Amina repeated. "I've read about that. It's very popular in romance novels these days, but…"

Given her expression he said, "You've never tried it."

"No, have you?"

"A few times. More as a way to spice things up for a night or two which was fun, I have to admit. I did date one woman who wanted it to be a more serious part of our relationship, but that wasn't my style so we went our separate ways." He was curious what Amina thought about it. "Would you like to try?"

She looked at him and thought for a moment. He wasn't sure of all the questions she was asking herself, but he could almost see them passing behind her eyes. "Yes," she said, "although I'm not sure what specifically I'd find exciting."

"Then this event is kind of perfect. They have lots of different toys and scenes set up and you can see what you like and what you don't. Shall we go and see what we discover?"

She agreed.

Amina changed before they left. She looked beyond lovely in a backless halter gown of black in some soft fabric with small clear sequins on it that caught the light as she moved. She seemed to have a thing for long dresses with high slits. Tonight she paired the dress with stiletto heels, also in black, which made her legs look even longer

Jonathan had no complaints.

In fact, his inability to form a coherent sentence a few moments after she stepped out in it amused her. He couldn't get over how it looked as though it were sheer yet nothing was really visible through the fabric.

And he did keep trying to look.

Every man they walked by tried too.

As the man who was supposed to be guarding her and the man sharing her bed, he was on alert at all times.

The sign in front of the room read Suadela's Dungeon Play Room. He'd always thought that a little silly and over the top, but since for many guests this would be the first time they saw or tried some of these things, anything that made it seem more like fantasy was helpful. This way if they were uncomfortable afterwards, they could say they simply got a little crazy on vacation and forget about it.

The resort used one of their larger event spaces for this because it was so well-attended, and divided up the space in to sections. Sounds of spanking and flogging were mixed in with moans of pleasure and squeals of pain along with a DJ playing music with a deep bass line.

In some areas there were bedroom scenes arranged. Others looked more like the playroom shown in the *50 Shades of Grey* movie. However, unlike that story, there were scenes of male and female domination, both of which attracted a good-sized crowd of spectators. In addition to some staff, there were several guests who agreed to "perform" in each of the areas. There was always a good list of people volunteering to help.

Each area was designed to highlight an aspect of power exchange. It wasn't extensive and Jonathan knew it wasn't even very edgy for some people, but it did build an air of excitement and for those who were newbies or had only tried a little, you could see curiosity turning to interest.

Some set ups were specifically good for those looking for an introduction, such as the use of blindfolds and softly bound wrists on a bed, and then there were the slightly more elaborate arrangements which included rope play tight enough to leave marks for a day and affect the color of the woman's breasts

187

and one of whipping which left marks that would last a lot longer. Jonathan doubted the woman in that scenario would be sitting comfortably for at least a day or two.

Neither would the man with his hands bound above him, ball gag in his mouth and his Domme walking around him wearing a long, black sheer gown and carrying a leather flogger. Sex swings, anal hooks, and violet wands were all in use and on display.

Jonathan and Amina walked slowly by each exhibition, not talking, but getting physically closer all the time. Jonathan found the scenes and the atmosphere arousing and clearly Amina did, too. What started with holding hands changed into Amina pressed against his side with his arm around her waist. She would place kisses on his neck when he wasn't expecting it and he, in turn, whispered in her ear, "if you like what you see, imagine yourself in that position and I will turn your fantasy into a reality."

"Promise?"

"Absolutely. At the back there's a place where we can buy some of the... toys you see being used. Whatever you wish, we will get."

"Then I better wish wisely," she said.

Eventually they made their way to the vendors in the back of the room where, as promised, a lot of the paraphernalia they saw were available for purchase.

"Choose carefully," said the person working behind the tables. "For obvious reasons, nothing is returnable."

Amina ran her hands over leather goods and others made of acrylic, glass and various metals. Some smooth, some studded, all designed to change and enhance the stimulation.

"What did you see that excited you?" Jonathan asked breaking into her thoughts.

"Definitely the blindfold. I know that's almost hokey, and of course you can just close your eyes, but I like the idea of knowing that even if I open my eyes, I can't see."

"I think that's part of the reason it's so popular. It immediately puts you at a disadvantage that also heightens your potential to enjoy what happens." Mentioning the disadvantage reminded him of something he knew he should ask her. "Have you heard about the importance of things being safe, sane and consensual?"

He didn't want to start anything that she wasn't completely comfortable with. This was only something he did occasionally for a little extra spice, not something he was hardcore about, but he knew it was important to have this conversation.

She nodded. "The characters in the romances with this type of play talk about this, but I've always thought it was so silly."

That was not the reaction he expected. "Silly? It's supposed to be a way of keeping things—"

"Safe, yes I get that, but the truth is this should be true no matter what type of relationship you have. After all, there's nothing safe or sane about opening yourself up to another person is there? Once you make that decision, there's always the chance of getting wounded, usually not physically but emotionally, right?"

"Yes, that's true."

"What is safe about caring for someone? What is sane about trusting someone? I mean, basically you are walking into a situation and announcing—here I am and I am willing to be vulnerable, I am willing to be hurt. Not harmed, of course, that's never the intention, but it occurs. No one is perfect and things happen when you're with someone that are not your intention or sometimes out of your control."

"I never thought about it that way. I think what they mean is that you shouldn't put yourself in a situation with another person who you have doubts about, who you don't feel you can trust."

"I completely agree with that, but isn't that the case no matter whether you want to be kinky or, what's the phrase, vanilla?"

She was right. He hadn't thought about it that way.

"And as for consensual," she continued, "that has nothing to do with BDSM. That's true about everything in relationship. Shouldn't you always get consent from your partner no matter what you're doing?"

"Absolutely."

"So why are these so called rules only applied or talked about when it comes to BDSM? It confuses me."

He thought about it for a minute and then answered, "I think the concept of consciously giving up control, of willingly surrendering to another person can be very scary for a lot of people. When you have a list that can be used like guidelines it feels safer."

"Safer," she said with a laugh. "There's surrender and power exchange in every relationship, and not only in romantic ones. People need to accept that, not try to put rules or guidelines on it.

"It does seem rather ridiculous now that you say it. Does that mean you don't want to pursue this?"

She kissed him fully on the mouth, teasing his lips with her tongue before pulling away and saying. "Not at all. I'm curious about so much of this. I've never been tied up or blindfolded and seeing it all was very exciting. I think it could be quite delicious. With the right person."

The blood rushed straight to his cock, and he was glad he was wearing black pants in a darkened room. She was always so surprising. "So, do you want to pick a safe word for our play?"

"You choose."

He looked at her and thought for a moment. "How about mermaid?"

"What? Why?"

"I don't know. When you first fell down the stairs and Carlos radioed to tell me what happened, he said there was an injured mermaid in the lobby. I can see why he called you that," Jonathan said running his hands through her beautiful long hair. "There's something about you, something that almost seems like it doesn't belong here."

She didn't answer, just looked at him.

"Did I say something wrong?"

"You don't think I belong here?"

"Oh, my beauty, of course not. You definitely do, and you belong with me." He kissed her. "Preferably in my bed, well your bed. You just have a certain quality that's hard to define and… Rare."

She nodded. "Okay, 'mermaid' is the safe word. Although something tells me I won't need to use it."

"I hope not. I want to thrill you, excite you, and

maybe push you to a new height of pleasure you've never reached, but I definitely don't want to scare you or do anything you don't like." He kissed her. "Let's choose some toys and see if I can't get you to scream so loudly you lose your voice."

Amina smiled at his comment and thought of the most famous of the human tales about mermaids. She supposed there were a few circumstances where it could be worth it to lose one's voice. Screaming with pleasure sounded as though it should be on the top of that list.

And she was already turned on by all they had seen. She would have been completely overwhelmed by this room had her gift not been dimmed. It was one of the reasons she got so much of her information through books rather than experiences.

Places with too many people gave her too much input and she quickly became overloaded. A few weeks after her bonding ceremony with the band she collapsed at a function when a fight broke out between several people because their emotions became too much for her to handle. Eventually she learned to shield herself or to drink what she thought of as a "lessening" tea so that she wouldn't be caught unprepared if emotions flared.

This room, filled with strangers growing hungrier and needier by the minute, with everyone becoming more turned on and more adventurous, would have either knocked her unconscious or given her an orgasm in the middle of the room.

Of course, looking at the choices of things to buy by while Jonathan traced patterns on her bare back, the public orgasm was still a possibility.

When he asked her if she wanted to check the event out, she'd had some reservations. She'd read enough to know that trust was an important part of this sort of sex play and she'd only met the man a few days ago. Yes, they spent a good deal of time together already, and yes, he was there to help her twice and yes, they'd already had sex—several times—but that didn't quite answer the core question.

Did she trust him?

Amina had to acknowledge to herself that outside of her family she didn't trust easily. Or maybe at all. There were some people who worked in the government compound for years who were very familiar to her and she supposed she trusted them, but only within the scope of their work and the interactions she'd had with them.

It was ironic to realize this form of sex play, with its awareness and need to talk about limits, made her realize how many constraints and limits she already placed on her life. For the first time she wanted fewer limits, fewer rules and less fear.

Yes, she trusted Jonathan. It was a wonderful, freeing thing to realize.

"So we're starting with a blindfold," she said. "Let's get something comfortable."

The vendor heard what she said and directed them to several types from leather with a fur side to be placed against the eyes, to satin ones that looked like oversized sleep masks. After running her hands along the different materials and textures, Amina chose one in black satin.

"And now," Jonathan prompted.

"You choose," she said, curious as to what might interest him.

193

"Cuffs. I like the idea of you being bound to the headboard, unable to stop me from doing all I want to please you."

"Can I turn the tables on you? Are you willing to try it as well?"

"Absolutely," he whispered in her ear and the intensity of the word sent shivers through her body and a rush of heat and wetness between her legs. For the moment she couldn't decide which she wanted more—to be bound or see him that way. How delightful this all was.

"Is there anything you didn't like," she asked."

"Gags of any kind. I want to be able to hear you when you moan and cry out and," he dropped his voice, "when you scream my name."

"How sure of yourself you are," she said, but he was right. She'd already called out his name when they were in bed. Tonight was likely not to be any different in that regard.

"Anything that's a 'no' for you?"

She thought for a bit back to the scenes she saw. "The full masks. I didn't like how impersonal that made the situation seem, and besides I think seeing the other person's facial expressions is both important and exciting."

"I agree," he said. "Did you notice the woman being whipped with the dragon's tail?"

"There was a dragon's tail?" Suddenly she wasn't thinking about sex anymore. Her world outside of the resort had made a second appearance in the space of a few minutes. Maybe she should take it as a sign. First he wanted "mermaid" as a safe word and now this. No one knew where she was, but perhaps she should consider leaving and finding a different place to stay until she got word it was safe to go home.

The thought of leaving Jonathan made her stomach flip. It had only been three days but so much had happened. Her fall, seeing him again, the attack in town and seeing him with Sofia. Knowing that she would be with him for the whole day was something she was happy about each morning when she woke up. It wasn't supposed to happen like this. She'd never cared about a human before. Now wasn't the time to start, but her emotions told her the choice was no longer hers to make.

"It was in the scene with the woman standing with her hands cuffed above her head. Her Master started with a flogger, making her ass red and sensitive, then he switched to the leather whip. That's the dragon's tail."

"Yes, I remember now."

"And did you see her face? The looks of pleasure and need?" Amina nodded. She flashed back to the image as he described it. "He saw every flinch she made and how she made it. When her squeals got to a certain volume, he'd stop and touch her. He'd caress her back, her breasts, and kiss her softly."

"That's right, I remember thinking his touches were such a contrast to the harshness of the whipping, but I could also see it was exactly what she needed, what she wanted."

"Yes. There's a great deal of intimacy and connection there."

She looked up from the table. "Do you know them?"

"They are regulars. They visit several times a

year and we comp some of their costs because they help us out at these events. They're quite popular."

"I can understand why."

"Anyway, I love seeing you react to what I'm doing, what you're enjoying. I would never want anything to cover that up."

"So," she said, "no gags and no masks. Is there anything else you want to try?"

"Ah, with an opening like that the list could go on and on, but since I know you mean I should pick out something else, there is one more thing I thought looked like a lot of fun." He reached out and picked up a beautiful rod in blues and greens that was ribbed and grooved over the length of the shaft. "A glass dildo. I've never owned one, but the thought of making it cold and using it on and in you when your body is hot and wanting sounds like it could be very pleasurable."

She couldn't speak for a moment. The sensations he was describing sounded so incredibly enticing. "Yes," she finally managed and he smiled at her breathless voice. "That sounds like a wonderful addition."

The vendor packed up their three purchases, careful to put the glass piece in its own soft cinched bag. "Enjoy," he said as he handed them a bag.

"I'm sure we will," Jonathan said.

"I think we should go back to the villa."

"You sure you don't want to look around more or…"

"Now," she said and then they both laughed.

"As you wish, my lady. I just want to make one quick stop."

His stop was to the front desk. He spoke briefly to

the woman behind the counter and then he rejoined Amina. "What was that?" she asked.

"You'll see."

They walked the paths to the villa quickly, stopping only to kiss every now and then. She needed to be alone with him.

When the got to the villa something was in front of the door. "Oh good, I hoped they'd be fast."

"With what?"

"A bucket of ice."

"To chill… water?"

"Perhaps, but my main thought was the dildo."

Amina let out a tiny "oh" that sounded almost like a squeal. She'd never done anything like this before, but it seemed as though it was a good night for firsts.

As soon as they walked in the door, Amina untied the knot at the back of her halter dress and let it slide to the floor. Since she wore nothing underneath, she was instantly naked.

"You are a goddess," he said as she took his hands and walked him into the bedroom. He got undressed quickly, if not as fast as she did and followed her, leaving his clothes where they landed. The room was dark, lit only by moonlight and the lights on the paths outside.

They were already so aware of each other, so ready. She wanted to touch him and be touched everywhere. She couldn't get enough.

"I think our purchases were a very good idea," he said.

"How so?"

"Because we both seem ready to rush to the finish, and these," he said holding up the bag, "are going to force us to slow down. If you are agreeable, for tonight I'd like to blindfold and bind you."

"Yes, I want that," she said. After her realization earlier of the constraints she put on her life because of her gift as well as because of her own fears and past losses, tonight she wanted to surrender completely. Surrender to pleasure, to whatever she might desire, and to him.

Just the thought made her wet. Wetter.

She walked ahead of him into the bedroom, turned on the nightstand light, and stared at the bed. The scroll work on the headboard, which she found beautiful and ornamental before, now looked different and she stared at it thinking of the possibilities.

"Yes," Jonathan said breaking into her thoughts. He pressed against her, softly caressing her breasts and letting her know he was naked as well, "I'm going to use that to attach the cuffs to you. You won't be able to touch me, help me, or stop me."

She leaned her head back and he kissed her. "Sounds perfect." She took his hand and they both got into the bed.

"Lie on your back," he said. "Arms up so I can see how far down you need to be so that your comfortably stretched."

She did as he said, then moved down the bed a little. He put two pillows under her head as he cuffed her wrists to the headboard.

"Comfortable?"

"I don't know if anyone can be comfortable with their arms like this, but I'm not uncomfortable. How's that?"

"It will do. You'll let me know if that changes."

She liked how he said that as an order, not a request. A little thing that felt like a big thing under the circumstances.

He reached for another pillow on the bed. "Lift your hips." She did and he placed the pillow beneath her ass then positioned her legs apart. "You are so unbelievably stunning." He stared at her for a long moment. She'd never felt more exposed or more beautiful.

"I'm going to keep all the lights on tonight."

"Why?"

"Because since you're wearing a blindfold they won't bother you, and I will have a chance to see you completely without you being able to do anything about it."

She shivered.

"And it reminds me of the day we met when the sunlight showed me all of you."

All Amina could do was nod.

He sat next to her on the bed and looked into her eyes. She loved how dark his were. "Ready for the blindfold?"

"Yes."

"And to simply enjoy all that I am going to do to you, for you?"

"Yes," she said, this time as a whisper.

"Then lift your head a little so I can put this on."

She did as she was told and her world went dark. She could hear him move around the room, then felt him get back on the bed. But because she couldn't see, she wasn't ready for his kiss. A simple, full mouth kiss sent a shock through her that was as unexpected as it was wonderful. If this is what a kiss could feel like, she could hardly imagine what was going to happen next.

199

As it turned out, she gasped against his lips when an ice cube was pressed against her nipple, instantly hardening the little bud into a sharp peak. When the heat of his mouth covered the cold skin the combination of sensations was incredible and again she called out. She heard him laugh softly at the sound.

"You, you…" she started.

"Is something wrong?"

"Not at all, but you may… regret not gagging me. I have a feeling I am going to be gasping and yelling a lot."

"Go right ahead, my Amina. The villa is isolated enough that we won't bother anyone, and if someone does hear, well I think they'll only be jealous." Now it was her turn to laugh. "Shall I continue?"

"Yes. Please." Two different sentences. Two different meanings.

As Jonathan continued to suck and kiss one nipple, he brought the ice to the other, bringing that one to the same hardness as the first. She moaned with each different sensation, enjoying them all, wanting so much more.

She pulled at the cuffs, not wanting to be free, but not knowing what do with all the pleasure rushing through her body.

He kissed her with cold lips and tongue and she responded a though she were starving. She was. She'd never experienced need like this.

He moved away from her mouth and she nearly whined. She heard the ice in the bucket then felt another cube on her skin. He must have had the ice in or near his mouth because as he made cold wet lines on her skin, they were followed by the heat of his breath, mixing the sensations and driving her wild.

He worked his way down her body and she lifted her hips in anticipation when he got to her pussy.

"So hungry," he said.

"Very." And then she squealed as a drop of cold water landed on her clitoris followed by another and then by the quick lick of a hot tongue. He didn't let her know the pattern, so she didn't know when she'd feel the water or the lick, or how long he'd lick before returning to the cold drops.

It was maddening. There was so much sensation and yet not enough.

And then he touched her tip of her hardened clitoris with the very cold end of the glass dildo. She screamed at the intensity of the sensation, her hands made grabbing motions but had nothing to grasp. She couldn't even pull away if she thought it was too much because he had one hand firmly on her hip.

"Tell me what you want."

"Don't stop," she said.

"Close enough."

Using the wetness of her body, he made agonizingly slow circles with the glass against her clit. She could feel herself getting more swollen, wetter. The touch was so focused yet so intense. Pleasure built in her, but only incrementally.

Until his tongue licked her pussy from the bottom of her inner lips to the top, and there he moved the dildo away so that he could lick her clitoris and give it an, oh too short, suck. The intensity was beyond words. All she could do was cry out her pleasure, although she did manage one word.

"Jonathan."

Chapter Eight

He had never heard anything as beautiful as the sounds she made as she became more and more excited, and hearing his name as he licked her got him harder than he already was.

He didn't know if this was torturous for her, but it was driving him mad. There was a part of him that didn't want to go slowly, that didn't want to take his time. He simply wanted to take all she was offering him. Her body was ready, her pussy wet and swollen. She couldn't stop him if he drove his cock into her immediately.

And yet...

Taking his time, seeing her desire build, knowing that he had all the control over her pleasure. It was a heady experience.

He continued to lick her, letting her body warm up while he placed the dildo on the ice-covered towel he'd brought to the bed. He listened to the sounds she made, watched how her body reacted—much like the couple they'd seen in the Pallas Room—and from this decided what to do, how to enjoy her.

Her legs were apart, but he wanted her more exposed. He stopped what he was doing to bend each of her legs back against her body, opening her more to his touch and gaze. He didn't know if he'd ever looked at a woman so closely, and he was sorry he hadn't. There was such beauty here, such... wonder.

Returning his attention to her pussy, he alternated licking and sucking, listening to what she liked, which seemed to be everything. Then as another gush of wetness ran from her, he added the dildo, pushing the slippery coldness into her.

"By the Goddesses," she screamed out.

Her body tensed then relaxed then tensed again. Once she had accepted the penetration, he continued to slide in and out of her as though it was his cock. Instantly it was slick from her juices. He loved seeing the lips of her pussy grab the sides, warming it.

And then something shifted.

He wasn't certain how he knew or what exactly the change was that came over her, but from one breath to the next he knew her orgasm had started. Maybe it was because he was watching her so closely, but he wanted her to climax more powerfully than she ever had. He focused on her clit with his tongue, slid the dildo in and out in time with the movements of her hips, responding to her body's natural rhythm so he could give her the most pleasure possible.

As promised, she did scream as she came. First his name and then nothing more coherent. The sound alone made him harder than he already was and the ache itself was exquisite.

Grateful he kept it close by and had already opened the package, he managed to put on the condom as he kept one finger on her pussy, stroking and easing her down from her climax.

Before she could completely catch her breath and without telling her, he sank into her wet, swollen pussy, making her cry out again.

"I wasn't expecting… I didn't know…"

"And yet it was exactly what you wanted."

"Yes," she said.

He knew it was because it was what he wanted, needed.

Craved.

She was hunger and fire and desire. She made him feel alive, excited, and powerful.

"I need to be deeper," he said.

"Yes. Yes, please."

"I'm going to undo one of the cuffs and then you are going to turn over onto your knees so I can fuck you from behind."

She nodded. There was something so exciting about her instant agreement, her clear desire.

He stayed inside her as he leaned over her and unclasped a cuff from the headboard. He left it around her wrist because it looked so damn sexy, then he moved her other wrist closer to the center of the bed, grabbed her by her hips, and turned her over.

She had the sexiest ass. He was usually so busy kissing her and enjoying her front, he hadn't taken the time to appreciate this side of her. He raked his nails down her back leaving mild red marks. She arched like a cat in response. He spanked her lightly and when she gave a small "oh" and a wiggle he did it again, a little harder.

After a few more slaps and sounds of pleasure, he slammed his cock back into her body without warning.

Her response wasn't small. Her pussy wrapped

around his cock tightly and he could feel her accepting him, wetting him. In this position he was so deep, every inch of his cock surrounded by her heat. He loved being able to dig his hands into her hips and bring her into him, pressing into her.

"I love feeling you so deeply," she said in a breathless stutter. He saw her free hand grip the sheet as though she would tear it in two from the intensity of her need.

He understood exactly what she was feeling.

He dug his fingers into her not caring—and actually hoping—there might be marks on her in the morning. He pushed himself into her over and over. He was so sensitive, even with the condom on he could feel her gripping him, holding him.

He was beyond thought, there was nothing but feeling. Need.

Fucking her. Making love to her. It rolled together until he couldn't do anything but push himself harder. He listened to them both, crying out. Wanting.

His release came over him like a storm, raging and taking. He had a moment to be grateful that she was as excited as he was, because he was going to explode and nothing could hold him back.

Blood rushing in his ears, his heart hammering like he'd run a marathon. He turned her over and fell on top of her, not even able to roll to the side for a while. He was so dazed he didn't even notice her unclasp her other wrist from the headboard until he felt the cool D-ring on his chest.

"So that's why they put it in romance novels. That's what the big deal is," she said.

"It is."

"And you know what?"

"What," he asked.

"It never occurred to me once to say 'mermaid.'"

* * *

"David, no!" Jonathan shot up in bed, heart pounding, instantly awake. He jumped when Amina put her hand on his shoulder. He was used to being alone after these nightmares.

"Jonathan?"

"I'm sorry. I'm fine. It was just a dream."

"I don't think 'just' is the right word. Do you want me to turn on a light?"

"No," he answered immediately. He stayed sitting, willing his breathing back to normal. Shit, this was unexpected and unwelcome.

"Will you tell me about it?"

He took a deep breath, grabbed an extra pillow and put it behind his head so he was raised when he lay back. She put her head on his chest and said nothing. He didn't either at first. He hadn't spoken of that day outside of therapy, and that's because it was mandatory. Maybe it was time.

"David was my partner on the NYPD, New York City Police Department. We'd been working together for almost four years. He took me on as rookie, poor guy. I totally lucked out. He was a great mentor. And friend. Three years ago we responded to a domestic violence call that devolved into a hostage situation. The guy had a gun on his wife and kids. And us. After hours of trying, David finally convinced the guy to let the kids go. David told me to walk them out and when

I did, the guy shot his wife, David, and then himself. It was over in seconds."

"I'm so sorry."

"Just an ordinary day. Anybody could have answered the call. It happened to be us. And when the shots were fired, it should have been me in that room. I should have stayed in the house."

"Why?"

"Then David would be alive. He was married. He had two kids, a boy and a girl. Me, I've got no one. No one would have mourned long. Three lives were ruined that day."

"Four," she said.

"Four?"

"Yes, yours. You're here because of that incident."

"I wouldn't say my life was ruined though."

"Oh no? I saw your apartment. It's bare, almost empty, even though you've been here two years. And what did you say about it being what you deserved?"

"That was a slip."

"A slip of truth."

He said nothing. "Maybe. I know in my heart I can't bring him back, but I guess I also still believe that I need to hold back because of what his family lost."

"You don't seem to be holding back with me."

"Yes, but you're different."

"Different how?"

"Because..." He stopped.

She looked up at him. "Because? Please finish your sentence."

"You won't like it. Hell, I won't like it."

"Is it the truth?"

"In this moment, yes."

"I know the truth can hurt, but I also know it has the power to heal."

"Because you'll be leaving and I'll be alone and heartbroken. That seems fair to me, since David's wife has been left in the same situation."

She said nothing, then asked, "How long do you think you'll keep living this shadow life?"

"What do you mean?"

"I think you know. If I met you three years ago, what would you have been like?"

He thought about it before answering. "Focused, interested in different things. Having fun. Actually, now that I say that, I've felt more like my old self these past few days with you. I *am* having fun, and I feel a connection with you. Even worrying about your safety has made me feel more alive and involved than I have in years. And last night was more than fun."

She smiled and kissed his chest. "Maybe it's finally time for you to let go of a situation that, yes, ended badly, but over which you had no control."

"A week ago I would have said, no, not yet."

"And now?"

"Now I'm starting to believe in possibilities."

She snuggled back against him and they went back to sleep. Or at least he tried, but his head was swirling with thoughts. As he held her, he thought about David. Not the day he died, which was the only thing he focused on for years, but the man who had been his friend and mentor.

David had wanted Jonathan to have a future like his, with a wife and kids. They'd talked about it one night while playing pool in David's basement. Jonathan was over there at least once a week for dinner for the company and the cooking.

"Jonathan," David said taking a swig of his beer then lining up a shot, "there is nothing like starting and ending your day with a woman who loves and accepts you. It's the greatest feeling in the world. And kids? They'll drive you crazy, give you gray hair and make you lose sleep and you'll be grateful for every minute. Don't let any of the other guys convince you to stay a bachelor. Find a woman you can love and you'll be amazed how life changes for the better."

He looked at the woman in his arms and thought about how in a few short days she had changed his life for the better.

* * *

I know the truth can hurt but I also know it has the power to heal. Amina knew that one all too well. Hearing herself say it, however, made her wonder if when she hurt others, she may have also given them a chance to heal?

She didn't have the answer to that yet. She was asking Jonathan to forgive himself for things out of his control. Maybe it was time for her to look doing so as well.

She snuggled closer, trying to fall back to sleep but something Jonathan said made her open her eyes again.

Because you'll be leaving and I'll be alone and heartbroken.

That was going to happen anyway, but hearing him say it was different. Yes, as soon as it was safe to leave or she was called to return, she'd disappear from his life and he'd have no way to contact her or find her. It's not as if she had a Facebook page.

Amina thought of her sister, Eden, and realized this was becoming an unfortunate pattern for her.

Those she loved, she lost.

Not that she loved Jonathan.

She cared about him, of course. He was strong, brave thoughtful and sexy as hell. And kind. Compassionate.

And she enjoyed spending time with him, wanted more time even, but caring, trusting and liking his company didn't mean she was falling in love with him.

She couldn't, wouldn't, be that foolish with her heart.

* * *

The next morning, they slept in and ordered a late breakfast. As Sofia set up the table, she took an envelope out of her pocket.

"Someone asked me to give you this," Sofia said.

"What is it?

"I don't know. Looks like a letter."

Amina couldn't imagine who would send her a letter. Surely the gangs didn't send threats that way. The paper was heavy, old fashioned. She opened it and read:

My messenger says you are never alone so he could not deliver this news to you. Fiero's reach grows, but he is not the true threat. There are others now in danger. Someone needs to help them. When you see your cousin next, it is time to come home.

Nerine

Amina was right to have told Nerine where she was. She was grateful the other woman reached out to give her this news. She still couldn't go home, but it was a relief to hear about Lyria.

"Is everything okay?" Sofia asked.

"Yes, why?

"You look concerned."

"Oh, it's just the real world, the world away from the resort, reminding me that eventually I'm going to have to leave."

Sofia stared at her with eyes so instantly full of sadness and regret that it took all of Amina's will power not to embarrass the girl by going over and giving her a hug. They both turned when they heard Jonathan in the bathroom, and the moment was broken. Sofia left quickly just as Jonathan stepped into the room.

They spent the day doing nothing, and it was wonderful. They read, swam, made love and slept. There was a moment with another pair of children trying to steal at the resort and Jonathan was concerned when they came close to where he and Amina were sitting, but his staff took care of it quickly and the possibility of danger passed.

She couldn't remember a more relaxing day.

"So," she said after dinner, "what shall we try tonight?" He did the eyebrow wiggle she was coming to know and expect. "Besides that."

"There's karaoke tonight at the Anthias Bar. That's always popular."

"What's karaoke?"

"People get up and sing to popular songs. The

lead vocal is taken out and they get to be the star."

"I couldn't do that," Amina said.

"Well, most people use several drinks for courage and most aren't very good."

"I really can't."

"But you're always humming. You clearly have a lovely voice. At least I think so. Look, I'll go first if that will make you braver. I'm lousy, but I'm loud."

"No, Jonathan. I don't sing. I never sing."

"There's more to that sentence. I can hear it."

She paused. Thought. She'd never talked about this with anyone but after his confession last night, she knew she couldn't hold back. "The last time I sang, my mother and my aunt were killed."

He came over and put his arms around her, pulled her to his chest. "I'm so sorry. How old were you?"

"Nine. And before you do the math, it was about 15 years ago."

"I'd never ask a lady her age. It's not polite. And it's dangerous. That's a long time to go without doing something you like."

"I was singing when we got the news. I swore to myself I'd never sing again. Besides, it reminds me of that night."

"I can imagine." He didn't say anything for a minute. "Did you like singing?"

"Yes, very much."

"Do you miss it?"

"I did at first, not as much now."

"What do you think would happen if you sang?"

She looked at him. "What do you mean?"

"Well, aside from bringing up difficult memories, which I assume happens whether or not you sing, and breaking a promise you made to yourself in a moment of grief, what would happen if you started singing again? Other than maybe having something in your life you enjoy?"

Amina said nothing. She understood what he was saying. She'd asked herself the same thing on occasion when she was younger, but now it had been so long she couldn't imagine singing. "My cousin, Lyria, and sister, Eden, lost so much that night other than our mothers, more than I did. I guess I thought I should give up something too."

"I understand the 'logic' of grief. I live here because I couldn't bear to do anything I once did in New York City. Living there and thinking about moving forward when David didn't live at all was too much for me." He kissed the top of her head then moved back so he could look at her. "Amina, this morning I woke up screaming because of nightmare that happened three years ago. Clearly, I'm not one to offer advice on how to move on from something. However, I do know that not finding ways to heal, not finding ways to forgive ourselves for situations we didn't create is not letting either one of us be as happy as we ought to be. David would hate it if he saw where I lived and how I haven't moved on. What would your mother say?"

"She loved hearing me sing." He kissed the tears that fell. "I don't know if I'm ready yet, if that's okay."

"It's more than okay. You don't see me running out to put pictures up on my walls or get decorative pillows do you? Let's just say we'll both try."

She nodded. "Guess some of that therapy paid off."

"Some. I'll have to send my old therapist a letter and let him know. In the meantime, didn't I hear you say something about liking the movies?"

"I love movies?"

"Well then for tonight, we'll reserve two floating lounge chairs, get ourselves some drinks and watch," he looked at the piece of paper that listed the resort activities, "*Dirty Dancing*. That's a classic. Have you seen it?"

"No, but it sounds good. "

"Fortunately, it's not one of the clothing optional pools. I don't love having couples groping each other next to me."

"I think I'd like to buy a new bathing suit for the night, if you'd like to help."

"I'd love to. I think it could be fun."

And it was. Especially since every time she came out in one he made sexy comments, until she chose a two piece in green that had ties in four different places. With that one, he came back into the dressing room with her, pressed her up against the wall and kissed her until they were both breathless. "Okay," she said. "I think I'll take this one."

The movie was fun and sexy. She liked being next to him, holding hands, teasing the skin on his arm and knowing there was nothing they could do or the floatation devices would flip them into the pool. She saw several other couples try this and fail.

Still, she couldn't stop thinking about what he said, and as they walked back to the villa. "There was a line in the movie that I really liked, she said."

"What was that?"

"Baby was talking about how she wasn't sure of

anything, of how she was scared of everything, but mostly she was scared of never having this feeling again. I think… that's one of the things I feel when I think about singing. When I miss it, I wonder if anything could ever give me that feeling again."

He kissed the hand he was holding and then, a few steps later, without letting herself over think it, she began to quietly sing Norah Jones' *Come Away With Me*.

He stopped at the bench they were walking by and sat in front of her as she continued to sing.

Tears came and she let them come. They weren't sobs and it didn't hurt. It was joy, simple and pure.

When she finished singing he said nothing at first, letting the silence of the night wrap around them. Finally, he stood and kissed her gently. "That, was the most beautiful thing I ever heard. On every level. I know that wasn't easy. Thank you for sharing that with me."

"It… felt wonderful. I thought I remembered what it was like to sing. I was wrong. I'd forgotten. I never imagined it would feel so amazing."

"It certainly sounded amazing."

"My mother would have loved that song."

"What was her name?"

"Zan. I know, it's unusual. Her twin sister was named Zia. Together their name means rainbow."

"That's beautiful." He took her hand and they walked the rest of the way back to the villa in silence.

In contrast to the passion and intensity of the night before, they made love slowly, tenderly. When he undressed her, Jonathan kissed her shoulders, inner arm and wrist, then spent time exploring the slope of

215

her waist, her hips and behind her knee, which turned out to be quite sensitive and almost ticklish.

She, in turn, did something similar, looking to discover new ways places that brought him pleasure. She reached around as they kissed to let her hands touch the base of his neck and top of his back, then his torso, and eventually kissed the tips of his fingers as she rubbed them on her lips.

Moans and sighs were soft. Their focus was on each other, pleasure was secondary, part of the experience rather than its goal. They reached for each other and found connection, understanding and love.

As she lay in her arms she knew the truth. Any defenses she might have had were gone, and any hope she had for not opening up her heart to him had vanished. So much for protecting her emotions. May the Goddess help her, she was completely in love with Jonathan.

Chapter Nine

The next night, after another relaxing day, Amina was becoming concerned about the amount of time she'd been at the resort. There should have been news by now, contact from someone, telling her she could come home. Once Jonathan was asleep tonight, she would head to the ocean, fin and swim out as far as she could to try to make contact with Lyria, or maybe Nerine. She didn't want to disappear on Jonathan, but she needed to know what was happening with the search for Fiero and the Stone of Love.

They were reading on the porch and had been talking about heading to one of the restaurants for dinner when there was a knock on the door that didn't stop. Frantic not professional.

"Amina! Mr. Barrett! Please, someone. Please be in."

"That's Sofia," Amina said, dropping her book and running to the door.

"Wait," Jonathan said before she could open it. "It could be a trap to get you to step out alone."

"We know Sofia."

"And I know crooks and gangs." She hated that he could be right.

He looked out the peephole then opened the door keeping the chain on. "Sofia, are you alone?"

"I am but I need your help right away. *Por favore.*"

"Let her in, Jonathan." The tone of the girl's voice and the fact that she was using Spanish for the first time had Amina's heart pumping fast.

Jonathan opened the door and Sofia ran in with tears running down her face and holding a piece of paper in front of her which she handed to Amina. "They've taken him. They've taken Raul. I don't know what to do. I don't know how we can help him. Please, he's everything to me."

Amina looked at the note and the crude handwriting.

We have your brother. If you want to save him bring the lady with the bracelet to the fountain at the Stall Market at 7:00. Come alone. No security. No cops. Tell no one or he dies.

"Oh no," Amira said. "Sofia, I'm so sorry." She opened up her arms and the girl rushed in. Amina held her close and walked her over to the couch where they sat. She gave the note to Jonathan. "Tell us exactly what happened."

With sentences broken by sobs, Sofia said, "I took the early dinner break for my shift, as usual, and got home around 5:30. Raul wasn't home, but sometime he's out playing with friends. He knows I can only stay about 20 minutes before I have to get back, so even if he's not home when I get there, he usually shows up a few minutes later. I put together what I had for dinner while I waited. 5:45 comes. No Raul. I don't want to leave without seeing him, but I don't want to be late. So, I get some paper to leave him a note. I sat down at the table to write it and that's when I found this."

"You have a routine they knew and could easily interrupt," Jonathan said.

"And Owen in the kitchens knows I've been to this Villa several times," Sofia added. "He knows I've spoken to you."

"I'm so sorry to have gotten you and Raul involved in this," Amina said. It was one thing having the sea dragon after her for the bracelet. It was something completely different to have these children in the crossfire.

"It's not your fault," Sofia said.

"It's because of the bracelet that this is happening."

"It's because of the gangs this is happening," Jonathan said. "I don't understand why the fountain. It's so public."

"Because I met Raul there when I went into town."

Sofia looked surprised. "That's not possible."

"I don't want to add to your concerns, but Raul has been cutting school—I don't know how often— and begging for money from tourists in town."

"No, he wouldn't do that. He knows better, that the gangs are there and they want little kids they can use and... *Oh, Dios mio.* Of course you are not lying. How could I be so stupid? How could I not know?"

"He wanted to be helpful, grown up. He made me promise not to tell you, and then with the attack on the way back, I didn't think of it again until now."

Jonathan said, "So they know him, saw the two of

you together because they arranged it, and know Sofia has a connection to Amina. I should have guessed they'd find a way to try again. Losing face by losing a steal is bad for a gang members' status. When you got away, it meant they needed to try harder, do something bigger."

"We can't sit here and do nothing," Amina said. "Raul's in danger, and it's almost 7:00 now."

"You can't give them the bracelet," Jonathan said. "Besides not giving in to gangs, it doesn't come off your wrist."

"I know that, but they may not know, and even if they've heard, they might not believe it's true. Who could imagine a bracelet with no clasp? I've got plenty of money with me. I'll bring it and use it as a ransom of sorts to get Raul back. It will have to do. They're not foolish. This is a business for them. I'll bring enough so that it's worth it for them to make the trade."

Sofia looked more panicked than before, if that were possible. "Amina, thank you, but if you do this… how will I ever repay you."

Amina took Sofia's face in her hands. "This is not something that needs repayment. This is a situation caused by people who feel entitled to take what they want and believe themselves above any consequences." An image of Wilmar and then Fiero came to her mind. She was not going to be the victim. And neither was Sofia or Raul. "We are going to correct the situation. More money can be earned. Raul is priceless, yes?"

Sofia nodded, couldn't speak.

"You are not going without me," Jonathan said.

"You can't come, my love. You saw what the note said. Just the two of us."

"And you're crazy if you think I'm letting you walk into a dangerous situation without my help. You are no match for them."

"I can bring a weapon. A knife or something."

"You don't know how to use it and if they find it, they will use it against you. Look, I'm a former cop, remember. I'm trained to do this kind of work. I won't arrive with you. I'll come up a different way and make certain to follow you. I'll only intervene if something goes wrong."

"You'll stay out of sight? You'll be careful?"

"Of course," Jonathan said. "You two will take a car into town. I'll leave before you do, take my bike, use back roads, and park a ways away. Then by the time you get there, I'll already be in place and watching."

It sounded as though it could work. Amina went to the bedroom to get her bag and made sure there was plenty of American money in it. That should make the deal even sweeter for the gang.

She came back into the living room to see Jonathan trying to comfort Sofia, who looked younger than ever. She'd seen too much in her short life.

Jonathan was such a good man. She was done denying and pretending. She was in love with him, damn her foolish heart. She had no idea what she was going to do with this new knowledge and acceptance of her feelings. Visit Jariz? Hope he never met anyone else? Bring him to her world? She had no answer.

And Sofia? She too had touched Amina. After this was solved she was determined to find a way to get Sofia and Raul off of this island. She had no plan for that either, but she was certain she could come up with something.

Taking a steadying breath for focus—one problem at a time—and hoping she appeared more confident than she felt, she said, "Let's go."

It was a quiet ride. Amina and Sofia stepped out of the taxi just before seven and waited at the fountain.

"I'm scared," Sofia said in a whisper.

"I know," Amina answered. She was too, and although sometimes stating the obvious helped to calm the nerves, this was not one of those times. Her heart was hammering in her chest as though she'd swum at top speed for miles. She knew Jonathan had followed them or, more accurately, arrived before them, but she couldn't sense him and she was worried about what would happen if he were spotted. She had to trust him, trust he was there and he wouldn't act before they had Raul.

A distant church bell started chiming the hour. Before the final ring three large men stepped up to them. "So good to see you on time."

"Where is he, Owen?" Sofia said. Amina didn't expect her to know these men. They were different from the ones who stopped her. Clearly he was one of the gang members who worked at the hotel.

"You didn't think we'd bring him here, where there could be so many witnesses? We needed to make sure you'd come and come alone as you were told. Don't worry, we have him in a safe place." Not worrying was not an option.

"I want him back."

"And we want that bracelet. If you do what you're told, everyone will get what they want."

Amina took Sofia's hand.

"Follow us," Owen said.

"Us?" Amina asked. More members of the gang stepped from the shadows. As if the situation weren't frightening enough.

"Come on. Elias is waiting."

Two men stood behind Amina and Sofia and one walked in front, a similar formation to the one used to stop Amina when she walked back from town. They left the Stall Market and walked into the residential part of town, passed houses where people closed doors and windows when they saw Owen and the others. Not a good sign. There would be no help there. Amina couldn't see Jonathan anywhere and hoped he wasn't far behind.

It wasn't long before she saw they were walking to the beach, although not as nice as the area that was part of the resort. This was for the locals only. There were no fire pits, no lounge chairs, and no witnesses. And even though it was still light out, it was deserted. Owen and his crew must have made sure to clear everyone out.

They neared the water line where there was a rock formation on one side. No telling how many more men hid there for additional muscle if necessary.

"Now, the bracelet," Owen said holding out his hand.

"I want to see my brother first," Sofia said.

"Yes, we won't turn it over without seeing that Raul is unharmed," Amina said.

"He is just fine," said a new voice. The man who stepped out was a little older, better dressed, and carried himself with an air of authority the others lacked. Even before Sofia whispered, "Elias," Amina knew this was the man who headed the gang. Next to him was a small boy.

"Sofia," Raul yelled and took a step forward. Elias' hand came down on his shoulder preventing him from moving.

"So this is the woman with the priceless bracelet that should have been mine days ago. It is rare for something I want to elude me."

Amina shuddered. There was nothing but cold in his voice. There was no way they were getting through this unharmed.

"Bring me the bracelet," he commanded." Amina stepped forward. "Not the girl. The bracelet only."

This is where it was going to get difficult. "The bracelet cannot come off," she said.

"Nonsense," Elias said.

"We told you," said Owen.

Amina stepped away from the others and held out her wrist. "There is no clasp, no catch. It is an unending loop. You can look for yourself." Elias motioned for someone else to keep a hold of Raul, and he came to Amina to check the bracelet. He spun it around on her wrist, looking for what wasn't there.

"So the rumors are true. And here I thought my men were exaggerating to cover up the fact they hadn't manage to take it from you yet."

"As you can see, there is no way for me to take it off. I can give you money instead. I brought more than the bracelet is worth in American bills."

"Of course there is a way to take it off," Elias said. "Owen, open the bag we brought and get me what I need." Owen did as he was told and Amina saw a long, wide knife. "If the bracelet has no opening, then we will have to take your hand. And the money you brought as a bonus for our trouble."

* * *

Following them from the beach without being seen was harder than Jonathan thought. He ran one street over and thanked his angels he never lost them. As soon as he knew the beach was their goal, he ran ahead and waited for them to arrive. He also made a quick call to Captain Givas, told him the situation and where he was. He didn't know if back up would arrive or if it would be in time, but he had to try.

As soon as Amina stepped up to Elias, Jonathan came nearer. He had never seen the gang leader, knew him only by name and reputation, but if he was directly involved in this, then it was a sanctioned kidnapping and the chances were good he intended to leave Amina, Sofia and Raul dead. Why deal with witnesses when no one will bring charges?

Because of the crime on the island he purchased a .9 mm gun shortly after arriving. but he never thought he'd use it. Tonight he had a feeling there was no way not to.

When he saw the machete he knew Elias' plan, how he intended to separate Amina—permanently—from the bracelet. There was no way he was going to allow that to happen. No one was going to hurt the woman he loved.

God, it felt good to admit it himself and as soon as this nightmare was over, he was going to tell her exactly how he felt. How she helped him to let go of the past. How he loved listening to her, being with her—even doing nothing but reading with her.

He didn't know what would happen after he shared his feelings. Could she stay here? Would she welcome him where she lived? It didn't matter. She had woken his heart. He could easily leave this behind. He would never let her go.

He moved in closer and took in the situation. There were plenty of gang members on the beach, the light was fading and all eyes were on Elias and Amina. He used that to his advantage to get close to one of members and cold cocked him into unconsciousness with the butt of his gun. He let the man stay where he was and stood in his position.

Amina was in front of Elias who had Owen on one side—that man was fired after this—and Raul on the other. Sofia was a few yards away, being held back by one gang member while another held a small knife to her throat. Small compared to what Owen was holding. Large enough to do some lasting damage.

Jonathan took a few steps forward.

"Hold out her arm," Elias said to one of the members Jonathan didn't recognize, "and Owen will relieve her of this terrible burden."

"Why me?"

"Because you were the one who told me about the bracelet, Sofia, and Raul. It's your responsibility. It seems only fitting you finished what you started."

It also meant that if there were arrests from tonight, Owen was the one thrown to the wolves. Elias could honestly claim he did nothing. Certainly nothing that anyone saw. Jonathan doubted the leader was the one to take Raul. Jonathan saw Owen hesitate. He wondered if the man knew how he was potentially being set up. Not that Owen had a choice.

Jonathan did.

He shot his gun into the sand. The noise was deafening and unexpected. Everyone looked for where it came from. Unfortunately, Owen grabbed Amina.

"Who shot that," Elias roared. "Who's there?"

There was madness as people scattered. The lesser gang members disappeared, not invested enough to stay if there was a gun involved. A few moved closer to Elias, showing loyalty and strength. Jonathan used the opportunity to move closer and hide behind a cropping of rocks.

"This is Jonathan Bartlett," he called out. "The police are on their way."

"Then we'll just have to get what we want and go," Elias said.

"Move even one inch toward her, Owen, and I will drop you where you stand."

"You're bluffing," Owen said, but there was no conviction in his words. In the next moment, sand blew into his face when a shot landed in front of him. Amina jumped but stayed silent.

"Fuck this, Elias. I'm not getting shot for you or some dumb tourist no matter what the take." He dropped the knife and ran. Jonathan wasn't going to need to fire him. Elias was going to make him disappear. Before Amina could move away, Elias grabbed her by the throat.

"Clearly she's important to you, Mr. Bartlett, but you are not the only one with a gun."

Jonathan had been moving closer, staying to the shadows, but he froze when another gang member pulled out a gun and handed it to Elias. He pressed it to Amina's side. "Her blood will stain the sand before you lay a hand on any of us."

"This isn't going to end well for you, Elias. Put the gun down and leave and there will be no one to press charges."

"And then there will be no one to get what we deserve from the tourists. Don't you know anything about how gangs are run? I am the leader and I will do what is necessary."

Jonathan had one chance and he had to move fast. Instead of shooting, which Elias expected, he ran and then lunged for the gang leader, throwing them both into the sand. The movement pushed Amina out of the way and from the corner of his eye he saw her move toward Raul. She was safe.

Elias landed a hard punch to his jaw and Jonathan saw stars. In the next moment he heard the click of a gun cocking. He reached out for Elias' right hand hoping to twist it and force the other man to drop the weapon. Instead, Elias' hand came between them as they continued to struggle.

When he heard the shot he had a moment to worry about Amina and then he was grateful, so very grateful, to feel the most excruciating pain.

* * *

"Jonathan, no," Amina screamed and ran to him.

"You shot the fucking cop," someone yelled.

"This is going to fuck us all."

"Do you hear that?"

"Sirens. Shit."

"Let's get out of here."

There were screams and running, but Amina didn't care. She looked around to see Sofia run to Raul and pull him close. She allowed herself a moment of relief then turned her attention back to Jonathan.

"Please be okay, please be okay." Her hand was warm. And wet. She moved it away and in the dying light she saw the blood. A stomach wound. There may not be many guns in her world, but she knew from Lyria that stomach injuries were serious and usually life threatening. "You're going to be fine. Sofia will call for help. Let her use your phone."

"I'm not so sure, my sweet, but it doesn't matter. This time the right person got shot."

"How can you say that? There's no such thing as 'the right person' when it comes to something like this. You can't die. I love you. You have to stay with me. I have to stay with you."

A heartbeat later she thought she'd been shot as pain lanced through her body. As she said the truth of how she felt about Jonathan out loud it was if the whole world started screaming. Everything in her body hurt. The noise in her head was overwhelming and excruciating.

At first she didn't understand what she was feeling, then she recognized it. Nerine's potion had worn off along with the side effects that kept her emotionally isolated for the past few days.

Once again, Amina was feeling everything.

It was a good thing she was already down on her knees or she would have collapsed. She could sense the fear of the gang members who were scattering, relief and love from Sofia and Raul.

"I love you, too."

"Jonathan," Amina cried. She situated herself behind him, with his head in her lap. "Hold on, please hold on." From him there were waves of love, more than she'd ever felt directed toward her, but there was also fear.

"I don't think anyone's going to get here in time, and even if they do, Jariz isn't known for its medical excellence. They aren't going to be able to help."

"No, I won't let you die. I won't let you leave me."

Melusine, give me strength! she called out.

And in the next moment there was a warmth at her wrist. She looked down at her bracelet and saw the Stone of Strength glowing. She had what she needed, a source of strength.

Lyria! she screamed both in her mind and out loud. She had no idea where her cousin was, if there was any possibility she could reach her, but if there was she had to try.

She focused on the glowing sapphire and called out again.

I hear you. I'm coming. Where are you? Is it Fiero?

She sent an image of where she was and a sense of its location in the Mediterranean Sea. *It's not Fiero. I'm fine, but I need you. You have to hurry.*

I'll be there as fast as I can.

She kissed Jonathan's forehead. "Help is coming. Hang on."

"It doesn't matter. You're safe.

"It does matter, you matter. You matter to me."

"Tell me again."

"I love you, Jonathan. I love how you make me

feel, how you let me be myself. How you don't mind my humming and my love of sitting quietly. I love how you listen to me, and talk to me, and kiss me and touch me."

"Damn, that sounds wonderful. My timing really sucks."

"No, it doesn't. You have to stay with me." The bracelet warmed further and Amina imagined its power, its strength enveloping them both. Keeping Jonathan from slipping away before Lyria could get there.

Sofia and Raul came over to them. The four of them were the only ones left on the beach. She heard Sofia mutter a prayer in Spanish.

"Your bracelet is glowing," Raul said.

"Yes, it has magic."

"Can it help him?"

"No, unfortunately not completely, but someone is coming who can."

Amina had no idea how much time had passed before she heard, *I'm here.* Amina turned and saw Lyria stepping from the water, already dressed and dried.

"She's a mermaid," Raul whispered.

"Don't be silly," Sofia said. "That's not possible," but her voice trailed off, clearly unsure.

"Actually," Lyria said, "the boy is right, but we'll discuss that later. What happened?" Lyria knelt next to Amina and Jonathan in the sand.

"He's been shot, Heal him, Lyria, please."

He's human.

I don't care, Amine said. *He's dying because he saved my life. And I love him"*

Let me see. "What's his name?" Lyria asked.

"Jonathan. Jonathan Bartlett."

"Yes, what?" he said when he heard his name.

"Jonathan, I'm Lyria, Amina's cousin. I'm here to help. I don't know if I can, but I will try. Do I have your permission?"

"Are you a doctor?" he asked.

"No, she's a mermaid," Raul said.

"Oh, in that case, go right ahead. And don't worry if you can't. Amina is safe. And so are Sofia and Raul. That's what matters. They are what matters. Are you really a mermaid?"

"He's delirious, Lyria. Hurry."

"Clearly you matter a great deal as well, Jonathan. And yes, I'm really a mermaid. So is Amina. Is that a problem?"

"Nah," he said and coughed. "I love her. And she told me she loves me. Isn't that wonderful?"

He slipped out of consciousness.

Lyria placed her hands on the wound. "Amina, I see him in our world."

"You do?" It was more than Lyria could have hoped.

"Will he want this? Will he accept it? I found my mate in a human and he, too, is now one of the merfolk. Will Jonathan be able to handle the change?"

Amina thought of the man she loved, the life he had here and the life she wanted to live with him. "Yes, he can handle it. Save him. Change him."

"Help me bring him to the water's edge. He needs to have his legs in the water during the healing and transformation." As Lyria worked on Jonathan, time seemed to stop. Amina wasn't certain she took a full breath as she watched her cousin. It wasn't until she saw his legs shift into fins that she knew Lyria had been successful.

She threw herself against him and held him close.

"We need to get him home before he wakes up. He can't stay here. He will need rest as his body continues the final healing process."

"You'll help me?"

"Of course," Lyria said.

Raul came to where they were and sat in the wet sand. Sofia joined him a moment later. "So it's really true. You really are a mermaid?"

"I am."

"And now Mr. Jonathan is too?"

"Yes."

"That's really cool." He thought about it for a moment. "Does that mean you have to go back to the ocean?"

When you see your cousin next, it will be time to leave.

She remembered Nerine's words. Apparently the warning was true.

"I do, Raul. I'm so sorry. I wish there was more I could do."

"What's that?" Sofia asked.

Amina looked to where Sofia pointed. This time it was Lyria's jewel that glowed. The Stone of Clarity gave off a shine like a beacon. "What's happening?" Amina asked.

"I'm not certain, but I have an idea. Come here, children. Tell me your names."

"I'm Raul and this is my sister, Sofia."

"Give me your hands," Lyria said. The moment they did, the Stone glowed brighter bathing the two children in light. Lyria looked at them, then closed her eyes. When she opened them she said, "You are meant to leave with us."

233

"What?"

"Are you serious?" Amina and Sofia spoke at the same time. "I thought you could only change children who were near death and taken by the ocean."

"I thought that too but the Stone of Clarity has shown me more than I thought possible, and when I touched their hands I saw them among our children."

"We get to be mermaids too?" Raul asked, clearly excited. "Well, I get to be a merboy, right?"

Amina laughed. It seemed impossibly wonderful. "Sofia, what do you think? I know this must come as a crazy, unbelievable shock to you, but I promise you it's all real. If Lyria says she can do this, she can and if you want it… You and Raul can come with me."

Sofia launched herself into Amina's arms and she hugged the girl close. "Yes, oh yes. Please let us be with you."

"Very well," Lyria said. "I do not want to make the transformation here and now. I'm hearing humans getting close, so this is what I'm going to do. I'm going to put both of you into a deep sleep. Amina and I will take you, along with Jonathan, to where we live and I'll complete your change there."

Both children nodded vigorously.

"If there is anything you want or need from this place, Amina can come back for it later."

"There is nothing here for us," Sofia said, and Amina knew it was true.

"Very well," Lyria said.

Moments later Sofia and Raul were asleep and the five of them were swimming to Amina's island off the coast of Brazil.

Chapter Ten

When Jonathan woke up, the first thing he noticed was Amina. Next to him, her head on his chest, her hand on his heart. Damn, that was the weirdest most vivid dream he could ever remember having. At least this time he didn't wake up screaming.

He kissed the top of her head and looked around the room. It was beautiful. White walls, a few stained glass windows, and a skylight above the bed.

This was not the bedroom he had woken up in yesterday.

This was not the Villa at the Suadela.

Last night was not a dream. Which means he'd been...

He sat up suddenly, pushed down the covers, then jumped out of the bed. "That's not possible," he said looking at his stomach.

"It is when you've got magic," Amina said. She gave him a sleepy look and a smile. She was radiant. The sun was coming in behind her from a window above the bed, her red gold hair messy and catching the light. "Come back to bed and I'll tell you everything."

"Last night wasn't a dream?"

"It wasn't, and it was two nights ago. You've been asleep for almost 36 hours."

"I was shot."

"Yes, and I almost had my hand cut off. You saved me, Sofia and Raul. We're all safe and you're in my home now."

"And you told me you loved me."

"I did."

"And… that you're a mermaid. I must have hallucinated that part. Loss of blood, thinking I was going to die." Amina said nothing. "Your cousin was on the beach. She helped me."

"Lyria, yes. She's a gifted healer."

His thoughts were jumbled as images and words played through his head. He looked down at his stomach. Only the smallest redness remained from what he knew was a fatal wound.

"Will you let me explain?"

He sat back on the bed. Amina took his hand. "Everything you think you remember is true. Raul was abducted, you saved me when Owen tried to cut off my hand. Elias got a hold of your gun and in a struggle, shot you. Now's were it gets unbelievable." She told him everything that had happened after the shooting and through to when he woke up in a new bed.

"You're a mermaid and now I'm a mer… man?"

She nodded. "I'm sorry if you don't want to be one. Lyria said she could see you living among our people. I love you and couldn't bear to lose you so I let her make the transformation. If you don't want to stay with me…"

He grabbed her and held her close then kissed her

until they were both breathless. "I love you too and if being with you means I'm a merperson—"

"Merfolk," she corrected.

"A merfolk then that is what I will be." He kissed her again to make certain she was real. "This is beyond amazing. And wonderful. And I love you too."

"I was so worried you might be mad, about the transformation."

"No, not in the least. I mean, it's going to take some getting used to, I'm sure, but we're together and that's better than almost anything." He was still in a state of stun, but happier than he could remember being in years. He remembered something else she said. "You said Sofia and Raul came with us. How are they adjusting to the change?"

"Other than the fact that it is nearly impossible to get them out of the water, they are great. My Aunt Betta has been staying here and looking out for them while I watched over you and took care of work that had piled up since I left."

"Left, holy shit. Brian. I disappeared over a day ago. What is he going to think?"

"I sent someone to deliver a note to him saying we'd gone to the mainland to explore for a few days. I didn't know what else to tell him."

"That works. We'll come up with something else later." He was quiet for a minute. "So, I have fins and legs."

"It's a lot to take in."

"Will you show me? Show me what you look like as a mermaid and how I make the shift?"

"Of course. You can shift anywhere, but it's wise to be in the water, at least knee deep. Once you learn what it feels like, all you will need to do is focus on that feeling and then…"

Before his eyes Amina's legs disappeared and in their place was a shimmering blue-green tail straight out of a fairy tale. She moved it to show him her flexibility and the light caught the scales.

"You are still so damn beautiful."

"Thank you. You can touch it if you want. That may help you when it comes time to consciously making the shift for the first time."

"Consciously?"

"You were in fin form when Lyria and I brought you here."

He reached out and stroked her skin starting below her breasts then continuing to where the scales began. They weren't rough or slippery like fish scales, although they were cool to the touch. He lay next to her, and continued to explore the different textures. With a wicked smile he moved his hand to the where her pussy would have been if she had legs in this moment.

In a teasing tone she asked, "What are you doing?"

"Just trying to figure out what is where."

"What you are looking for is not there in this form any more than your cock will be when you shift to a tail."

"Are the scales sensitive," he asked, stroking the sides as if he were touching her hip.

"They have some feeling, but not nearly as much as skin."

He lay there by her side and looked at his legs next to her tail and thought about the fact that he could now have one as well. As he tried to picture it, his legs started to disappear.

Amina brought her head up. "Stay with that thought, Jonathan. See your body looking like mine. Strong, muscled and able to swim for amazing distances at a time."

He let his mind accept what he was seeing and as he did, his legs were gone. In their place was a blue-gray scaled tale. "Mine's a different color."

She laughed. "If that's your first thought, you are going to have no trouble with this transition."

"What do most former humans do?"

She thought for a moment. "I'm not actually certain, but I know I've never heard of someone shifting for the first time on land."

"And how do I change back."

"Imagine yourself walking."

He did and almost instantly the tail was gone as though it had never been there. "Amazing."

"You're really not upset?"

He looked at her and saw the concern in her eyes. "Which part am I supposed to be upset about? That I'm still alive? That you love me? That I'm completely in love with you?"

"That I kept this from you. That I didn't expect to ever tell you. I was trying to figure how to tell you about my feelings and my heritage but then everything with Raul happened and... well, you know the rest."

"Why were you at the Suadela in the first place?"

She held up the bracelet. "This causes trouble wherever I go. There's a sea dragon after it. And me."

"A sea dragon? Clearly I have a lot more to learn about than shifting my legs to fins."

Amina told him of her Aunt Betta's prophecy and the current threat to her family and all the beings of the oceans.

"So, no idea where he is now or what he plans next."

"Unfortunately not. There's been no news since my near abduction and Lyria's temporary victory over him. We only know he's not going to stop."

"Is there anything we can do about this now?" She shook her head. "Then will you go swimming with me?"

"I'll do more than that, I'll teach you how to dry yourself as you come out of the water. You probably won't develop the full gifts of merfolk, but there are a few that come automatically."

He grabbed her hand, bounded out of bed and they headed to the water.

* * *

Amina's heart soared as she saw Jonathan easily adapt to swimming with a tail rather than legs. They went out deep and played in the shallows. After about an hour, he was ready for a break and she had something she wanted to share with him.

As they'd left the house, she'd brought a large blanket and as they walked onto the shore she spread it out. His first tries at drying himself weren't quite successful, but he was improving and she had no doubt he'd get the hang of it soon.

"I can't believe this," he said as he lay back and looked up into the cloudless sky. "A week ago my life was routine and predictable. And now—"

"You're in love with a mermaid."

"I'm in love with a mermaid. Who loves me back."

"Very much," she said and kissed him. His arms came around her and she wrapped her legs around him to bring him close. "There's something you should know about this island."

"What's that?"

"Sex on the beach is permitted."

"This is definitely my kind of place."

"And there's one other piece of good news," she said.

"Which is?"

"Mermaids track and take care of their fertile periods. So not only do I know that I'm not fertile right now, I can also tell you we do not and cannot carry the diseases of humans."

"Which means… no more condoms."

"I want you, Jonathan. I want to feel all of you deep inside of me."

He murmured her name and kissed her deeply, pressing himself against her, showing her how ready he was, how much he wanted her. His hands traveled down her back to her ass. He caressed her there, then moved around to her hips then between her legs. When he stroked her pussy, she moaned her pleasure. "God, you are so wet already."

"It's been too long since we've made love. I am aching for you."

"Don't you want me to—"

"No, I don't want to wait."

"But should I just—"

"Stop teasing me, Jonathan."

241

"Very well," he said and didn't wait another moment before sliding into her.

"Goddess, yes," she called out and brought her legs around his hips, drawing him closer, bringing him deeper.

"It feels like it's been forever since I've been inside of you."

"It has been. It was another lifetime," she said and as they moved together, she realized it was.

The last several days were so full of emotions, everything from deepest love to the worst fear she'd ever experienced. She'd understood where she hadn't forgiven herself for the times her gifts hurt others and how she'd been carrying that with her. She allowed herself to offer love, holding nothing back and not knowing what the other person might feel in return. She'd offered Jonathan her biggest fears, her secrets and her love.

He'd accepted it all.

Now she looked up at him, moved with him and marveled at how far she—and they—had come. With him she could imagine a life she'd only read about before. And even when it wasn't easy and fun, which would have to happen, she trusted he was a man who could help her and stand by her.

He bent his head forward and, knowing what he wanted, she arched up, taking every inch of him, and allowing him to lick and suck at her breasts. Her nipples hardened and became sensitive at his touch. He bit her gently, and she cried out.

"I am going to spend a lifetime finding new ways to please and excite you," he said.

"Then I am going to have enjoy every moment of that."

His pace increased and she matched his thrusts, needing not only the pleasure but the connection. He was safe, alive and all hers. He knew her truths and he loved her still.

"I'm so close, Amina. Let me bring you with me."

He pulled back a little so he could find and tease her clit. Her pussy clenched around his cock along with a rush of wetness which made him moan. Knowing that touching her meant he couldn't go as deep, she put her hand where his was. "Allow me," she said as she stroked herself.

"God, that is so sexy," he said watching as she played with her clit. The visual was clearly too much. Moments later his strokes became harder. She grabbed his ass with her other hand, widened her legs and moved her finger faster.

He screamed her name as his orgasm hit, and she followed him into her own climax. Feeling him cum inside her, no barrier, added to her pleasure, and she hoped to his.

His head dropped and he kissed her. She slowed her own pleasuring then brought arms around him and held him close. He fell against her, and she reveled in the feel of his weight, the exhausted bliss.

A moment later he rolled to the side and brought her with him so she was now on top of him, the sun warming her back. She put her head on his shoulder and listened to his heartbeat, as loud and strong as the tides that surrounded them.

She had never been happier.

"I just thought of something," he said.

"What's that?"

"We're going to need a new safe word."

* * *

Hand in hand, Amina and Jonathan walked back to her home, got dressed and enjoyed something to eat, all the while talking about things he needed to learn and what, if anything, he wanted to get from Jariz and bring back.

An hour later Sofia and Raul came over and regaled them both with stories of all they'd been discovering and the other merfolk adults and children they'd met. It was clear they were picking up the magic and the methods of this world faster than Jonathan and easier than Amina could have imagined.

Raul convinced Jonathan to go swimming with him, and after promises from both that wouldn't go far, they left. Sofia asked to stay behind to talk to Amina.

They sat down on the couch, and Sofia took Amina's hands in hers. "I wanted to tell you thank you. Those words have never seemed so small to me, or meant so much," she said. "I can't imagine what would have happened to us if we had stayed. We were witnesses to everything on the beach. There's no way Elias would have allowed us to live."

Amina pulled Sofia close. It felt so good, natural. She'd wanted to do this since she'd met the girl. "There's no need to think of that anymore. It's over, and you're here. I was drawn to you immediately and clearly there was a reason. I kept feeling that I wanted to help you, needed to help, and that was without any additional input from my gift."

"Your gift."

Amina explained about her empathic abilities and

her work among the merfolk because of it, and because of the Stone of Strength.

"That glowed the other night on the beach. Lyria's too."

"Yes, I'd never seen either of them do that before, but Lyria said hers did when she faced the sea dragon."

"There's a sea dragon?"

Amina kissed Sofia's forehead. "It's not for you to worry about, but yes, you haven't suddenly joined a Utopia. There are good Oceanides as well as bad, and one in particular who wants to amass power and rule the seas."

"You're going to stop him, right?"

"That's the intention." She couldn't say plan. They didn't have one yet.

Raul and Jonathan came back a little later while Amina and Sofia were still talking. Both children had endless questions, and Amina did her best to answer them. Jonathan was as rapt as they were. Amina realized it was new for all of them. She wondered how Drew, Lyria's mate managed the transition a few days before, but they hadn't met him yet. Perhaps tomorrow.

Without warning, a pain lanced through Amina that brought her to her knees and she cried out and dropped to the floor.

Jonathan was by her side in a heartbeat. "What is it? What's wrong?"

"I don't know," she said breathlessly. She'd never felt pain like this. It started in her head and radiated through her body. She was still trying to get her focus and catch her breath when she heard her name.

Amina, a voice called.

I'm here.

Do you feel that?

What is going on?, she asked. The voice was familiar but she couldn't place it. Not Lyria, but... Another wave of pain raced through her and she yelled again. *Who is this?*

Nerine.

Do you know what this is?

It's related to Fiero, but worse.

Worse? What could be worse?

I've been trying to find him since you left. I heard a rumor and it appears to be true. Fiero's uncle, Balban, is going after the heirs to the Stones.

The heirs?

The girls who are to wear them next. He is going to capture them, then kill you and Lyria. As soon as you're dead, the bracelets will go to the girls who will already be in his control.

What can we do? Where is he?

Closer to you than me. You need to get to an island off the coast of Argentina.

I don't know how to find him, Amina said. Her heart was beating so fast she thought it would burst.

Swim south. Follow your feelings. Ask the Stone for help. Go now!

Nerine was gone from her head but the pain continued. As best she could, she explained to Jonathan what happened while making her way as quickly as possible to the water's edge. "The girls are in danger. I have to go."

"What girls? How can I help?"

"You can't. I'm going to try to reach Lyria as I

swim but if you see her before I do, please tell her what I just told you. I love you."

"Come back to me," he said.

She ran into the water and finned as soon as she could.

She tried to contact Lyria telepathically but couldn't. That concerned her. Lyria wasn't far away. Her call should have reached her cousin without a problem. Could Fiero or Balban have found a way to interfere with their connection?

There was no way to know, no way to find out and it didn't matter. She needed to stop him from getting to those girls.

She'd never swam so fast. She did what Nerine suggested, she thought about the pain, focused on where it was coming from and when she did she knew, somehow, where to go. And she called on the Stone of Strength to help her. The warm glow on her wrist told her she was being supported.

Hundreds of miles later, the feeling shifted and Amina swam for the surface. She looked around and saw an island in the distance. Like Nerine's it seemed to waver, but the cloaking spell wasn't as strong. Amina headed straight for it.

When she got close, she swam around the island looking for signs of life. The pain was still there, throbbing within her. She tried to use it to find the source. Finally, she saw a large home set back from the beach. She shifted to legs as soon as she could, then crept toward the building. If Balban lived here, he must have thought he was well hidden. There were no sentries anywhere on the grounds.

There was also no sign that either Balban or Fiero

were here. She went back to the beach and as she came around some rocks, she saw a cavern with a large opening—and light coming from within.

Amina walked in, hugging the walls and moving slowly. She didn't know if she'd come across someone and wanted to stay hidden as long as possible. She was several yards in when she heard voices.

"Uncle, please." She recognized Fiero. "You were the one who drilled into me the importance of calm and well planned leadership. What kind of leader will the people think I am if I take power by kidnapping children? We will turn all of the merfolk against us. I don't want to start by having to put down a rebellion from the largest Oceanide race. There will be no winners."

"You won't have to do anything of the sort. I promise." Amina had never heard—or seen—Balban. He sounded calm, frighteningly so.

Amina peered in and took in the details of the cavern. Clearly this was where Fiero, and his uncle, had been working on the magic that had tracked and harmed her and Lyria. There were shelves on the wall with bottles and jars with visible dry ingredients. There was a large work table with things scattered across and at the back, a raised, stone cone with water bubbling in it, almost like a small volcano, but with the ocean feeding it rather than lava.

"This is not necessary. Amina has returned to her home. Look, the tracking spell we put on her necklace activated yesterday." Amina put her hand to her throat. She needed to get that back. It was bad enough it was in his hands, but to know he was using it to get to her—and possibly Jonathan and the children—was not acceptable. "I'll know where she is and by tomorrow, at the latest, she'll be ours."

"What good is one? We must have three. You know that." Amina heard contempt in Balban's voice. She wondered if Fiero did as well. Now that the pain had receded, she reached out with her gift. Fiero was worried and confused. Balban was angry and determined. No, it was beyond anger. There was a ferocity and cruelty to his feelings Amina had rarely, if ever, felt.

"Having Amina will draw Lyria to us. You said so yourself."

"Yes, and you have no way to get near that one's stone. It repelled you when you tried to take it from her. The stone's power has been magnified and she's protected by it. Once they know we have the girls, both of them will come looking for us and we'll let them find us. With any luck by that point they will have found the third mermaid and bracelet as well. Then, we kill them all and raise the three girls to follow orders and do as we say.

"But what about the merfolk. They will come after me."

"I told you. You have nothing to worry about."

"How can you be so sure?"

"Because you are not going to be alive to see me take over the Oceans."

Before Amina could react, Balban shot out a stream of magic that looked similar to what Lyria described as having injured her when she fought against Fiero. Like a bolt of lightning, it struck the man square in the chest and sent him flying backwards until his body hit a stone wall. As he dropped to the ground,

Amina could see blood on the wall where he hit his head. He lay, unmoving, in a broken heap.

Balban walked over to his body and cut a piece of skin off Fiero's arm. Amina flinched at his callous action. "Sorry, nephew," he said the word with distain. "Did you really think I'd let you have this power and let you rule? A mermaid mix-blood? My brother and his son would have come back from the dead if I allowed that. Mermaid blood needs to be eradicated in all forms, especially mixed races. Let them try a rebellion. They will discover how many enemies they have made over the centuries."

Amina didn't know which part of what she heard was most upsetting. This was only partially about gaining power and reorganizing the seas. It was also about one man bent on genocide, although, she supposed, other Kelpies could be involved.

"And now, to complete the Angler Witches magic."

He returned to the stone cone and dropped in the piece of Fiero's flesh. Then he picked up three strings, each with a charm at the end and held them over the water as he began to chant:

One for clarity, strong and clear
One for strength, powerful and dear
One for love this makes three
Daughters of Melusine, show yourselves to me

When Balban started the chant for a second time, Amina knew she needed to act quickly. It was a thrice-spell, one that required being repeated three times for it to work.

She had to do something, but she had no idea what. Like when she was stopped walking home from the Stall Market, she had nothing with her to use as an offensive weapon.

Except the Stone of Strength.

She needed to tap into that power. She thought of Jonathan and of Lyria. Then of Sofia and Raul, children liked the ones who were in danger because of Balban.

With that thought, the Stone began to glow.

Amina sent out a prayer of thanks and focused on the stone and the power radiating from it. She thought about what she most desired, what she wanted to accomplish. She promised Jonathan she'd come back so she needed to be protected. With that thought she sensed a shield around her, fortifying her.

Next, she needed to be able to stop Balban. She didn't necessarily want to kill him, that wasn't in her nature, but she had to be able to do something that would get him away from the cauldron-like cone and stop him from completing the spell. With those thoughts she detected a change in her body, as though she could lift anything she wanted, move or deflect anything in her way.

As Balban started the chant for the third time, Amina stepped fully into the room.

"Stop," she said, her voice louder than she expected and echoing throughout the chamber. She might have thought she imagined it, but bottles on the walls shook. It was enough to make Balban turn and look at her.

"So, my foolish nephew was correct about something. You've come to protect your precious, prejudiced world."

"I think it's you who has the prejudice."

"Only someone who lived with privilege could say that. You have no idea what it is to grow up as a lesser race."

"There are no lesser races. That is something you see, you believe."

"Really? How many kelpies are permitted to work in your uncle's government? What positions of authority do naiads or selkies hold?" Amina had no answer. She didn't want Balban to be right, but in this instance there was truth to his words. "This is why so many were willing to join our cause. To follow and listen to Fiero. Even some of your own kind. It was easy to convince them to turn on you. Your uncle, his lineage, and those like him around the globe have no idea what it is like to be treated as less, as an outsider. But that is going to end. When merfolk are gone, the rest of the Oceanides will take their rightful place."

"With you as their leader."

"Of course. I'm the one who will give them their freedom. And if they don't do as I say, well, there are ways to keep people in line." He glanced over at Fiero's body. Yes, if he was willing to kill a member of his family, there was nothing he wouldn't do, of that Amina was certain.

Amina wasn't certain what to do next. At least for now the process of the incantation had been broken. Balban would have to begin from the beginning to make the spell work, which gave her some time to come up with a way to stop him. She needed to get the charms away from him and she needed to make certain he couldn't finish the curse.

And then she knew.

As long as he couldn't start the chant again, as

long as he couldn't complete it, the girls would be safe.

She laughed to herself. Sometimes, the clichés worked. She threw out her hand and reached as if to grab him by the throat. A line of magic wrapped around his neck and stayed there for only a few seconds, but it was enough.

When he tried to yell at her, his mouth moved, but no sound came out. The horrified and shocked look on his face would have been worth it if it weren't followed by a look of such anger that Amina took a step back. She didn't know what he could do to her, but she didn't want to find out.

She focused on the shield that felt like a coating on her skin and, pouring her thoughts into it, made it stronger.

Balban was frantic. He looked around the room, pulling things off the shelves, and tossing them aside. Finally, he grabbed several bottles and threw them into the water cone, which exploded in every direction, soaking the ground and widening the opening. He then slammed another bottle on the floor which resulted in a sound wave that pushed her back and knocked her off her feet. It probably would have thrown her against the wall, as he'd done to Fiero, if it weren't for her shield.

Unfortunately, it gave him enough time to do what he wanted. By the time she looked up, he'd shifted into his kelpie form and, before she could stop him, he dove into the water and was gone.

Her ears were ringing and her head and heart were pounding. She searched for the charms that supposedly connected him to the mermaids he wanted to kidnap, but she couldn't find them. Furious, she tapped into the power of the Stone one more time and destroyed everything that remained in the cavern. If Balban came back, there would be nothing he could use.

"Amina?" came a voice from the cavern opening.

At first she thought it was Lyria, then realized her mistake. "In here," she called back. The dark haired mermaid stepped into the room. Would Balban want her destroyed as well, even though she was a mixed blood and lived cut off from her people. She gave her head a slight shake to get rid of the thought. Now was not the time.

"Nerine, how did you get here so quickly?"

"Not as quickly as I wanted, or quickly enough," she said looking around. "I created a portal, but the pain blocked and slowed my abilities. I use them to get from one part of the ocean to another when I, or my assistants need to. I had hoped to get here sooner. Clearly you didn't require my help."

"I'm not so sure about that. The process of finding and getting the girls has stopped for now, but Balban got away. I believe he still has part of the potion and charms that will allow him to find the heirs. I don't know if he has enough to try again. And he turned on his nephew," she said and motioned to where he lay. "Fiero is dead."

Nerine rushed to Fiero's side and placed a hand on his heart. "Thank the Goddess, his heart still beats, although it is faint."

"He tried to stop his uncle. This wasn't something he wanted. He didn't want the girls hurt. I didn't expect that."

"There's good in him. It's been corrupted by years of influence and lies."

"So I heard. Balban said some awful things to him." Amina understood something in that moment. "You know him."

"I did. We lived on the same island when we were children. He hasn't seen me in 20 years. I'm not sure he even remembers me." For the first time Amina received emotions from Nerine and could clearly feel how much the other woman cared for the sea dragon.

"What can we do for him?" Amina asked.

"You, nothing. I am going to bring him back to my home. If I can heal him, maybe I can also get him to understand what's been done to him and earn his help."

"It would be wonderful if you could. Fiero knows Balban better than anyone. He could be key to finding and stopping him."

"Help me bring him to the water's edge."

"Let me get one thing." When Fiero was struck, he dropped her necklace with the charm Lyria gave her from the Stone of Clarity's bracelet. She picked it up and put it back on. It was comforting to feel it there again.

Together they carried him and as they placed him in the water, Nerine magically shifted him to fins. "Good luck," Amina said. "Please let me know if you need anything or if something goes wrong."

"I will."

Nerine pulled him into deeper water, finned and dove beneath the surf. As she did the light caught something Amina hadn't noticed before.

Nerine wore the Stone of Love.

Chapter Ten

In the early evening, Amina walked with Lyria on the shore of their island. Jonathan was up at the house talking with Drew and the two men were getting to know each other. From her brief acquaintance with him, Amina already liked Lyria's mate and she loved how her cousin glowed with happiness when they were near each other.

"Can you explain to me what happened?"

"As far as I can tell, as soon as Balban tried to activate the potion he was given by the Angler Witch all three Stones were affected."

"That's when we both felt that awful pain. I don't know how you could stand it."

Lyria had lost consciousness when the pain hit which was why Amina was unable to reach her telepathically. "I think it's probably a combination of being an empath and the Stone of Strength. I've dealt with strong emotions before, and that is what the pain was like. As if the potion tapped into the emotion of the girls who were at risk and broadcast them out."

"And Nerine felt it—"

"Because she wears the Stone of Love. I'm not certain how she was able to withstand it, but that's why it reached her."

"How is it that she wears the Stone?"

"I have a feeling Uncle Costin has some things he either hasn't told us about or doesn't know about his father. Remember, there was speculation that there was a child from an affair."

"Which means we had an aunt of sorts we didn't know about."

Amina nodded. "I suppose so. Every family has its secrets."

"This is kind of a big one, don't you think."

"I do. I told you, though, when I first met Nerine there was something about her I really liked, something that made me feel that I wanted to know her better. She was well shielded from my gift, however, so there's no way I would have guessed what she was hiding."

"You didn't see the bracelet when you met?"

Amina thought back. "No, she wore a shawl that covered her arms completely. I assumed she was cold. She did use temperature to keep intruders away."

"And you say she knew Fiero when they were young."

"Yes, I asked Aunt Betta about this. It took her a while to admit, but apparently there are islands where mostly mixed race Oceanides live, especially those who have been ostracized by their communities or families."

Lyria winced. "That's terrible, but I guess I'm not surprised."

"Lamia-mermaid. Kelpie-mermaid. I'm sure there are other combinations which aren't supported as well. Neither Nerine's nor Fiero's mother could have been in those relationships without being censured," said Amina. "I think a lot of Fiero's, well Balban's, followers come from this group of Oceanides."

257

"And here you and I have mated with humans. Yes, they've been transformed, but there was a time that would never have been accepted. There was a time I wouldn't have accepted it," Lyria admitted.

"After we finally end this threat, and clearly Nerine is a part of making that happen, we need to look in to the offspring of mixed race relationships. Nerine is amazing and from how she looked at Fiero, there is more there than we could have imagined. We need to make some changes going forward."

"Agreed," Lyria said. "I hope Nerine is safe with him."

"Something tells me she's going to be fine. More than fine."

* * *

Jonathan watched as Amina and Lyria walked in the door. From the looks on their faces he could tell the conversation had been serious, but when she caught his eye, the strain melted away as a smile lit up her face. He would give a lifetime to always be able to do that for her.

And that is exactly what he had. Thanks to her cousin's magic, he had a lifetime ahead of him with the woman who had brought him back to life.

As Lyria went to be with Drew, Amina stepped into Jonathan's arms and he kissed her with all the love she had drawn out of him.

"Everything okay?" he asked as they walked to her living room to sit. She curled up against him and he pulled her close.

"For now," she said. "We're a few steps closer than we were. We know what Balban is trying to do.

Unfortunately, we don't know where he's gone or how long we have before he tries again to find the bracelets' heirs."

"Well, whatever it takes, I'm here with you and for you."

She looked up and kissed him. "I know, and that means the world to me."

"So mermaids really do sing."

She laughed and shook her head. "I know, it's terrible. I'm the living cliché, although after what happened, I'm starting to embrace the stories told about us."

"Yes, but this time the mermaid took the voice from the wicked witch. Wicked king?"

"He certainly wants to be king. He's not done. He's going to come after us again."

"Well from what I learned from Lyria while you were gone and from you since you came back, it sounds like he's no match for the two of you."

"Three of us. There's a third bracelet and I know who wears it and where it is."

"That's good, right?"

"It is, although it means the final battle is coming, and coming soon."

"You're scared."

"Yes. For my people, my cousins. For us. Even humans could be affected. Balban is a power hungry maniac. He has to be stopped."

Jonathan took her hand in his and kissed it. "Then he will be. We're all with you on this. Me, Drew, yes we're new but you're our family now and we will do whatever it takes to keep us safe."

Amina kissed him and when he deepened the kiss

she allowed herself to fall into his love. She could never have imagined when she went to hide on Jariz that she would find someone so precious, so wonderful and so completely right for her. That being without her empathic gifts could gain her so much. She'd taken risks she never had before, opened herself up not only for him to see, but so that she could understand herself better.

And now, not only did she feel more capable than ever of being able to defeat Balban, she knew she was capable of loving passionately and being loved in return.

It was the greatest gift of all.

Read on for an excerpt from the final book in the
Melusine's Daughters Series,
Waves of Seduction,
Coming August 2017.

Chapter One

Present Day

"Who are you?"

Someone who loves you, thought Nerine with her foolish heart and her fangirl head. Now was not the time to be thinking about human movies. "A friend," she said instead. "My name is Nerine."

He continued to look at her as though she were a complete stranger, and although that didn't surprise her, it still hurt.

It had been two days since Fiero was nearly killed by his uncle, Balban, and Nerine was worried. Today was the first day he'd regained consciousness long enough to speak, and his major wounds—one to the back of his head and one to the abdomen—were healing too slowly. The laceration on Fiero's arm where Balban had cut off a piece of his skin in order to activate the potion was also slow to repair, but it wasn't life threatening as the other two injuries were.

When she arrived at Fiero's island off the coast of Argentina her heart had nearly stopped when she saw him lying bloody and unmoving on the floor of the cavern. Amina had just destroyed the place after temporarily defeating Balban and keeping him from enacting his plan to find the heirs to the three bracelets that made up Melusine's band. Up until that point, Amina and Lyria and many others believed Fiero was the one in control, the one trying to take over the Seas, but Balban showed his true colors that afternoon and willingly used his nephew as a sacrifice to get what he wanted.

For the last two days Nerine felt Amina trying to reach out to her and knew her new-found cousin—she had no idea how she and Amina were related, but the fact that Amina wore the Stone of Strength and she wore the Stone of Love meant they had a familial connection—wanted to find out how Fiero was doing.

Nerine was tempted to respond. Lyria, who was Amina's first cousin, wore the Stone of Clarity and was the greatest healer in their world. However, Nerine also knew that less than two weeks before, Fiero had attacked and seriously injured Lyria, even using Lyria's blood from the attack to create a tracking potion so that he could find and capture the other mermaid. Nerine was certain Amina had told Lyria what had happened in the cavern and how Fiero was manipulated and influenced for years, but she couldn't trust Lyria to help Fiero. Not yet.

Amina told Nerine of the prophecy seen by Betta 15 years ago that predicted Melusine's daughters—the three mermaids who wore the bracelets made from the necklace—would need to unite in order to save the Ocean from a terrible threat. Amina and Lyria thought Fiero was that threat, and even though they knew they were wrong, it would naturally take time to change their perceptions of Fiero.

The man Nerine loved since she was a child.

If Fiero didn't improve soon, however, she might not have a choice about asking for outside help. It was unlikely they had much time before this ultimate danger came to pass.

Balban was out there with the charms to find the heirs of the Stones and a spell to help him do it. When she faced him in the cavern, Amina had robbed Balban of his voice and destroyed his workshop, but none of them had any idea of how long they had before he tried again.

Or tried something worse.

"I know you?" he asked, his voice hoarse from lack of use.

Nerine's heart tightened at his words. He didn't know her. She knew he'd forgotten her, been made to forget her, but hearing it was so very hard. Part of her hoped that her voice or presence would wake up his memory.

Apparently not.

"I'm Nerine. We knew each other a long time ago." She wanted to tell him more, but she could see how agitated he was and didn't want to add to it.

"I don't remember."

"That's okay. Don't worry. You will in time."

"Where am I?"

"You are in my home which is on an island in the Aegean Sea." Humans had no idea how many cloaked islands there were in the world that appeared on none of their maps. Oceanides had even learned how to magically block them from the satellites humans set up. Nerine had thought of bringing him to Azov, but she had better access to her magic here and on Azov there was always someone wanting her attention. Here there was the privacy she wanted.

"I ache in so many different places I cannot even separate them out. What happened?"

"You were injured. Your head and your stomach as well as a gash on your arm. I brought you here to help you heal."

"How was I…?" As Fiero looked at the bandage on his head, his eyes widened and a touch of red appeared in his irises. That was new since they were children. She'd only seen adult kelpies with that red. "Balban," he finished in a flat tone.

He screamed so loudly the walls shook and Nerine feared his heart would burst from the pain and anger that raged through him.

* * *

He'd been betrayed.

Completely betrayed and fooled by a man he thought believed in and championed him. More than half his life Balban had been a parent, mentor, family.

No, Balban only acted as though he was. Now, Fiero knew the truth.

Fiero remembered every moment in his uncle's workshop. The man was manic and driven, determined to find the young mermaids who were the heirs of the three Stones of Power, and then he was going to abduct them and their families and force them to do as he wished. Fiero had been against the idea from the beginning. One of his only childhood memories was being taken away from his mother. He couldn't allow his uncle to do something similar to other children.

"Uncle, please, you were the one who drilled into me the importance of calm and well planned leadership. What kind of leader will the people think I am if I take power by kidnapping children? We will turn all of the merfolk against us. I don't want to start by having to put down a rebellion from the largest Oceanide race. There will be no winners."

"You won't have to do anything of the sort. I promise." Fiero watched as his uncle continued to work having laid out three crystals—one clear, one green, and one pink—on a table. Around each was a circle made from something granular that looked like sand, but Fiero doubted it was.

"This is not necessary. Amina has returned to her home. Look, the tracking spell we put on her necklace activated yesterday." He was feeling more and more desperate to change his uncle's plans, but he knew he had to keep his worry out of his voice or his uncle would dismiss him completely. Weakness and uncertainty were unacceptable. "I'll know where she is and by tomorrow, at the latest, she'll be ours."

"What good is one? We must have three. You know that." Fiero heard contempt in his uncle's voice. He understood the other man's frustration, but this was not the solution. Fiero was certain.

"Having Amina will draw Lyria to us. You said so yourself."

"Yes, and you have no way to get near that one's stone. It repelled you when you tried to take it from her. The Stone's power has been magnified and she's protected by it. Once they know we have the girls, both of them will come looking for us and we'll let them find us. With any luck by that point they will have *found the third mermaid and bracelet as well. Then, we kill them all and raise the three girls to follow orders and do as we say.*

"But what about the merfolk? They will come after me."

"I told you. You have nothing to worry about."

"How can you be so sure?"

"Because you are not going to be alive to see me take over the Oceans."

That was the last thing he remembered hearing. Next there was a flash of magic and a pain beyond anything he'd ever imagined possible.

Then nothing.

Fiero wasn't supposed to survive to live with the truth. Balban used him to gain power and position. He'd pretended to encourage Fiero's goal of overthrowing the merfolk and creating a new ruling class.

His goal?

Was it?

Fiero tried to think back to when he first started on the path that led him to try to obtain the Stones of Power and rule the Oceans. Sifting through the fog in his brain made his head hurt. It didn't matter. He didn't need to remember.

He knew.

Everything had been his uncle's idea. Everything had been a lie.

"I am such a fool." Fiero tried to sit up but a pain in his gut stopped him and he roared again, this time in frustration.

"Please, I know you're upset, but- "

"Upset," he said through gritted teeth, "doesn't begin to cover it."

"You can chose another word another time. You need to calm yourself."

"I am a world away from calm. My uncle," he said the word as though it were poison, "tried to kill me."

She put her hands on his shoulders. "I am aware of that. I arrived not long after he attacked you."

"I need to track him down. He needs to be stopped. I need to kill him. My priority is to eliminate him, however I can."

"I can understand why that's your first reaction, but you have other priorities right now."

"Such as?"

"Getting stronger. Your uncle knew what he was doing with the magic he chose, and you are not close to being healed yet. He was very nearly successful. If I hadn't gotten you out of that workshop, you would have died there and if you do not find a way to relax—for now—he will succeed belatedly."

Fiero was about to yell again but something about her made him stop. He stared at the woman who'd been helping him. Someone he couldn't remember was doing something kind for him. There must be something in it for her, he thought. He knew from experience—some quite recent—no one did anything without a motive and something to gain. Still, she was caring.

And beautiful.

Now that he looked at her more closely, he couldn't remember ever seeing a woman more beautiful, more compelling. She had the fairest skin of any creature he'd ever known. It was tinged with a soft blush in her cheeks that deepened as he reached out to

269

touch her hair, which was long, wavy, and black as a starless night. He moved a strand away from her face and felt the need, for some reason, to tuck it behind her ear. When he did, he saw that hers came to the gentlest of points at the top. It would have looked unusual on another, but seemed right on her. Exotic. Sexy.

Her eyes, which never left his, were as black as her hair although as he stared into them he though he noticed a ring of violet near the center. He'd never seen a color like that, eyes like hers. Then his gaze dropped to her mouth. Full, red. Needing to be kissed. A moment ago he wouldn't have thought anything could distract him from his anger, but looking at this woman had done just that.

"You're holding your breath," she said, breaking into his thoughts. "You may want to release it." He did as she said. "Good. Try another slow breath, you probably can't breathe too deeply because of your stomach injury, but try. I know it's cliché, but it also works."

He did as she asked. "You said you knew me, that we were friends."

"Yes, when we were children."

"Were you this beautiful then?"

She blushed more. "I don't know if I can answer that, but you always told me I was pretty."

"You are much more than pretty. Why don't I remember?" Her eyes broke away from his. She looked toward the bedside table and reached for a glass.

"You should drink this, Fiero. You've been unconscious for most of the last two days and it's been difficult to keep you hydrated."

He winced and pushed himself up higher on the pillow. "Why don't I remember you, Nerine?" he repeated. "Tell me."

"Drink this first." He was about to argue, but the thought of the liquid, of drinking something cool, was too tempting, so he did as she said. "When you were 11 years old and I was six, your father came to take you away from your mother. He wanted you to live with him."

"That I remember."

"He didn't want you to have any ties to your past or to the mermaid part of your heritage so," she paused and he stiffened. Great, he thought, more bad news. "On your first night with him, he drugged you with a potion that took away virtually all of your childhood memories."

Fiero stared at her and let the words sink in. "And how could you possibly know this?"

"Your brother, Yacopo, used to come visit me every year on the day you were taken away. At least for the first five years, then he didn't come again."

"He was killed."

"I assumed something happened to him. I never knew what."

"It was my fault."

"That doesn't sound possible. You wouldn't have been more than 16. How was it your fault? Did you kill him?"

"My actions. Well, my agreement. We went somewhere we shouldn't have."

Nerine placed her hand on his face. Her touch was cool, calming. "I knew your brother and, I may have been young, but from things he told me, he had a wild side. I would guess it was his idea."

271

"It was, but I could have said no." She raised one eyebrow. It made her face more striking, more interesting somehow. "Fine, he was persuasive and I always wanted to do what he did. I was glad he invited me instead of one of his peers."

"Will you tell me what happened?"

His heart clenched. Fiero never spoke to anyone about that day, but Nerine was different. She knew Yacopo, seemed to care about him the way Fiero did. When she took his hand, he started. "I never asked him why, but he wanted to get close to the Leviathan."

When he was done with the story, the tears falling silently down her cheeks told him more than words could. "I'm so sorry, for you both." Never had anyone offered him words of consolation or sorrow on Yacopo's death. Anger, disappointment, fury. Those he was familiar with. Her kindness, while welcome, was also disconcerting.

She reached out and traced one of the small scars that covered his arms. There were more over most of his body. To the kelpies scars of battle were a symbol of honor and strength. To him, they were a reminder of one of the worst days of his life.

"I'm going to get you more to drink and maybe some broth. You need to get your strength back."

And quickly, the thought, because he needed to find and destroy Balban. He looked at the scars on his arms and though about his brother. He thought of waking after the attack and learning Yacopo hadn't survive. He remembered his father's anger and grief, the way he self-medicated away the pain. The overdose that killed him.

As he thought back, he realized something else.

Yacopo's death and Sevuk's lack of acceptance of his half-breed son was likely when Balban must have started his plan of influencing and using Fiero. His anger started to burn again.

"Your eyes get some red in them when you're angry," she said as she came back into the room with a tray.

"Be grateful then that I am a half breed and they aren't entirely red."

"I know there's nothing I can say that will make any of this any better."

"Not unless you can tell me where Balban is and give me what I need to kill that scum."

"No, I don't, but when the time comes, I will not stand in your way. That man deserves to pay for what he has done to you and others." She handed him more liquid and he drank. Then remembered something else. The reason they were in the cavern in the first place.

Others! "Did he succeed? Did Balban find the heirs to the Stones? His plan was to kidnap and control them."

"No, when he started to work the spell he was given, all three wearers of the Stones of Power felt a wave of pain. It knocked Lyria unconscious. Amina's gift enabled her to withstand the pain and get to the cavern and stop him. I arrived after he fled her attack."

Something about what she said bothered him. He couldn't figure out what it was. She mentioned Lyria and Amina who wore two of the Stones, but she also mentioned all three wearers.

She sat with her left side to him, her right he didn't see. She'd reached with her left hand to give him things and touch his scars.

"You wear the Stone of Love."

She brought out her right hand and placed it on his chest. There woven into the most beautiful piece of jewelry he'd ever seen was a pink sapphire.

"I do. And we are going to have to work together with Lyria and Amina if we are going to stop your uncle and save the Oceans from what he wants to do."

About the Author

A Jersey Girl trapped without good diners or boardwalks in New England, Rachel Kenley is a novelist, workshop leader, and co-founder of the Writers Business School (www.writersbusinessschool. com). She speaks nationally on writing, business, and her personal passion—how to connect with your heart's desire.

Rachel's first romance novel was published in 2007 when the e-book world was new. Since then she has had seven novels and numerous short stories and novellas released, with many reaching her publishers' bestseller lists. She is a member of the International Women's Writers Guild, Essex Writers and Artisans Guild, the Vice President of Broad Universe, and Vice President for Events of the Independent Publishers of New England.

When she is not writing Rachel is homeschooling her sons, trying unsuccessfully to keep up with laundry, and laughing as much as possible. She believes in shameless flirting, never missing the chance to watch *The Wizard of Oz* and the emotional and economic power of retail therapy. Please don't talk to her before her morning cup of coffee.

She enjoys hearing from readers. She can be found on Facebook at www.facebook.com/authorrachelkenley and on her website www.rachelkenley.net where you can sign up to receive a free story and other goodies!

If you liked this, you might like these other titles from Riverdale Avenue Books

By Rachel Kenley:

Waves of Pleasure
Book One of The Melusine's Daughters Series

Her Beastly Stepbrother:
A Once Upon a Stepbrother Novella

Her Stepbrother's Christmas Gift:
A Once Upon a Stepbrother Novella

Her Frozen Stepbrother
A Once Upon a Stepbrother Novella

Her Stepbrother, The Wolf

The Glass Stiletto
A BDSM Fairy Tale

And:

Her Stepbrothers' Demands
By Trinity Blacio

Her Stepbrothers are Aliens
By Trinity Blacio

Her Stepbrothers are Demons
By Trinity Blacio

Her Stepbrothers are Blood Suckers
By Trinity Blacio

Her Stepbrothers are Angels
By Trinity Blacio

Her Stepbrothers are Saber Tooth Tigers
Book Five of the Masters of the Cats Series
By Trinity Blacio

Trinity Blacio's Paranormal Stepbrothers Omnibus:
Volume One
By Trinity Blacio

The Red Shoes
By John Stewart Wynne